It Happened on Thunder Road

by

Susan Antony

It Happened on Thunder Road

Cover Art by *Kim Mendoza*

The Wild Rose Press, Inc.
PO Box 708
Adams Basin, NY 14410-0708
Visit us at www.thewildrosepress.com

Publishing History
First Edition, 2021
Trade Paperback ISBN 978-1-5092-3532-2
Digital ISBN 978-1-5092-3533-9

Published in the United States of America

I hadn't expected that. And I wasn't sure I wanted to respond. The old me, the good girl from New Jersey, wouldn't have choked. She would have told Charlie to take a hike. But the new me didn't want to let him go.

What was it about this strange boy with greased hair that attracted me so?

"What's the matter, New Jersey? Cat got your tongue?"

My face flushed. "Why don't you quit asking me ridiculous questions and do something that you're good at?"

"What's that?"

"Drive, Teddy Boy."

One of Charlie's brows tipped upward in a cocky salute. His knuckles whitened as he gripped the T-shifter, while rivers of veins formed on his muscular forearm. With a look of steely determination etched on his face, he slammed the shifter into first gear and jammed the accelerator pedal to the floor. The car rocketed forward. My head slammed against the seatback, and I dug my nails into the black tuck and roll upholstery.

"You scared, New Jersey?" Charlie asked, his eyes aflame.

"No," I said as the blood left my face.

"Then hang on, baby, 'cause you're about to go for the ride of your life."

Praise for Susan Antony

It Happened on Thunder Road ~ First Place in the Southeastern Writers Association Annual Contest.

~*~

Other Books by Susan Antony

Cherokee Summer

Dedication

This book is dedicated to my friends from Chatham Township High. Thanks for the memories. And to Diane Meigel Pittman, my dear friend, thank you for being my biggest cheerleader.

Chapter 1
Moncks Corner

Sunshine stood in the crowd just beyond airport security. I couldn't miss her. No one could miss my mother. She wore her skirt of many colors—as I called it—a skirt she made years ago out of old bandanas. It sagged toward the floor like a tattered battle flag which had clearly seen better days, the longer pieces grazing the tops of her ankles. And, if the skirt wasn't weird enough, she had flowers in her hair. Literally.

Her eyes widened, and she threw her hands in the air, waving frantically. "Over here!"

Everyone turned to look. I ducked my head and rushed to her. Not only because I was mortified, but also because my legs shook from the bumpy flight back to South Carolina. Sunshine didn't wait but ran to me with open arms.

"Emerald, look how much you've grown."

No one but my mother called me Emerald since elementary school. I shortened my name to Emmy Russo because it sounded normal. She squeezed me tight like I'd been gone for years rather than summer break.

"Oh, Emerald, you don't know how much I've missed you. How have you been, baby? How was your flight?"

"Scary turbulent, but I'm okay."

I wiggled out of her embrace and focused on a kid and woman racing to greet a man with a briefcase. A real family. The kind I wanted.

"How's your father?"

"Are you really interested in how Dad is?" My tone sounded mean, even to me, but I couldn't help myself. She was to blame for their split.

"Of course, I am. Just because we're not together anymore doesn't mean I don't love him."

What kind of person would leave someone they loved? Dad fell to pieces when she left, plagued by a case of the blues that settled deep into his eyes, leaving him with a continual far-away look. I'd never let Sunshine know how badly she hurt him.

"He's doing great."

"I'm glad. Your father deserves to be happy." She managed a tentative smile.

Not sure how to respond, I stared at the unpainted toenails sticking out of her leather sandals, while I tried to come up with something snarky to slay her. My mind drew a blank. If the humiliating greeting was an indicator of what my life was destined to be for the next year, I was in big trouble.

Rain poured in my window as we drove from underneath the covered parking lot. I cranked it up despite the fact the inside of Sunshine's prehistoric hippy microbus was blistering hot. I dabbed at the beads of sweat on my temples with the bottom of my shirt.

"Don't you think it's time we got a car with air-conditioning?"

"Emerald, 'The Dub' runs great. I'll never get rid of it."

"You're holding on to it like it's your mother."

Sunshine's expression grew distant. Her mother deserted her when she was a child. All she had left of her was the van. *If the earth opened up and swallowed me whole, it would still be too good for me.*

"Sorry. That was mean."

She sighed. "Don't worry, *Emerald.* I'm over it."

But she wasn't, which is why she emphasized my real name. Oh hell, I deserved it, but it couldn't hurt to reiterate my request.

"Call me Emmy, please?"

"Emerald is a beautiful name, and I'm not going to butcher it. So, deal with it."

"Do I have a choice?"

"No."

She hadn't changed one iota over the summer. Nor had I. It was hopeless. The two of us would always be sparring partners, forever doomed to get on like oil and water.

"And, by the way, I love your nose jewelry." She poked the side of my nose with her pointer finger. "When did you get it?"

I twirled the little emerald stone between my fingers. "A few weeks ago."

"Well, I absolutely love it." Of course, she would. Dad hated my pierced nose, which is why I'd gotten it after he took a job in Iraq and told me I couldn't stay in New Jersey. I promised I'd finish my senior year while I took care of his house, but he said I was too young to live alone. That didn't make sense since both my parents had practically allowed me to raise myself over the years.

Sunshine veered off the highway toward Moncks

3

Corner. We hadn't forged onward long before I came to the conclusion nothing here had evolved while I was away. To my right, the tractor dealer stood sandwiched between a ramshackle trailer and a rotting house with the Christmas lights still hanging on the eaves. The cinderblock liquor store with three hand-painted red dots, steel bars on the windows, and portable air-conditioning sticking out of its sidewall had failed to crumble. And just beyond the watering hole, Baptist churches continued to sprout out of the ground every mile or so.

Why had a Buddhist and former thrill-seeker like Sunshine chosen to leave my father to settle down here?

She pushed a faded tape in the eight-track player on the dash and sang, accompanied by Joni Mitchell and the *swish-swish* of the wipers. I settled back in my seat, closed my eyes, and listened to the sound of her singing Joni's song in an almost identical reedy voice.

A sudden jerk brought me to attention. I must have dosed off because we were now in the center of Moncks Corner. We passed the fifties-style, generic-named department store, the antique shop, and then the barber/beauty shop the size of a small garage. A wide smile spread across Sunshine's face while a frown spread across mine.

What was it about this town she loved so? For most of her life and a few years of mine, Sunshine moved around from city to city. She only stayed in New Jersey for more than a minute because of a drunken one-night stand gone awry—the one-night stand being my father and the awry part being me.

We turned down our tree-shaded street, and a few mailboxes later we were home. Loose gravel crunched and spattered under the weight of the tires as we rolled toward our tiny, yellow house—a smidgen of the sturdy brick home my dad owned in New Jersey. Viewing our home through the rain-teared windshield didn't hide the fact it was in desperate need of a paint job. Maybe I'd take on the task next spring, before I left for college.

Sunshine slapped my knee. "Come on. The rain won't stop anytime soon. Let's make a run for it."

I covered my head with a Buddhist magazine I found on the floorboard and ran behind her onto the side deck. The door thudded against the mint green stove wedged in between the opening and the short counter housing our rust-stained ceramic sink. The large mustard-colored refrigerator at the other end had greasy fingerprints around the handle. Maybe Sunshine had changed this summer—and for the worse. Our stuff was old—vintage as Sunshine put it—but she'd always lovingly cared for it.

Then I spied a third mismatched chair pushed under our crushed-ice vinyl table. Before I could inquire about the curious addition, Sunshine slid open the pocket door separating us from the adjoining cracker-box-sized living room.

"Sid, can you fetch Emerald's bags from The Dub?"

A giant of a man with shoulder-length hair and an unruly red beard was sprawled on our plush orange sofa, covering every bit of cushion space and both arm rests. The wooly-bully snorted. When he caught sight of Sunshine, he vaulted to his feet and planted a kiss right on her lips. He took a step toward me, beer-belly protruding, arms spread open. My jaw dropped, and I leaped out of his reach. The beast's arms fell to his sides and wiggled as if he were trying to find something else to do with them.

"You must be Emerald," he said in a gravelly voice.

"Emmy," I said.

"Okay, Emmy, it is."

Sunshine shot him a hip-cock pose. "Don't you dare. Her name is Emerald by prophecy."

Sid scrunched his face and uttered an articulate, "Huh?"

Sunshine responded as if reading a newsreel. "A few weeks before Emerald's birth, I sought the advice of a fortuneteller. She told me my baby would be perfectly healthy and that I should name her Emerald."

I shook my head. She hated it when I challenged the reliability of her fortuneteller, but someone had to.

"Come on, tell him the rest. The part where she said my name should be Emerald because my eyes would be green like yours."

He bowed to my level and squinted. "Your eyes aren't green."

"Exactly my point. The psychic was wrong."

By the time my eyes changed from the smoky blue color most newborn babies have, I had a head of mousy brown hair and umber eyes like my dad. I didn't inherit Sunshine's emerald orbs, her strawberry-blonde hair, or her carefree attitude either. The only things the two of us shared were a fine, straight nose with a slight button on the tip and a dusting of sun freckles across our cheeks.

Sunshine pulled back her shoulders. "I'm not going to discuss this subject any further. Your name is prophecy, and that's that." She dusted her hands together.

Sid undid the top button of his sleeveless, flannel shirt and scratched his hairy chest. "Well, tell me, little lady, prophecy aside, how was your trip?"

Oh no, he didn't. The dude did not just call me little lady. I answered him anyway.

"Apart from the fact that I arrived in a torrential downpour, it's hot as hell, and I really miss my *dad*, it was fine, thank you very much."

Sid raised his arms in a *don't-shoot* position. "Whoa. Take a chill pill, Emmy. I was only asking."

Sunshine grabbed my shoulders and cranked me around. "Come on, *Emerald*, you must be tired."

She guided me down the hallway, the wood floor creaking beneath our feet, and stopped in front of my bedroom. Then she pushed me inside, shutting the teal green door behind us. Why was she angry? The right to that emotion belonged to me, not her.

"Who is he?" I whispered.

"I told you about him. He's the mechanic who keeps The Dub on the road. We got together while you were away this summer. It just seems right. Him being here, you know. He's my soul mate."

If she'd have slapped me, it would have hurt less.

"You mean he lives here?"

"Yeah, didn't Frank tell you?"

I shook my head. Dad was obviously a big fat chicken. A tear rolled down my cheek. Sunshine wrapped her arms around me.

"It'll be okay, baby."

The scent of lavender soap wafted from her. My traitorous body sank into her embrace, and I cried ugly—until the image of Sid rematerialized in my mind. Our home. My home. The place that was supposed to be a haven had been invaded. Anger from the pit of my gut roiled upward, and the F-bomb trembled on the tip of my tongue. I pushed her away and raked away my rogue tears.

"Hook up with him if you want, but he can't live here. He's a biker."

"I raised you better than to judge someone by their appearance. He's not leaving, Emerald. I love him, and I know you will too if you give him a chance."

Oh, no. This wasn't happening. Next thing I knew, I'd tossed out an ultimatum.

"If he stays, I go."

The corners of Sunshine's mouth drooped. Divots formed on either side of her chin, accentuating the fifty-five long years she's spent on the planet.

"You're free to do as you wish, but I assure you, there's plenty of room for both of you in my heart. I'll be in the living room with Sid. When you've calmed down, you can come in and join us."

My mother had chosen her boyfriend over me. My stomach wrenched, but I held my stoic expression until she disappeared from view.

Then I threw myself on the bed and cried some more.

Chapter 2
Lords of Purgatory

The next morning, dragging from lack of sleep, I grabbed the jar of forbidden instant coffee I'd stashed in the top of my closet and made my way to the kitchen. If I hurried, I could drink my brew in peace without a lecture from my mother on the dangers of caffeine and avoid the wooly-bully in the process.

I slid open the pocket door and entered the kitchen. The butterscotch sun burned through the picture window, ravaging my tear-stung eyes. Through the haze that had become my vision, I made out Sunshine sitting shoulder-to-shoulder with Sid at our table.

"Good morning," they said in unison as if they were in a breakfast cereal commercial.

"Oh, I forgot something."

I hid the coffee behind my back, then bolted to my room and shoved my stash under the bed. With my heart pounding in my chest, I stalked back to the kitchen and sat at the table.

Sunshine pushed a bowl of granola in my direction. "It's fresh. I made it last night after you went to bed. It's much healthier than caffeine."

I could never fool her. I retaliated with a diversion. A box of soy milk sat on the Lazy Susan in the middle of the table.

"Do we have any real milk?"

Sunshine blinked rapidly. "No. Soy milk is healthier. Little saturated fat, no cholesterol."

The milk wasn't the real issue, nor was my lack of caffeine, but I didn't have the strength for a confrontation about our present living arrangements, and frankly, I had nowhere else to go. So I poured the soy into my bowl and took a bite.

"Mmmm, this stuff sure is good," Sid mumbled.

Specks of oat and grain spattered out of his mouth, nesting in his beard and dropping like wet, gooey bombs all around him. Sunshine batted at the sleeve of her T-shirt to get rid of his crumbs.

My stomach twisted, and half-chewed branny clumps lodged in the back of my throat. I jerked to my feet, sending my chair flying, and bolted to the sink to gulp water straight from the faucet.

Sunshine sprang to my side and pounded on my back. "Are you all right?"

I wiped my chin with the back of my hand, my gaze fixed on the wall behind her. "I'll be fine, Sunshine. I always am."

She draped her arm over my shoulder, and I maneuvered out of her grasp, using the momentum to flee the room. I slid to a stop outside of the kitchen. Sunshine spoke too low for me to decipher what she was saying, but Sid's raspy voice came across loud and clear.

"Give her time. She'll come around."

I had a plan, and it didn't involve me coming around. I rushed to my room to text Dad. If anyone could put an end to this nightmare, he could.

—*SOS. Sunshine is living with one of the Lords of Purgatory bikers.*—

Maybe Sid didn't belong to the LP gang, but he looked like one, and he rode a big old motorcycle, so my text wasn't a complete lie. I stretched out on my bed and waited for Dad to respond. Five minutes passed, and nothing. Maybe he was in the shower.

No sooner had Sid's motorcycle roared out the driveway when Sunshine called, "Hurry up, Emerald. You'll be late for school."

I rolled out of bed and stuffed my phone into the front pocket of my backpack. Then I plodded into the kitchen, my sneakers slapping against the cracked linoleum. Sunshine stood ready, hand on the doorknob. She'd slipped out of her T-shirt and into a pair of patched blue jeans and a smock shirt. A bandana tied over her head like a bonnet kept her strawberry-blonde mop in place while tangled tendrils—a notch away from full-blown dreadlocks—hung halfway down her back.

Though never a conventional mom, her appearance had become even more bohemian since she moved to Moncks Corner and became a writer. Four whole years and her memoir remained a work in progress. Surely the trust fund her grandparents left her had to be depleted unless the wooly-bully was kicking in. That reminded me…

"Someone left the toilet seat up."

Sunshine propped her fists on her hips. Her breasts jiggled under the thin gauzy material of her shirt. "Just put it down."

"I already did."

She rubbed the back of her neck. "Okay, so now that you've gone potty, we can leave for school."

Sarcasm was her weapon of choice when she

wanted to avoid the real issue—her live-in boyfriend. She opened the door and gestured for me to walk through.

I dug my feet into the floor.

Sunshine stifled a laugh. "You know, you remind me of myself when I was your age. You've got the whole package, rebellious attitude and all."

I held my breath as fury burned the back of my neck, then willed my feet to move and brushed past her as if I didn't care.

We weren't alike.

Not one bit.

Chapter 3
Charlie Fields

After a short but silent ride, Sunshine pulled up in front in a spot marked *Reserved for Teachers* and cut off the engine. I'd hoped maybe she'd obey the rules for once, but no.

"You can't park here," I said.

"Quit worrying. No one will care."

"Is that the same thing you thought when you moved Sid into our home? Well, I care."

"Emerald, did you think I would stay single forever?"

"If it's money, I'll give you my weekly paycheck. That way, we won't need his help."

"It's not the money. This time, it's forever. Sid and I don't have the kind of love that makes me weak in the knees. I despise being wobbly on my feet. It's much deeper. If I could have anyone I wanted, I'd still choose him."

Did she really say that? Words escaped me, and even worse, the muscles between my shoulders ached from the silence. Nothing was forever to Sunshine, and it never would be. She was fooling herself and wrecking my life in the meantime. This was one situation I couldn't wait to correct itself.

I reached into my back pocket for my roll of antacids, bit one off at the end, and stuffed it in the side of my cheek with my tongue. Maybe she didn't care what I thought, but she'd have to listen to Dad, or he'd come to get me.

"I've got to go," I said.

"Call me if you need a ride."

I climbed out of the microbus and pushed the door shut without saying goodbye.

The Dub puttered off, the motor chirping like a bird. Two sophomores ran by, tossing a football. One missed a catch. The ball bounced off the pavement, and I dodged it, narrowly missing getting beaned.

I grabbed the ball. As I rose, the sun glinted off the roof of a cerulean car in the back of the lot, parked next to my friend Keir Harper's old copper-colored Mustang. It seemed oddly familiar, yet I couldn't place it. I tossed the ball to the closest guy, stepped off the curb, and walked closer to get a better look.

The car was large and boxy by today's standards, with tinted windows and a SS logo on its chrome grille. It was awesome enough to have been showcased in one of those auto magazines Dad's mechanic kept rolled up in his back pocket. The only thing missing was a couple of girls in bikinis sprawled across the hood.

The bell rang, reminding me the time for gawking at old cars had passed, and the nearly empty parking lot indicated it must have been the second bell. Damn. I was late. Good thing I'd memorized my new schedule.

I jogged across the parking lot, burst through the doors, and set off down the empty hallway. When I passed the auditorium, I hugged a corner and *smack*!

"Ow," a deep voice said.

I stumbled backward, helpless to stop my fall. A large set of hands caught me before I hit the floor and pulled me to my feet. It was a guy, and he smelled good—like cinnamon.

"Whoa, baby. What's your rush?"

I blinked to clear my vision. He wasn't alone. Five guys surrounded me. I recognized all of them but one, the tallest of the group. The one who had stopped my fall. A sleeve of tattoos decorated his left arm, and a mound of slicked dark hair lay atop his head. He hooked his thumbs in his pockets and hunched his shoulders. I followed the line of his long, blue-jean-clad legs, stopping at his black, steel-toed boots. He cleared his throat. My gaze shot up to meet his. A lopsided grin stretched across his face.

"Like what you see?"

"Yes—I mean, no—I mean I'm late to class."

I tried to step around him, but he blocked me. I moved in the opposite direction, and he cut me off again. The guys with him tightened the circle, and like a gang of sexist thugs, commented on my appearance. My ta-tas, to be specific.

My cheeks burned. "Haven't you idiots heard of the Me Too movement?"

The tall one cut in. "She's right, you scumbags. Shut your traps." As if a switch had been flipped, the others fell silent, and the tall one said, "Why don't you let me walk you to class? Little-big girls don't need to be wandering these halls all by themselves. It might not be safe."

"I'm perfectly fine on my own. Thank you very much." I blasted through a small space between him and Chuy, a black-haired kid I knew from one of my classes. I'd barely noticed Chuy until now.

"Don't go, *chica*," he cooed. "Stay and talk to us."

My level of adrenaline spiked. I upped my pace.

"What's the matter? You too good for us?" another one called.

I darted inside the washroom and sagged against the door. There were never gangs in our school before. Who was that guy? And why the hell was I hiding? No matter how intimidated I was, I couldn't let them know. I had to do the mature thing: face the jerks and insist they leave me alone.

I cracked the door and peeked out. The thugs were nowhere in sight. It was as if I'd imagined them. With my gaze focused on the end of the hallway, I double-stepped to history class.

An hour later, when the bell rang to change periods and with a strange gang still on my mind, I checked out the hallway before leaving class. They were nowhere in sight, so I threw back my shoulders and continued onward.

"Hey, girl," someone shouted.

I hesitated while my brain registered the high-pitched words. Jade. I breathed out then back in. While my friend's voice hadn't changed, she certainly had. Her usually unruly brown hair hung in silky strands to the middle of her back. Gone were the oversized tee-shirt and bargain store jeans, replaced by a navy blue and peach flowered, button-up shirt and matching peach pants. The heavy make-up coloring her eyes made her look at least two years older. A few months ago, we'd have laughed at someone with so much paint on their face. Bombshell wannabe. That's what we'd have called them.

"Wow, you look, ah..." The words escaped me for the second time today.

"A lot better, huh?"

"Yeah." My ears burned liar-hot.

Suddenly, something felt wrong, and it had nothing to do with my best friend looking like she'd been captured by pop-culture aliens and recreated. It was as if the body-snatching aliens had their sight set on me, too. With every step I took, my heart rate increased.

And then I spied him. The thug who'd frightened me earlier. He leaned against a locker a few yards ahead, chewing on a toothpick. His lips twitched, working on a grin. I pretended not to notice him, but it was clear he didn't buy it. He swiveled his head as I passed, impaling me with his gaze.

I moved closer to Jade. "Who's the new guy with the greasy hair?"

"Oh, him. That's Charlie Fields. Stay away from him." Her voice was laced with an underlying tone of disgust. "Over the summer, he swooped in and assembled all the losers in school and formed the Back Lot Gang."

Referring to people as losers was far from Jade's nature. At least it was until now. I'd call her out on it later, but there were more important things I needed to know.

"Is Charlie dangerous?"

Jade scrutinized me, obviously unimpressed with my naiveté. "Aren't all gangbangers?"

I shuddered, remembering my run-in with him and how he and his friends had given me a major case of the creeps. "Has he ever threatened any girls?"

Jade paused a moment. "Not that I'm aware of. But take my advice and stay far away from all of them, or you'll get yourself labeled Back Lot property."

"I don't understand."

"Girls who've been used by the gang, if you know what I mean. No decent guy will ever touch you if you're infected with their cooties."

"Thanks, I'll keep it in mind," I said, grateful for the heads-up.

"There's something else I need to tell you."

Her frown indicated I might not like it too much.

Ashanti Stephens, the head cheerleader, waved and skipped in our direction. I looked over my shoulder, expecting to see one of her friends behind us. Then out of her mouth came the loud and proud shout: "Jade!"

Jade turned to me. "Look, I've got to go. We can meet up later and talk then. Okay?"

"Sure." I swallowed down the sting of her dis.

Then Jade flitted off with an uncharacteristic bounce.

What had happened to Moncks Corner?

Chapter 4
Just a Boy or Two

To my relief, the rest of the day passed without incident. I stepped into my last class, grinning not only because Art was my favorite but also because in one short hour, all the stress would be behind me.

Instantaneously, the tiny hairs prickled on the back of my neck, and the same unrest I'd experienced in the hall earlier struck me. It took only seconds to spy Charlie Fields in the back of the room, his foot propped on the corner of the table next to a cup of sculpting tools.

I tripped over my feet and bumped into the teacher's desk. My schedule slipped from my grasp, fluttered through the air, and landed face-up on his personal planner. I rubbed my injured thigh. Diverted by the pain, I skirted entering full panic mode.

"Ah, Ms. Russo," said Mr. Hart, a spindly man with a toothpaste smile. "Nice to see you back this semester."

I secured his nameplate that my clumsiness had left dangling over the edge. "Thanks."

He handed me my schedule and flicked his hand. "Take a seat. Your choice."

I froze. Of the two seats available, one was directly in front of Charlie. The other was beside him. The sudden rush of blood racing to my brain nearly brought on a migraine. I had to break my bad habit of always arriving late.

Mr. Hart looked at me, then beyond me. "Mr. Fields? Do you mind removing your foot from the table?"

Charlie bared his teeth in a predatory smile and thumped his black boot on the floor. I scuffed to the back of the room and slipped into the seat I perceived as the lesser of two evils—the one in front of him. I nodded at the girl dressed in solid black occupying the other seat at the table. She stabbed a pencil into a lump of clay. I presumed she was new, too, since I'd never met her either. I arranged my supplies then settled in my seat, with my arms crossing my chest.

A cloud of hot breath tickled the back of my neck. "So, we meet again."

Ugh. If I didn't have bad luck, I'd have no luck at all.

He tapped me on the shoulder. "What's your name?"

I ignored him.

"Come on, baby, don't make me beg."

I shushed him.

My table mate shot me a look. "Get over yourself."

"Excuse me? Are you talking to me?" I asked.

She looked me up and down and cocked an eyebrow. "Or do you prefer girls?"

"No, sorry." I smiled to show her I was cool with being friends.

She scowled and stirred the clay with her pencil.

Mr. Hart cleared his throat. "We are studying Michelangelo today."

He held a statue of David over his head with a fig

leaf of yellow sticky papers in front of his private area. The room erupted into whistles and hoots.

Charlie's table squeaked and bumped against the back of my chair. "Come on, bae, what's your name?"

I hooked my left arm across the backrest and twisted around. "Would you be quiet?"

"Not until you give it up." He poked his finger through a hole he made with his other hand, with his forefinger touching his thumb.

I wrinkled my nose. "Pig."

"Don't get your panties in a wad. I'm only kidding."

"Well, you're not funny." I spun and faced the front of the room.

Charlie's table squeaked again, and my hair moved. I swatted his hand away. But seconds later, he was back. Twisting and twirling, twirling and twisting *my* hair. Maybe if I ignored him, he'd give up.

I waited. And waited.

It didn't happen.

Instead, the light touch of his fingers triggered goosebumps on my arms. Oh, hell no. No guy would make me feel something I didn't want to. I grabbed the edges of his desk.

"Listen, if you don't stop, I will report you for harassment."

"Take it easy. I'm just having a little fun. If you really want me to leave you alone, all you got to do is say the word."

"I want you to leave me alone," I emphasized each syllable as if talking to someone who spoke a foreign language.

"Okay. From this moment forward, you don't exist."

Charlie's face went blank, his dark eyes vacant. Apart from the dusting of dark stubble on his chin and a scar next to his right eye, he had the face of a boy, a crude but handsome boy. I opened my mouth to apologize but realized how ridiculous that was. The last thing I wanted was to strike up any kind of relationship with someone who viewed girls as property. So I left Charlie Fields in his comatose state and forgot all about him.

Almost.

When the bell rang, I ran outside to distance myself from Charlie as soon as possible. Hopefully, he'd get the hint to buzz off, as confrontation had never been my thing.

Once I was sure the coast was clear, I fished out my phone to see if Dad had texted me back. My screen lit up void of messages. Maybe he'd called Sunshine. I had to get home.

On the far side of the parking lot, opportunity awaited. Keir opened the door to his prized Mustang. I weaved between the cars lining up to leave school, shouting his name. He glanced over and waved. I raced to him.

"Hi, can I get a ride?'

"I haven't seen you all summer. Don't I get a hug first?" He opened his arms.

"Of course."

I threw my arms around his waist and squeezed. Not only had he grown taller, but his doughy middle had hardened to muscle, and stubble darkened his formerly smooth chin.

"Wow, you've changed. You're bigger."

"It's still me." He squeezed me tighter.

We'd hugged many times, but his new body threw me. My armpits dampened, and a tiny buzz swirled in my stomach. I wiggled out of his arms.

"You were fine the way you were."

He frowned and rubbed a spot on the hood with the bottom of his shirt.

"Whatever, Em."

Em, geez. He was the only person I allowed to call me that. To everyone else, I was Emmy, except for Sunshine, who, despite my pleas, refused to call me anything but my given name. Keir had been my best friend since the eighth grade, so he got a pass.

I settled in on the familiar brown vinyl seat of his hotrod. Though clean, the cab smelled of must mingled with a hint of raw fuel and pine from the can of air freshener he kept under the seat. Once we were seatbelted in, he turned the key. The engine roared to life, and the floorboard rumbled under my feet. We pulled out of the parking lot.

"You working tonight?" he asked.

"Yeah. You?"

"Want a lift? I'll come a few minutes early; I have something I want to talk to you about." He blushed.

First Jade, now him. Why did everyone I knew have something to talk about? I'd only been away nine weeks. Then our awkward hug popped into my mind. Maybe he wanted to be more than friends. Oh no. He meant too much to me. I'd be damned if I'd let him ruin everything.

"Sunshine's driving me."

"Then let's go get a soda and talk now."

He wasn't making this easy.

"I need to call my father. Family business."

23

His face fell hard, and he shrugged. Why did guys always have to make things so difficult? I explained to him about the predicament with Sid, but that didn't seem to make him feel any better. So we rode in silence the rest of the way while I stared out the window, longing for freedom from the change that had plagued me since I'd returned.

When we reached my house, the crape myrtle in the front yard with its summer blooms wilting left me with little hope. The few short months I'd been gone might have well have been ten years. Keir deserved an honest conversation, but at this moment, all I managed was a forced smile before I bolted from the car.

I confronted Sunshine as soon as I got inside. She swore my father hadn't called her. So I locked myself in my room and adjusted the portable AC window unit a few degrees cooler. Then I settled on my bed and opened my laptop while musty manufactured air filled the room. A message appeared in my recently empty email box. It was from my father. My heart thumped as I stared at the blank subject line. I took a deep breath then pressed the track-pad.

Emmy,

I know you are upset with your mother. Lord knows she has some off-kilter ideas, but she loves you, and she'd never do anything to harm you.

As far as Sid goes, quit freaking out. I had a background check run on him before I agreed to let you go home. His record is clean. While I cannot attest to his appearance, you can rest assured he has no affiliation with the Lords of Purgatory. Next summer will be here before you know it. In the meantime, if you need anything, clothes, money, whatever, I'm a phone

call away.
   Love you always,
   Dad
I clicked the browser closed. A screen saver of Dad, Sunshine, and me when we were still a family filled the screen. Instead of a family, I was stuck with my mother and her live-in boyfriend for another nine months.

My hands trembled as I deleted the photo.

Chapter 5
The Back Lot Gang

The cool air blasted me as I walked through the front doors of Big George's Groceries. While I didn't make a lot of money, I loved my co-workers and the camaraderie of working in a family-owned grocery store. Keir offered a wave as he breezed by with a broom, whizzing in and out of the checkout aisles, collecting old receipts and dust bunnies.

The office door swung open. My manager, Miss Iola, flew out and accosted me with a boney hug.

"Hi, Sugar, welcome home," she said in her thick Southern accent.

I stepped back and smiled. The scent of her sweet perfume lingered in the air around me. Until Miss Iola, I'd never had a friend over eighteen. She had to be near seventy, but she wasn't old-old. She wore her bangs poofed-up, eighties-style, and the rest of her strawberry-blonde mane sat atop her head in a high ponytail. Energy radiated off her, making the grocery store's fluorescent lights seem to burn a tad brighter. Iola grinned.

"I'd love to lay idle and catch up, but we got to git to work, girl. It's fifteen minutes 'til the late afternoon rush."

Her words were prophetic as usual. After a short lull, customers swarmed the registers. Iola got on the central microphone and called all the cashiers to the front. Keir dropped his broom and raced back and forth like a pendulum gone wild, chasing prices and locating forgotten items in between buggy trips to the lot. Before I knew it, the clock struck nine, and it was quitting time.

Keir stopped at my register. His jaw twitched.

"Is something wrong?" I asked.

"Do you need a ride home?"

The words flew out his mouth so fast it took me a moment to mentally translate them. My skin turned all clammy. I wasn't ready to have *the conversation*. Why couldn't boys just be happy with being friends? The idea of coming up with an excuse to avoid him was inviting, but we had to talk sometime. Now was as good a time as any.

"A ride? Yeah, sure."

And the two of us headed for the employee parking lot.

A single streetlight flickered around the side of the building, casting shadows off five figures emerging from two vehicles parked on either side of Keir's rod. The doors slammed shut, blasting the quiet of the night with something that sounded like a three-gun salute. Even from a distance, one of the guys was unmistakable. Charlie Fields hopped on the hood of the boxy ride and lay back, using the windshield as a pillow, his arms crossed behind his head.

The situation with Keir had just become a small problem. I rooted my feet to the pavement and threw my arm out to stop him.

"Watch out. The Back Lot Gang has your car surrounded. Let's go inside and wait until they leave."

Susan Antony

"You're not afraid of them, are you?"

"Aren't y-you?" I stammered.

"Naw."

I grabbed his elbow. "There's more to this than you know. Charlie Fields gave me a hard time at school, and I threatened to report him to the principal for harassment. He'll probably beat you up just for being with me."

Keir threw his hands in the air. "No one is going to beat anyone up. It kills me how people are always ragging on Charlie just because he's different. You have nothing to be afraid of."

"How can you be so sure?" I frowned.

He took a deep breath, and his brows drew together. "Because I know him. Well."

I stepped away from him. "You've joined a gang. I go away for a summer and—"

"Em, stop. I haven't joined anything. But I've known Charlie my whole life. He's my brother," he said half-aloud.

He'd mentioned a half-brother that he rarely saw. But *Charlie Fields*? The best friend bubble burst in my head, and I shook away the suds.

"If this is some kind of joke, it's not funny."

I spun on my heel, ready to take flight. Keir caught me by the wrist.

"Calm down. You've got it all wrong. Charlie's a good guy. They're all good guys. They won't hurt you."

I wanted to believe him, but there were many unanswered questions. Keir stood motionless, his chest rising and falling beneath his green Big Georgy G's polo. I swallowed. "You never told me he was coming."

"I didn't know. His dad died suddenly, and he had

nowhere else to go."

"I thought he was older than you. What's he doing in our grade?

"He is a year older, but he failed once in junior high."

Keir's birthday was in December, so Charlie must be eighteen, like me. Still, I was unsure. I stared at the check pattern on my slip-on sneakers until the squares merged.

"Em, my brother has had a tough life, but he's not dangerous. I wouldn't bring you anywhere near him if I thought he would hurt you. Do you want to meet him, or would you prefer to believe the stupid rumors?"

Charlie had set me on edge in the hallway, and he'd annoyed me a bit in art class, but he hadn't done anything to harm me. Maybe if Charlie knew I was friends with Keir, he'd leave me alone. I took a deep breath and steeled my nerves.

"Okay. Let's go."

Keir held out his hand, and I took it. As we moved forward, his firm grip distracted me from any fear I had of Charlie Fields.

Almost.

When the gang members noticed us approaching, they craned their necks, like a pack of wolves catching the scent of prey.

"Hey, Charlie," Keir called.

Indifferent thus far, Charlie propped himself on his elbows. "Well, well, well, if it ain't my little bro. What's up, hot stuff?"

"Not much," Keir said.

His eyes gravitated to our clasped hands. "I see your *not much*. Who's the lady?"

My cheeks burned, and I wiggled my hand free. For some reason, Charlie pretended he didn't know me, despite the unmistakable glow of recognition that shone in his eyes.

"Charlie, you know Emmy. You met her today," Keir said.

In one fluid movement, Charlie rolled to a sitting position and hopped off the hood. His heavy boots thudded against the pavement. "I don't remember."

Charlie—the big fat liar—offered me his hand. Though the urge to slap it away crossed my mind, I took it, and he curled his calloused fingers around mine. The streetlight flickered, and a sudden burst of static electricity zapped me. I jerked free.

He flashed a smug grin. "Hey boys, this is Emmy."

The gang members circled me, the same way they had in school, playing along with Charlie's sham.

A car door flew open. A tall girl with spiky, black hair with blonde tips emerged, followed by a short girl with wavy black hair and bumper bangs. They sauntered over. Both had gone to Moncks Corner High but had graduated a year or so ago. I didn't remember their names. The tall one snaked her arm around Charlie's waist, causing the thorn tattoo on her biceps to grow larger.

"Turn me loose, woman." Charlie busted out of her grip. "It's too hot out here for this."

She jutted out her lower lip, exposing the pink gums below her blood-red lipstick.

Keir frowned, and his posture stiffened. I stared at Keir, wondering if rude behavior like Charlie's ran in the family? The short girl picked at the tip of one of her red fingernails. Even the gang members shifted uncomfortably.

"Chuy," Charlie shouted, slicing through the silence like a switchblade. "How about you get the brewskies from The Ghost?"

"Sure thing, boss."

Everyone seemed to relax. Everyone but me.

While the gang members busied themselves cutting up, I busied myself fretting about getting busted for underage drinking. And what in the hell was "The Ghost?"

Chuy crawled into the trunk of the blue car— evidently The Ghost—emerging moments later, juggling four cola cans in his hands, much to my relief.

"Here Emmy, ladies first."

I sniffed the lid. "This smells like beer."

"Very observant," Charlie said.

A roar of laughter followed. Keir snatched the can out of my hand and tossed it on the ground.

"You ready to go?"

He was offering me an out, and I was more than willing to take it.

"Yeah, if you are?"

Slick, a lanky guy with a complexion problem, stared at the ground as sudsy liquid formed a small puddle. "Hell, Keir, what'd you do that for?"

"I'm not wasting words explaining. See you guys later."

Keir ushered me away while the gang mewed sarcastic goodbyes. Safe inside his car, I melted so deep into the seat, it was if the vinyl and I were one. Keir turned the key in the ignition, and the car burst into a rumbling idle. Pop music blasted from two speakers in the back. He pumped the gas pedal until the engine ran smooth.

"Sorry. I didn't know they'd be partying."

First gear. I faced him.

"He's your brother. Don't you know his habits?"

Second gear.

"They usually party in Jake's Garage."

"And he lets them?" I asked.

Third gear.

"Not exactly. Charlie works there, and Jake gave him a set of keys in case he wanted to use the shop to work on his car after hours."

He swung out on the main drag and shifted into fourth.

"Look, I've got nothing against Charlie and his friends, but drinking in the parking lot of Big George's isn't cool, nor is taking advantage of your boss."

His expression flattened. "I agree. How about we quit talking about Charlie? I'd rather talk about you and me."

Did he say you and me? I'd almost forgotten he wanted to change our relationship dynamic—the perfect one he only stood to ruin. My heart thumped like the backbeat of a snare drum in a rock and roll band. I needed more time. The only way out was to play dumb.

"What's there to talk about?"

Keir shook his head. "Forget it, Em. It's nothing important."

Well, that stung. Perhaps I misread the situation entirely. I wished for a *How to Understand Guys* manual to materialize in my hands, pronto.

We pulled up in front of my house, and he parked behind a large crape myrtle tree, so we were obscured from the view of the front door. Then he fiddled with the radio dial until he found a station playing country tunes.

Now what?

"Em," he finally said, "Want a ride to school on Monday?"

Monday sounded like a long time away since we usually hung out on weekends. Maybe it was for the best.

"Sure. See you then." I reached for the door handle.

"Wait. Don't go yet."

Uh, oh. I couldn't look at him.

"You know, I really like you, even though you're real different than most girls."

I picked at my cuticle. "How so?"

"You act more like a guy."

What? Now he felt the need to tell me he didn't even think of me as a girl. I fought the urge to pinch him and flung open the door.

"Thanks a lot."

"I'll call you tomorrow."

"I won't be home. I've got plans."

Anger simmered in the pit of my stomach. By the time I made it inside, I was boiling hot. Sunshine greeted me at the doorway.

"Emerald, I've been waiting for you to call."

"I got a ride from Keir." I pushed past her into the house.

"What's wrong? Did you two fight?"

"I'll say. Boys are jerks. They say one thing but mean something else. They think they're complimenting you when actually they're insulting you. And then they're too dumb to know the difference. I'm never ever going to have a boyfriend. It only leads to disaster."

Sunshine cackled. "Good girl. Men are not worth it."

A deep moan came from behind the sofa. Sid's head popped up from its constant state of horizontal.

"Hey. What am I? Chopped liver?"

"I wasn't talking about you, baby."

Sunshine rushed to him and stroked his hairy cheek. Then the two of them commenced to gazing lovingly into each other's eyes.

"I think I'm going to be sick," I muttered before marching to the bathroom to wash the boy germs off my hands.

Chapter 6
Relieved or Reprehensible?

By Monday morning Keir still hadn't called, and my anger had faded into regret. I'd always been challenged in the temper department, and often it came back to bite me. How long would it take me to get to school on foot? Thirty minutes? One thing was certain. Walking a mile and a half-beat listening to Sunshine and Sid's bed squeak until it was time for her to drive me to school.

I stepped onto the porch and eased the door closed behind me. The sky burned hazy pink. The sun was a bright orange blob on the horizon. Birds twittered shrilly from their perches in the trees, each one warning the next of an intruder in their paradise. Me.

In the distance, the sudden roar of a familiar engine grew louder, drowning out the tweets. I forgot about bird watching and ducked behind a post. Keir's copper brown hotrod zoomed up and screeched to a halt in front of my house. He lowered his head as if he were reading something in his lap. Seconds later, my phone buzzed. I pulled it out of my pocket and glanced at the message.

—*Need a ride?*—

I jumped from the porch, crept across the lawn, and pounded on the windshield. Keir bounced off the seat, and his phone tumbled to the floor. He picked it up, examined it, and when I didn't get in, cranked down the passenger window. I bent sideways, my long hair hanging like a stringy brown curtain. Unlike Keir, the humidity in the South was unforgiving.

"What are you doing here?" Since he'd come, I could afford to be smug.

"I offered you a ride today, and I'm a man of my word. Will you get in, please?" He gestured to the passenger seat.

I waited just the right amount of time not to appear anxious, then got in and adjusted my backpack between my ankles. I used my remaining grain of smugness to stare him down.

"Truce," he said, his hands flying up in front of his face, his fingers forming a cross.

I snickered. "Okay, truce, but first we need to get something straight."

He flinched. "Oh boy, here it comes."

I held up the finger that would surely have gotten me suspended from school if I'd done it there. "I promise to hold my temper if you promise not to compare me to a guy."

His lips stretched into a triumphant smile. "You got a deal, Em." We shook on it. "Can I ask you something?"

I nodded.

He unthreaded and rethreaded the gearshift knob two times before he spoke. "I need to know something upfront."

"What?" I asked, turning to face him.

"Do you think someday you might give me a chance to be more than just your friend?"

Bah, boom. My heart lodged in my throat.

"I did a lot of soul-searching this weekend, and I think that someday I might like the same thing, but I'm not ready yet. Right now, I just want to be friends, if that's okay."

"I guess that's better than nothing." He squirmed behind the wheel. "We better get going."

I fell against the seatback and let out a breath. He cranked the car, and we rolled forward.

First gear. Well, that went better than the last time.

Second gear. At least we're still friends.

Third gear. He doesn't seem too bugged about my suggestion.

Fourth gear. Now, he was ignoring me. Dealing with boys was so complicated.

We passed the gas station and Big George's and then continued down the main street until we reached school. He downshifted into the parking lot and maneuvered into the space next to Charlie's car. He still wasn't speaking, so I would. Nothing like a little small talk to break the ice.

"What kind of car is The Ghost?" I asked.

"It's a '67 Chevelle Super Sport."

I traced the little chrome horse on Carl's glove box with the tip of my finger. "Is it a Ford, like yours?"

"No, Em. It's a Chevrolet."

His mouth twitched. I could tell he was trying not to laugh, but the gleam in his eyes gave him away.

"How am I supposed to know?"

"If you're going to be 'just friends' with me, you're going to have to improve your girly knowledge of cars."

"Is that so?" I said, copying his slight Southern drawl.

"I don't sound like that."

"Do too."

"Never mind my accent." He squeezed the back of my neck, playfully. "Cars are serious business where I'm concerned. This summer, I spent most of my Saturday nights hanging with Charlie and the boys out on Thunder Road. We made a ton of money street racing."

"Isn't that illegal?"

"Yeah, but the cops don't come out that far often."

"Okay, well, maybe, but you promised you didn't join Charlie's gang."

He brushed a flyaway strand of hair off my face, leaving tingles where his fingers touched. "I'm not, but I like to drag race. Sometimes I need to cut loose. It gets tiring being the good kid in the family all the time."

I supposed there were much worse ways to be bad than street racing. I laced my fingers together, twisting my hands outward. "You know what? I'm tired of always being good, too. Will you teach me how to race?"

"You have to have a car first. Until then, you're stuck watching me." He tickled my ribs.

I swiped the keys from the ignition and twirled them around my finger. "Don't leave these lying around, Hot Rod, or you may get left in the dust."

His eyebrows quirked up, and he grabbed for the keys. I tossed them in his lap and sprung from the car, leaving the door open wide. Pleased with the bold new me, I exaggerated the sway in my hips as I sauntered away.

"Hey, wait for me," he shouted.

I kept my pace.

****

During lunch hour, Jade dragged me into the cafeteria and led me to the popular kids' table. She patted the space next to her. "Sit here. Dylan's sick today."

I'd never been invited to sit with the popular crowd before, but I shrugged and took the spot anyway. Laura Mobley, the editor of the school newspaper, sat on Jade's other side. Across from the three of us was Ashanti, her boobs swelling beneath her cheerleader's sweater, and Melissa Kraus with her ever-present boyfriend, Marcus Dobbs. The conversation had risen near delirium as everyone tried to persuade Laura to use her clout as editor to petition for two no-homework-days a week.

Keir entered the cafeteria and waved. I rose on my knee and motioned for him to join us. He strode toward us, arms swinging, and slid into the sliver of a spot next to me. The table crashed into silence.

"Hey, Keir," Marcus finally said, adjusting his wire-rimmed glasses on the bridge of his nose.

Ashanti and Melissa whispered amongst themselves. The only noise at the once lively table was the clinking of flatware against the white cafeteria plates. Keir's expression changed from wary to haunted. He stood.

"Where are you going?" I asked.

"I need to get some lunch before I starve to death."

As I watched him make his way to the line, I said, "What's wrong with you guys? Why were you so rude?"

Ashanti shot a snide glance in Keir's direction and

leaned across the table, resting her chin on her fist. "Do you know who his brother is?"

"Yes."

Jade grabbed my forearm. "This is what I wanted to tell you earlier. You've got to stop hanging out with Keir. His brother is no good. His whole gang drinks and does drugs."

I focused on Melissa feeding Marcus a fry from her tray. "Lots of kids in high school drink and do drugs. You're not warning me about them. Keir's my friend. He's your friend too. You know he's clean."

Ashanti flipped her hair. "Look at the facts. Keir's brother is a thug. His father is MIA, and his mother is poor. She's a waitress at a diner, for God's sake. Keir has to help support her."

"You're saying I shouldn't like him because he's poor?"

Ashanti turned to Jade. "She's *so* not getting it."

Jade nodded, her expression grave.

My patience vanished into a rising wave of anger. "*What* don't I understand?"

Ashanti squinted, her smile hard. "It's simple. All we're saying is that if you want to hang around us," she jabbed a manicured finger at me, "you need to choose your friends carefully."

Melissa, suddenly interested in something besides hand-feeding Marcus, rumpled up her nose. "She's right, you know."

Alarm bells sounded in my head. If they found fault with him because of his family, what would they think if they ever met Sunshine or Sid?

The entire table stiffened. A set of strong hands rested on my shoulders. I craned my neck to see who was behind me.

"Oh, Keir." I blushed, ashamed of the conversation I'd been a part of seconds earlier. "Where's your lunch?"

"I left it over there." He pointed at a table two rows behind. "I promised Nero I would meet him to discuss video games."

Nero brushed his shaggy bangs to the side and waved.

"Do you want to join us?"

My new friends glared at me with *don't-you-dare* eyes.

I lost my voice.

Keir let out a long breath. "I'll catch up with you later."

"Oh…all r-right," I stammered.

He squeezed my shoulders once, and then he was gone. I felt as if I'd taken a test I was sure I'd ace and then failed. My lunch looked as appetizing as dog poop. I pushed it away.

"Good riddance to bad rubbish," Laura muttered to Keir's back.

I wanted to shove a fry up her nose. How could I have been so stupid? Keir had been more of a friend to me than any of this snotty crew. I rose from the table and bumped my shin on the attached bench. It hurt like hell, but I didn't care.

"Go on. Sit with him," Ashanti grumbled. "Ruin your reputation if you want, but you're not going to ruin ours."

I thought about slapping her with a snappy comeback but changed my mind. Sometimes it was better to take the high road.

Though I didn't deserve it, as always, Keir welcomed me with a smile.

****

So far, my day had been so-so, but soon it skidded to an abrupt halt. Art had always been my favorite class. Now it was the bane of my existence. I took a deep breath and stepped into the classroom. My anti-social tablemate was absent, but Charlie Fields wasn't. Nerves in my brain crossfired, and my head spun as I toe-heeled it to the back of the room. I slumped in my chair.

Hot breath tickled my neck. "Well, well, well, if it isn't Miss New Jersey in the flesh."

How did he know where I was from? Keir must have told him. And apparently, knowing I was friends with his brother hadn't changed a thing.

"Cut the bull, Charlie. You know my name. Your brother introduced us. Remember?"

"I sure do. Your name is Emerald, like that sexy little jewel you're sporting." He stretched across his worktable and reached for the side of my nose.

I leaned back so he couldn't touch me. "I'd prefer you call me Emmy."

"Whatever you want, hot stuff." He licked his finger, touched my shoulder, and made a sizzling noise.

"Just so you know, I'm not intimidated by you and your cliché display of machismo. Your tactics don't work any longer," I lied.

"Oh, yeah." He kneeled on his chair and leaned over until our noses were inches apart. He smelled like cinnamon gum.

"You can quit with the tough guy act. Keir's told me you're really a sheep in wolf's clothing."

"Keir? And you believed him." Charlie fell back in his chair, laughing.

Several students gawked at us. Mr. Hart banged his pointer on the edge of the Smart Board.

"Miss Russo? Mr. Fields? Do you have something funny you'd like to share with the class?"

I swung around and faced sixty probing eyeballs. "No, sir."

"Then how about you and your pal keep it down back there?"

Terrific. Now I had the teacher inferring we were buddies.

Charlie yanked a strand of my hair. "Emmy and Charlie sitting in a tree," he sang under his breath.

"Quit being a jerk," I whispered over my shoulder.

He kissed the air between us. I fondled the blob of clay lying on the center of my desk and contemplated shoving it in his mouth.

"Listen up, people," Mr. Hart said. "I want you to take note of the index card I placed on your table. Scribble down a word, any word. Then fold the card in two. I'll come around to collect them in a minute." He held up a plastic milk container he'd manufactured into a canister.

"What kind of word?" several voices chimed.

"Anything you want. But be kind. One of your neighbors will have to sculpt it."

After a few groans, the sound of pencils scratching on paper dominated the room. Mr. Hart circled, collecting the folded cards, occasionally shaking the contents of the jug. When he reached the last student, Tre'von Phillips, he invited him to select a card and circled back around the room, requesting each student to do the same. Some students cheered, some laughed, and others moaned as they read the word that would become their assignment.

By the time Mr. Hart reached my desk, there were only two choices. He allowed Charlie to pick and handed me the last. I unfolded my card. Scrawled in capital letters was the word *penis.* I folded the card, opened it, and reread it, and folded it again.

Charlie tapped me on the shoulder.

I mouthed. "What now?"

"You got my word." I looked at the small piece of paper and back at Charlie. He winked.

Of course, it was *his* word. How could it not be? And, in a sleight of hand, he made sure I'd gotten it. I ripped the card into tiny pieces and scattered it on the ground. Then I ground them into the floor with the ball of my foot.

"If you weren't Keir's brother, I'd turn you in."

Charlie's table bumped against the back of my chair. "I guess I lucked out twice, then?"

"What do you mean twice?"

"You're giving me a pass because of Keir. That's lucky. And you ripped up my word. That's really lucky."

"Why?" I'd already regretted asking.

"There's not near enough clay on your desk to do my junk justice."

"Pig," I said.

Charlie chuckled. "You're right. That last comment was rather boorish of me, but I'll make it up to you."

"Don't bother." I reeled around to face the front of the room.

Charlie ran his fingers from the base of my neck to

the roots of my hair. Ah, the old hair twisting game. I shifted positions, first crossing and then uncrossing my legs, hard-driven to ignore him. Undeterred, he walked his fingers downward and kneaded my shoulders. Flesh bumps shimmied down my arms, and the tiny hairs rose on the back of my neck. A boy sitting in the aisle next to us nudged his tablemate.

"Feels good, don't it," Charlie said in a throaty voice.

I couldn't lie to myself. His touch felt good. In fact, it felt better than good. I closed my eyes and gave in to the sensation, allowing my body to rock to the rhythm of his motion, my muscles melting like marshmallows over a blazing fire. Images appeared in my mind, flashing like a movie on fast-forward skipping frame to frame:

Charlie stood below a giant oak tree, a cigarette burning between his lips. A girl in a full skirt darted toward him. He flicked his cigarette and opened his arms. She crushed her body into his, flattening his back against the tree. He moaned and used her ponytail as a lever to ease her head back. Her lips parted, and he covered her mouth with his, devouring her with passion. I circled the trunk of the oak, desperate to see the face of the girl, the one who beguiled him so.

The girl was me.

I gasped, and my eyelids shot open. "How did you make me see that?"

Charlie fell back into his seat. His brows scrunched together. "See what?"

Telling him what I saw—or more like what I daydreamed—would be the same as handing a key to my heart to a lothario. I rubbed my temples.

"Do me a favor; don't touch me again."

"You sure? You seemed really into me."

"I could never be into you."

I scowled at him to show him I meant it. But as much as I wanted to deny it, as much as I told myself it wasn't so, Charlie was right. His touch had bewitched me.

And I hated myself for it.

Chapter 7
Dancing With The Devil

With a little ingenuity, I'd managed to avoid Charlie Fields for the rest of the week. It involved taking different routes in the hallway and cutting one art class, but it was worth it. The farther I stayed from him, the less he weighed on my mind and my emotions. Friday night was a few hours away, and I'd made plans.

None of them had anything to do with Charlie Fields.

****

Sunshine placed the platter of vegetarian lasagna in the center of the table, beside the organic greens. She settled in next to Sid. The two of them nuzzled together, acting like a couple of lovesick teenagers. I stared at them from the opposite side, consoled by the fact that I was genetically linked to only one of them. Whatever magic Sunshine saw in him, I didn't, but moping around and slamming doors hadn't changed anything. The wooly-bully was here to stay, and he treated me well, so I had no choice but to make the best of it.

Sunshine cleared her throat and cocked her head. From a peripheral glance, I noticed her staring at me. I ignored her and stuffed a bite of lasagna in my mouth. She placed both elbows on the table and rested her chin on her fists.

"Come on, Emerald, spill it. You know I can

always tell when you're hiding something."

Having an intuitive for a mother stunk.

"Keir is on his way over to pick me up. We're going to a party at Nero's house."

"I can see I'm going to have to drag it out of you." Sunshine clapped her hands. "Wait a minute. I've got it. You and Keir are dating. I should have known. No boy drives a girl to and from school and work every day if he isn't interested."

Sid dropped his fork. It clattered against his plate.

"Looks like Emmy's got herself a boyfriend."

"Quit it, Sid."

He tapped his finger on his temple and grinned. "What was it you were saying last week? Something about how you didn't want nothing to do with no man? What happened? Did *love* change your mind?"

"Shut up. He's just a friend."

"Okay, kiddos," Sunshine said. "I've had enough of this." Her green-eyed gaze darted between us. "Sid, you stop teasing Emerald. And Emerald, you treat Sid with the respect he deserves."

"Sorry," I said.

Sid dipped his head. "Sorry, Emmy."

Sunshine nodded once. "That's better." After a minute, entertained only by the sound of clanking forks, she raised her eyebrows a trifle. "Has he kissed you yet?"

I rolled my eyes. If Dad thought Keir was my boyfriend, he would have insisted on knowing his full name, rank, serial number, and where he bought his underwear. Sunshine only cared if he'd kissed me. Next, she'd be inviting him to crash in my room. My whole body flushed at the thought of it.

"You both need to stop. He's my best friend, and the last thing I want to do is mess that up."

Sunshine leaned back in her chair and gnawed on her lip. Most likely, she was using her psychic-voodoo-mind-reading thing to try to kidnap my thoughts. Her omniscient gaze set me on edge. If she thought I'd tell her about Charlie Fields, she had another thing coming. Besides, he was old news now.

Sid elbowed her, knocking her out of her trance. "Hey, I just remembered something. A friend of mine has a car for sale. It's a fixer-upper, but he's only asking seven hundred bucks for it. What do you say we buy it for Emmy? You'll like it, baby. It's a Bug."

Had I heard right? "You want to buy me a car?"

"Would you like that?" Sunshine grinned.

"Who wouldn't?" I pulled my plate back in front of me.

"Okay. We'll go check it out tomorrow," she said.

Wow. And after all the bratty things I'd said about him. "Thanks, Sid. That's nice of you."

"I ain't done nothing yet." He smiled so wide his lips disappeared in his beard.

The doorbell rang. In my excitement over the car, I'd forgotten about Keir.

"I'll get it."

Sunshine raced after me, reaching the kitchen archway at the same time, and after a struggle, she passed through first. Defeated, I leaned against the jamb and hid my eyes in the crook of my arm. She barreled through the living room and flung open the front door.

"Come on in."

"Thank you, Mrs. Russo," Keir said.

"Call me Sunshine," she cooed.

If she weren't so hung up on Sid, I'd have marched right in and accused her of flirting. Keir did look kind of hot in a gray hoodie, covering a wide-striped, blue and white shirt, and dark, cuffed, blue jeans resting atop his steel-toed boots.

"Hi, Emmy." His brows rose, and a broad smile stretched across his face.

Sunshine winked at me, and his smile widened.

Oh, no, she didn't just do that. I imagined strangling her with her dreadlocks.

Sunshine looped her arm through Keir's and tugged. "I have a lasagna in the kitchen. Would you like some?"

I wagged my head behind her back.

"Sure. That sounds great," he said, ignoring me.

Sunshine led Keir into the kitchen. Sid stood and offered him his gargantuan hand.

"Hi, buddy."

Keir accepted it. "Is that your bobber out there?"

Bobber? What's a bobber? Maybe it was something I could use to chop Keir's man-bits off if he didn't start listening to me.

"Bought it other day," he answered proudly as if were his first-born.

"Man, it's sweet. Is it a '69?"

"Yep. You really know your motorcycles, kid."

I sighed. The bobber was a useless motorcycle.

Sunshine thudded a plate of lasagna on the table and gestured for Keir to sit. He draped his hoodie over the back of the chair and settled in beside Sid. Between bites, the two of them conversed about Sid's new bike and every other motorcycle on the planet. Twenty minutes passed, and they were still yakking. I grabbed my thrift-store army jacket from the hall closet and tapped Keir on the shoulder.

"If we don't leave soon, it'll be time to come home before we even go out."

"Oh yeah, right, the party," he said, sounding disappointed.

I shuffled him through the goodbyes before he had a chance to back out, and soon we were on our way. Keir weaved through the neighborhood at a snail's pace, but when we reached Main Street, he stomped on the gas. We cruised through a few green lights and right past the street where Nero lived. I strained against the seatbelt and did a double-take.

"Hey, you missed the turn."

Keir pulled at his collar. "Charlie's having a party at the shop. He invited us to swing by."

Perspiration formed on my upper lip. "And when were you going to tell me?"

"I was working up the nerve. I know you don't like to hang with him and the boys."

"You're right. And I don't think it's a good idea to go tonight."

In fact, it was a horrible idea. Keir might be blind to Charlie's antics, but I wasn't, and I suspected the invitation was more for me.

"Tell you what. We'll stop by, say hello, and let him know we can't stay. I have to at least show my face. He's my brother, and he asked me to come."

I could see he was hellbent on going. Besides, how much harm could Charlie do in a few minutes? I would go. But only because Keir wanted me to. At least that's what I told myself.

"Since it means that much to you. Okay."

"Thanks, Em," Keir said as if I'd really done him a favor.

By the time we reached Jake's garage, it was full dark. He tossed me an apologetic look and opened his car door.

The sensible side of me thought to remain in the car and not pit brother against brother, but my other side—most likely inherited from my mother—was intrigued by Charlie's world. We got out.

The bass from the music inside buzzed against the bay doors. Keir pounded on the metal until it flexed and shuddered under his fist. Seconds later, the latch clanked, and the door flew up. Charlie stood before us. He wore a white T-shirt stretched across his well-defined chest. A tiny ache twitched in the pit of my stomach.

"Hey, little bro. You brought Emmy," he shouted above the music. "Come on in."

The shop was close to how I'd imagined it. Large toolboxes, steel workbenches, and metal cabinets lined the side and back walls. The Ghost sat between the two lift posts, illuminated by the florescent lights from above. Charlie lowered the door behind us and twisted the latch. The boys rushed Keir, shouting a chorus of "Hey, mans," and "long time no sees." Then they wrestled him to the ground.

Charlie grabbed Chuy by the belt and tossed him to the side. "Get off him, you lugs. You want to scare him off again?" He kicked Slick in his butt with his steel-toed boot. "Go on, get out of here."

Slick and a stout buzzed-haired guy named Shorty scrambled to their feet and strutted to the back of the shop. They joined Jason—the largest of the gang members, and the raccoon-eyed girl—the one I'd seen in Georgy G's parking lot. There were two other girls I didn't know: the first a slightly chubbed-out, faux redhead with bumper bangs, and the second, a heroin-thin blonde with pink-streaked hair and boobs bigger than mine. They lit up cigarettes. A hazy cloud of smelly smoke surrounded them.

Charlie offered Keir a hand up off the floor. The music changed to an up-tempo rockabilly song. Chuy flung his leather jacket on a workbench and dragged Charlie's girlfriend, Melody, to the center of the shop. They held hands and shuffled from side to side. He wound her in a tight counterclockwise circle, caught her by the lower back, and spun her out wide. Specks of crushed oil-dry dusted the air below their knees. He whirled her in a wide spin, and she grazed the top of his pompadour, leaving a few greasy, black locks hanging down on his forehead. Though vertically challenged, he led Melody through the dance as if he were six-foot tall.

Charlie pulled three beers from a mini-fridge. He passed two bottles to Keir and then peeled the cap off of the third with his teeth. In a move worthy of a frat-boy, he tipped back his head and chugged the entire beer in one gulp. Keir used the edge of a workbench to pry off the tops of the other two beers. He passed one to me.

"You don't have to drink this if you don't want to."

Charlie scrutinized me as if he were waiting for me to fail another of his tests. For reasons I couldn't explain, I longed to impress him, so I took the beer. Charlie's face lit up with a smug glow of self-congratulation. I wiped off the lid with my shirt and checked the bottle's lip for chips before drinking. The

53

bitter brew tasted terrible, but as the liquid went down, a wave of warm pleasure went straight to my brain. So I took another sip. Charlie walked to the back of the shop and whispered something in Shorty's ear.

Shorty scuffed over with his stubby legs and punched Keir in the arm. "Dude."

Beer splashed out of the neck of the bottle in Keir's hand. He brushed the drips off his shirt.

"Watch it. Will you?"

Shorty laughed. "A little suds never hurt anyone, sissy-boy."

Keir gave him a schoolyard shove. "Don't you have anything better to do? Like, get your butt out of here."

"No, seriously, man. My rod's idling rough. I'm going to get whiplash from all the bucking if I don't do something about it soon. Think you can help me out?"

"Can't you bother someone else?"

"I could, but you're the best." He slapped Keir on the shoulder.

Never in a million years did I think Keir would fall for Shorty's false flattery. But then his eyes glistened, and he said, "Pull it in."

"No can do," Shorty said. "Charlie don't want no more cars in here 'cause of the party. We got to go out to the lot."

Keir squeezed my elbow. "Want to come with us, Em?"

"You can't go anywhere without your mommy?" Shorty held his hands in mock prayer. "Please, please, *please,* can Keir come out to play?"

Shorty may have conned Keir but didn't fool me. He and Charlie were up to something. However, I was an independent woman. Anything Charlie could dish out, I could handle. I took a long swig of my beer, polishing it off, and wiped my mouth on the back of my hand.

"You two go ahead. I'll be fine."

Keir glanced back at me on his way out. I waved him forward, hoping I was truly as strong as I believed.

Chuy danced past with Melody and almost ran into me. I skipped to the side to avoid a collision and rocked back a little, my head spinning from the sudden movement. I found a tall stool in the back of the shop, climbed up, and rested my elbows on my knees. The music stopped.

Charlie stood at the boombox, fiddling with some CDs.

Melody braced her hands on her hips. "Hey, why'd you do that. It was a good song."

"I've got a better one," Charlie said. "This one's dedicated to Emmy."

Melody's face fell, and as if on cue, she stalked out of the shop. A door slammed from somewhere in the lobby. Any normal person would have felt sorry for her. I wanted to, but I enjoyed the attention Charlie afforded me. Why? I didn't know. I wasn't even sure I liked him.

The play button on the boom box clicked. Slow bluesy music with a sexy rhythm bled from the speakers. The skinny girl with the pink bangs slithered up to Slick and hauled him over to a darkened area on the far end of the shop.

Charlie swaggered across the floor in my direction, not stopping until his thighs were butted against my knees. My heart jumped, sputtered, and blasted off to the moon.

He snatched the beer out of my hands and set the empty bottle on the floor. "Come on, snake, let's rattle."

"Huh?" I coughed.

"Let me rephrase that for you." He held his hand out in front of me, palm up. "Miss New Jersey, may I have the pleasure of this dance?"

I swayed backward and grabbed the bottom of my stool to keep from falling. "I don't know how to dance."

"Don't worry, baby. I'll teach you."

My mind screamed, *Run away*! But my legs refused to cooperate. My mind screamed. *Tell him to get lost!* But I forgot how to speak. It was as if he were master of the universe, and I was his pawn. Everyone was. I could see through him but couldn't resist him. I didn't want to.

So I allowed Charlie Fields to drag me into the center of the shop.

We faced each other for a beat or two. Then he placed his arm around my shoulder and took my hand in his, positioning his body a respectable distance away. We danced, slow and reserved at first, but as the singer's wails intensified, so did Charlie's moves. His hips swayed from side to side, and he inched closer to me, smidgen by smidgen, until his pelvis ground against my hipbones.

Our bodies melded, moving together in perfect synchronicity. Side to side. Back and forth. He moved his hand to my lower back and pulled me closer. I took in a quick, sharp breath. He smelled of cinnamon and motor oil, and I had to make a concerted effort to breathe again.

"You know, baby," he murmured, "You and me have more than chemistry. We have fire. Not the easy kind of fire you can make from a box of matches, but the kind of fire you get when you rub two sticks together. I'm all yours if you want me."

The world around me blurred as if I were watching it through thick lenses. I imagined Charlie's lips against mine. I imagined him shirtless, propped above me, his triceps bulging as he slowly lowered his chest—mine rising toward his, beckoning him closer. He groaned a low animal-like sound. It drew me to him.

And I wanted him bad.

I wanted our bodies to burn in Hell together for all eternity.

What was happening? Had I lost my mind? I wasn't ready. Was I?

No.

Spasms of panic surged from my loins to the deepest recesses in my brain. In a sharp snap, the imaginary lenses cracked, and through the broken glass was a clear image of a boy with kind eyes and a halo of yellow hair.

Keir was my angel, and I was dancing with the devil. A devil who would betray his brother. A devil who would convince me to betray him as well.

I shuddered and pressed my free hand, fiercely against his shoulder. He clutched me tighter.

"Charlie, please. We can't do this."

"Why not?" he demanded.

I took in a long, ragged breath. "Because I don't want to hurt Keir. He likes me."

He forced a laugh and loosened his grip. My hand slipped from his, and he leaned toward me. His chin brushed against my cheek, and flesh bumps shimmied down my spine.

"That was the right answer, New Jersey," he whispered in a throaty voice. "Welcome to the gang."

Chapter 8
Don't Blame Emmy

Welcome to the gang? I took a quick step back and stared at Charlie. Surely, I'd misunderstood him.

"Don't look so doe-eyed," he said. "I can tell by the way you dance you ain't no goody-goody."

From where I stood, Slick and the skinny girl were barely visible in a darkened corner of the shop, but Melody stood in plain view. She locked her gaze on me. Had she seen us dancing? I'd screwed up and allowed Charlie to touch me again. Only this time, it was right in front of his girlfriend. Remorse washed over me like lava, scorching my skin, penetrating my every pore, and leaving no part of me guilt-free. Charlie seemed unfazed.

A ringtone sounded. Charlie pulled his phone from his back pocket. "What's up?" He paused while the caller's voice buzzed in the receiver. "Okay. Give me a half-hour, and I'll be there."

He left me in the center of the shop under Melody's seething glare while he went to work under the hood of The Ghost. I willed my legs to move and sought refuge on the same stool I'd used before.

Melody tramped over to Charlie and snuggled him from behind. He spun around, dipped her back like a tango dancer, and planted a sloppy kiss on her mouth. She giggled and smirked at me as he righted her.

My cheeks burned, and so did what was left of my ego.

"Go on, baby, scoot," Charlie said. "I'm trying to work."

He spanked her on the butt, and she flitted off and sat on a nearby workbench. Then, he looked at me and winked, his eyes glinting with wolfish inquisition. A sense of humiliation hit me, and I rubbed my cheek with my middle finger. He smirked, most likely taking my gesture literally, and turned back to the engine.

Charlie Fields was trouble. A big, fat, over-stuffed garbage bag of trouble. How could I have let him hold me that way? My heart ached with regret. So why did the thought of him kissing Melody piss me off?

The bell on the front door jingled. Seconds later, Keir jogged into the shop. He glanced about, searching. When he noticed me, his face slackened, and he hurried over.

"Was I gone too long?"

"No, not at all." I faked a smile.

Charlie walked in our direction. What was he up to now? I hopped off the stool and positioned myself closer to the door.

"Keir," Charlie said, "There's been a change of plan. We're moving the party to Thunder Road. You and Emmy should join us." He looked at me and grinned. "I'm racing Swartz and a few other saps from Huger. I'll give you a cut of the action."

Keir hesitated. Was he considering the invitation? If he agreed, I'd insist he take me home. I'd had all I dared of Charlie Fields for one night. Keir must have read my expression because he shook his head.

"Emmy and I already have plans."

Charlie threw his hands up and let them slap against his thighs. "Okay. Your loss." He looked directly at me. "And yours."

I gave him a dirty look.

"Lock up for me, would ya, Keir?" He dropped the keys into Keir's waiting palm. Then he cupped his hands around his mouth, creating a bone and flesh megaphone. "Time to agitate some gravel."

Gang members ran from every direction. Chuy and Shorty got into a shoving match over who had called shotgun first. Charlie slung his arm over Melody's shoulder and led her out, with the rest following close behind. The sound of gunning engines screamed the news of the gang's departure to anyone in a quarter-mile radius. The once lively shop stood empty except for Keir and me. He lifted my chin and turned my head from side to side.

"You look flushed. Are you okay?"

I rested my hand over his heart. The gentle thumping grew louder.

"I'm fine, just a little out of sorts."

"Let's go to Nero's," he said.

Even driving alone with Keir, I couldn't stop my mind from traveling to his brother. "Can I ask you something?"

He swerved, narrowly missing a pothole. "Sure."

"Why does everyone at school hate Charlie?"

"Not everyone hates him, Em." Keir sounded politely exasperated.

"Okay, let me rephrase that. Why do ninety-two percent of the student body hate him?"

We stopped at a traffic light.

"Maybe it's because he's not a follower. He

61

doesn't care what people think of him, and I don't either. One day he'll do good things with his life. I can feel it."

The sincerity in Keir's voice cut through me like a knife. How could I ever tell him what Charlie—what we'd—been doing behind his back.

"You really love him, don't you?"

"Why wouldn't I?"

I opened my mouth but shut it again. Some things were better left unsaid.

"He cares about people. Take Chuy, for example. He used to get picked on all the time. This year no one has the guts to mess with him.

"That's a good thing."

"He helped Slick too. Remember, Slick the loner, dressed in black, lurking in the hallways, not saying a word? Everyone joked he'd come to school one day with a shotgun in his hand. Hell, even we used to call him psycho."

I squeezed the armrest as Keir accelerated. "Yeah. I feel bad about that."

"Well, Charlie saw the good in him and took him under his wing. Now he even has a girlfriend."

"Are you saying Charlie is like a champion for the underdogs?"

"Yep."

I rolled down my window an inch to get some air. "Jason seems pretty normal. What's his story?"

"Two years ago, he got busted for breaking into a neighbor's home. His parents refused to pay for a lawyer, and the judge threw the book at him. When he got out of juvie, his parents sent him to Moncks Corner to live with his grandmother. Charlie met Jason at Lake

Moultrie. Jason had a gun ready to blow his brains out, and Charlie talked him out of it."

I shuddered. "That's horrible. Is he getting help?"

"Don't know. But he seems okay now."

"What happened to the gun?" I asked, hoping it wasn't lying somewhere waiting to go off.

"Charlie said he chucked it into Lake Moultrie so no one would know."

I turned and faced him, wide-eyed. Keir exhaled.

"He had to. It was stolen."

How low had I sunk? I was drinking and cavorting with criminals.

"I'm almost afraid to ask about Shorty."

"Nothing to speak of. He was like, invisible."

That was true. I'd seen him around for three years, and I didn't even know his name. Keir shifted, repositioning himself in his seat.

"The people who hate Charlie don't know him. Underneath that tough guy act is a heart of gold."

"The way you rave about him, you make it sound as if he were on a mission to save the world. Are you sure helping people is his only motive?"

"What else could it be, Em?"

I could think of a few things like manipulation, the need to be worshiped, or the desire to rule the world. But most disturbing: why had Charlie chosen me? What was my flaw? My parents' divorce? My mother's freakiness?

Me in general?

Chapter 9
The Invitation

The next day, Keir and Sid returned with my car—which I christened Baby Dub—and went to work. Sunshine and I sat at the kitchen table sipping herbal tea, watching the two remove sooty, black pieces of metal from the engine and replace them with shiny new ones. The clouds shifted, allowing the dull sunlight to breakthrough. Sid and Keir stopped what they were doing for a moment and looked at the sky.

"They work so well together," Sunshine said. "Sid thinks the world of him."

"He's a good friend."

She pinched my cheek. No matter how many times I'd told her differently, she believed Keir was my boyfriend, so I gave up trying to convince her otherwise.

"Come on. I've got an idea you're going to like."

Sunshine dragged me to the kitchen door, poked her head outside, and summoned Keir with a curl of her arm. He wiped his hands on a rag and jogged to the foot of the deck.

"What'd you need, Miss Sunshine?"

"I'd like to invite your family to dinner next weekend."

Keir's grin faded. His gaze flicked down to the ground and back up again. "We won't be able to make it. Mama's shift at the diner doesn't end until eleven."

Sunshine's brows furrowed. Seconds later, she slapped her thigh and broke into a smile.

"We'll have dinner at eleven fifty-five. That will give your mama plenty of time to get a shower and change. Bring Charlie and his girlfriend too. There's nothing better than a midnight meal."

"That sounds great," he said. "I'll have her call you tomorrow to confirm."

Sunshine side-hugged me and said, "Having your family here will make Friday special for us.

"Thanks, Miss Sunshine. That's really cool." Keir gave her a two-finger salute.

The idea of watching Charlie with his girlfriend all night was about as appetizing as dog poo, but the wide grin on Keir's face made it almost worth it.

****

That evening, after cleaning up Sid's tools, Keir and I headed back to Jake's Garage. I sensed we were making a gigantic mistake, but Keir loved his brother, so visiting the garage seemed like a small sacrifice. Who was I kidding? I wanted to see Charlie Fields, too.

When we arrived, he and the boys were gathered under the hood of The Ghost, elbows deep in grease. Melody and Jason's girlfriend, Layla, were sharing a cigarette and bottle of beer in the back seat. Apart from a few distracted nods, no one paid much attention to Keir or me.

The Ghost's massive engine looked like a naked letter W, more ferocious but less complicated than the high-tech bundle of steel and wires crammed into my dad's newer model car.

Keir nudged Charlie. "Getting her ready for a race

tonight?"

Charlie scratched his nose with his wrist. "Yep. I picked up a new set of high-performance springs. Maybe now I can get in a few good runs before the cam chews them up."

He squeezed the trigger on his impact gun, and a high-pitched squeal whirred through the shop. Charlie had yet to acknowledge my presence, and it ticked me off.

I cleared my throat. "How does an engine chew up springs?"

Charlie sighed and rolled his eyes. "Explain it to her, will ya, bro?"

"The cam lobes open the valves. The higher the lift, the more air/fuel mixture in and more exhaust out, which means more power, but also more stress on the springs…" Keir stopped short.

My lack of knowledge about cars must have been apparent.

"In other words, stock springs break."

"Oh. Makes sense," I said, even though it didn't.

Sid's muscle car magazines had sat on the end table, untouched by me for too long. I'd have to start reading them if I was ever going to fit in with this crowd.

Did I just consider fitting in with The Back Lot Gang?

What was wrong with me? A few short weeks ago, I hated Charlie Fields. I still wanted to loathe him, but for some crazy reason, I was drawn to him and his motley pack of greasers. And, whatever the reason, it was surely more than just a need to please Keir.

Chuy poked his nose out from under the hood.

"Charlie's going to kick butt tonight."

"Who's the victim?" Keir asked.

"Tell him, Charlie." Chuy rubbed his greasy palms together.

Charlie straightened and stretched his back. "Paul Middleton."

My jaw dropped. "He's the captain of the football team. He'll be kicked off the team if he gets caught."

Charlie exaggerated a yawn, patting his mouth with his hand. "Keir? You better move your beauty queen away from The Ghost. She might get grease on those designer threads of hers."

The boys snickered, and an overwhelming sense of pride rose inside me. How dare they laugh at me?

"I'm not worried about a little grease. I'll prove it to you. Put me to work."

Keir stared at me as if I'd lost my mind. So did all the boys. Charlie's lips sputtered as he coughed out a laugh.

"You? Work on a car? I bet you don't even know what a wrench is."

He was challenging me, and if I backed down now, I'd be fodder for his jokes for the rest of the evening, and possibly for all eternity.

"Of course, I know what a wrench is. I used to help my dad change the oil on his car."

"Then go over to my toolbox and find a 9/15 inch boxed-end."

My stupid pride had gotten in the way of my sanity. Unwilling to back down, I threw back my shoulders and walked to the enormous red toolbox, determined to impress all of them with my knowledge of tools. I rooted through the drawers until I found a line of uniform, multi-sized metal contraptions that matched a long-forgotten mental image of a wrench.

"There's a 9/16 here, but your 9/15 is missing."

A rumble of laughter formed a cloud of ridicule above me. My cheeks burned.

"What's so funny?"

The boys hee-hawed louder, holding on to each other for support. When my traitor best friend's lips twitched upward, it dawned on me. I'd been set up. I braced a hand on my hip and glared at the lot of them.

"I get it. There is no such thing as a 9/15 wrench. I knew that. I just forgot."

Charlie laid a hand over his heart. "From unborn to newborn in sixty seconds. What an accomplishment. Bring the 9/16, baby, and I'll give you your first job."

I hesitated. Was he actually going to make me use the thing? Charlie summoned me with three slow curls of his finger. I picked up the greasy wrench and edged toward him, taking care to stop a safe distance away. He shook his head, grabbed hold of me, and spun me around, pinning my hips against the fender cover. Then he draped his arm over my shoulder.

"Do you see that bolt on the alternator bracket?" He pointed to a round contraption with a metal fan thingy on the front.

"Yeah, the alternator, right," I said.

"Break it loose."

I stretched across the fender and locked the round end of the wrench on the bolt. Then I licked my lips and tugged. It didn't budge. Everyone snickered, including Melody and Layla, who'd abandoned their bottle of cheap ale to watch the show. I yanked harder, grunting with the effort. The bolt, still frozen, snickered at me too. Charlie stretched across me, covering me like a blanket.

"Let me help you with that."

My skin tingled as if I were ensnared in a static-charged cobweb. Was he aware of how seductive he sounded? He cupped his hand over mine and positioned my fingers around the neck of the wrench.

"Now, when I say three, pull hard with a quick counter-clockwise jerk."

"Okay. A counter-clockwise jerk." My voice had gone all screechy.

He let go of my hand and straightened up, leaving his pelvis pressed against my rump. My breath hitched and flowed out jaggedly. Where was Keir? Had his *brother worship* dazzled him into denial? I dared not look, nor complain. The waves of shimmering tingles shooting through my entire body encouraged me not to.

"Alright. Go on the count of three," Charlie said. "One." He pulsed against me. "Two."

He pulsed against me again. Determined not to let him get to three, I mutinied and yanked the wrench with all my might. The bolt broke loose. My knuckles scraped against the jagged blades of the alternator fan, and the wrench clattered to the ground. I clamped my injured fingers with my good hand and jumped backward, knocking Charlie out of the way.

"Damn, damn, damn, that hurt."

Keir grabbed my wrist and tried to pry my hand open. "Hold still, let me see what you've done to yourself."

"No. I'm afraid to look," I said.

"Em, please? I need to see how bad you're hurt."

I loosened my grip. Two slimy, red, mangled flaps

of skin hung from my second and third knuckle. My knees buckled, and Keir grabbed me around the waist. I dangled like a rag doll while the world faded to hazy yellow. After a few forced breaths, everything came back into focus.

"You'll be okay," Charlie said. "It's only a few busted knuckles."

"Thanks to you," I snapped.

Charlie picked up the wrench. "Hey, Slick. Grab me an alternator belt from the cabinet, will you?"

I imagined snatching the wrench back and bopping him between his eyes. Before I got a chance, Keir escorted me to the sink in the men's room. He stuck my hand under a stream of warm water. I gritted my teeth.

"Thanks for helping me."

"Charlie's gone too far. I'll have a serious talk with him."

About me? If anyone told Keir what, if anything at all, was going on between Charlie and myself, it had to be me. I struggled to pull my hand free.

"No, don't. I mean, I don't want to cause trouble between you and your brother. He didn't mean any harm."

"Calm down. We need to clean your wound."

"Please, Keir. Don't start anything with Charlie."

"Okay, if you don't want me to, I won't. Just hold still."

I took a deep breath and let it out. Keir examined my fingers.

"Don't mess with wrenches anymore, okay, Em? You don't belong under the hood of a car."

Something about not belonging under the hood struck a flat note. Between Charlie's antics and Keir's over-protectiveness, I felt rather insignificant.

"Are you saying I'm not capable of working on cars because I'm a girl?"

His eyes widened, and his mouth opened and closed a couple of times like a goldfish gulping air. "I never…It's just that girls—"

"Geez, Keir, give me a break. Everybody knows women can do anything men can." I wrapped my fingers in a paper towel and headed into the shop with Keir following at my heels. I ignored all the stares from the boys, spun around to face him, bracing a fist on my hip. "Unless you think I'm too dumb?"

"You're about as dumb as a fox in a chicken coop," Charlie muttered from under the hood of The Ghost.

"Lay off her," Keir growled. "Haven't you done enough damage for one night?"

Charlie stepped back from the car and straightened. "Ah, little bro. Always trying to be the knight in shining armor."

I glared at him. "Why don't you shut up? You're just jealous because Keir is a gentleman."

As soon as the words left my mouth, I realized my mistake. This wasn't the crowd to appreciate that sort of sentiment.

"Ain't that sweet," Shorty cooed.

Melody and Layla looked at each other and giggled. The boys removed their ballcaps and bowed. Keir's cheeks reddened. I'd embarrassed him in front of the whole gang. I owed him an apology, but first, I had to fix my mangled hand.

"Where are the bandages?" I asked.

"They're in the medical cabinet in Jake's office. I'll show you," Keir said.

"No, stay here and help your brother. He'll need all he can get if he wants to impress me at the race tonight."

The boys looked at me, gape-mouthed.

Melody huffed. "Like he wants to impress you."

Charlie's wrench clinked against the metal frame of the car. "You want to go to Thunder Road?"

"I sure do."

Keir's face lit up like a birthday cake for a centenarian. "That's great, Em,"

Charlie blinked a few times, and for the first time since I'd known him, he appeared anything but one-hundred percent confident.

"All righty then. We'll see you at Thunder Road at nine."

Chapter 10
The Race

Following the parade of Back Lot gang cars, we exited the main highway and turned onto a two-lane road lined with live oaks. The tree's massive branches, twisted and bone-like, stretched and strained to form a cathedral of bark and leaves above us. The tunnel lasted for at least two miles before we reached the clearing on Thunder Road. Charlie got out and paced the yellow line with tomcat grace, the three-quarter moon casting a bluish aura about him.

A case of fleeting jitters traveled down my spine and settled in my stomach. Part of me felt terribly out of place attending a street race on a desolate road, where I was on the wrong side of the law. At least for the night.

Keir got out and opened my door.

"I can do that myself, you know," I said, still stinging from his macho girls-can't-be-mechanics comment.

"I was raised in the South, ma'am. You'll have to get used to it." He bowed and offered me his arm. Playing along, I accepted his help, and daintily climbed out. Then I stomped on his foot as I brushed past.

He caught me by the elbow. "Watch it, lady."

A long, loud screech pierced the foggy night. Shorty's Chevelle headed straight for us. Keir yanked me off the road and into the brambles. Charlie ran in front of The Ghost and spread his arms wide, positioning himself as if he believed he had the power to fend off a four-thousand-pound machine. The car fishtailed once, spun in a half-circle, and came to a halt with a set of wheels on either side of the dotted line. Shorty rolled down the window.

"Where do you want me?"

Charlie smoothed his hair and pointed into the distance. "You be my eyes tonight, 'kay, Shorty?"

"Sure thing, boss." He turned the car around and gunned the motor.

Clouds of burning rubber wafted off into the field and burned my nasal membranes as we climbed back onto the easement. Shorty stopped about a quarter mile down, just beyond the edge of the clearing. His rod's round headlamps stared at us like two yellow cat's eyes in the darkness.

Charlie returned to pacing, his long shadow dancing along beside him. Back and forth, back and forth, he strode, his breath heavier with every pass. Abruptly, he circled The Ghost and threw open the passenger door.

"Melody, get out."

"Wait a minute, would you," she said, with her cell phone glued to her ear.

"I said, *now*. Go yak in Keir's ride."

"Whatever." She rolled her eyes, then turned to Keir.

He tipped his head, and she shambled to the Mustang and closed herself in.

"Middleton's late," Charlie growled.

I glanced at my cell. "It's not nine yet."

"Well, I'm too hyped to stand here any longer. I'm

taking a ride. Come with me. I'll show you what racing is all about."

"Me?" I gulped.

"Yeah."

The chance to ride in the cherished passenger seat of The Ghost overrode any thoughts I had of danger.

"Yeah, I'll go," I said, lowering my voice to exude confidence.

"Your chariot awaits." He opened the door and gestured for me to get in.

Keir latched onto my wrist. "I don't know. It's kind of dangerous."

Charlie stepped toward him; his chest puffed out. "Don't be a jerk. Emmy says she wants a ride, and I'm going to give her one."

Keir tightened his grip. "I don't like it."

His voice was strong yet pleading. If it were more than just the ride's danger that worried Keir, he certainly didn't say so.

I glanced at my wrist—the one he had the garrote-like hold on. "Do you mind?"

He held tight. Charlie pursed his lips, looked at the heavens first, down to hell second, and finally straight at Keir.

"Listen, little bro; I'm not sadistic. I won't open it wide with your beauty queen in the front seat."

Keir's face contorted. "You really want to ride with him, Em?"

The reckless genes I'd inherited from Sunshine begged for satisfaction.

"I've come all the way to Thunder Road. I might as well get the whole experience."

"Fine, go." He turned to Charlie. "You better take

it easy."

Charlie slapped his back. "You got no worries. I'll take care of her."

Keir loosened his grip, and with my heart pumping, I stumbled forward.

Forward toward fear. Forward toward excitement. Forward toward Charlie Fields.

The Ghost reeked of cigarette smoke. Still, I slammed the car door before Keir or Melody, or my better judgment could stop me. Charlie ambled around the car at his usual pace, somewhere between languid and cool. He slipped in the driver's seat and positioned himself behind the wheel.

"Put your seat belt on."

I laughed. "If you're such a good driver, why do I need one?"

"Cut it out, New Jersey. Buckle up, or hop out."

I pouted, toying with him, but Charlie's dark, unyielding gaze bored right into my psyche, making me feel naked inside and out. I mocked him under my breath and then groped around on the floor until I found the buckle and fastened it across my lap. Charlie cranked the car. The engine roared like a tortured demon. Blood thrummed through my body. He slipped the shifter to D, and The Ghost rolled onto the highway. The floor pan rumbled, sending vibrations through the soles of my feet to my knees.

As we crept forward, Charlie rattled off the unwritten rules of street racing.

One, don't drive drunk.

Two, don't race when your gut says no.

Three, don't race in town where there's traffic on the road.

Four, never assume the other driver is on the up and up.

And number five, always, always, always have fun.

At a speed barely above an idle, we rolled past Shorty's car and entered the darkened tunnel of trees on the other side of the clearing. When we were out of view from the crowd, Charlie stepped on the brakes. We were alone in the dark. Every nerve in my body combusted.

"You know, New Jersey," he said. "Most of the time, you act all sensible and stuff, but you have a wild streak. I can smell it. The first time I saw you, I said to myself, now there goes a lady who's looking for trouble." He sniffed the air. "Yep, cinnamon and ashes, the scent of trouble, that's what you smell like."

Cinnamon? How weird. That was his smell.

I opened my jacket and sniffed my shoulder. "I smell like laundry detergent, and I never look for trouble. Perhaps you don't know me as well as you think you do, Charlie."

He rested his arm on the back of my seat and eyed me as if I were a cherry tart he wanted to gobble up. "Oh, I *know* you, all right. I bet I could read your mind if I tried."

"In your dreams," I said, though I doubted him not.

Charlie pinched a lock of my hair and twirled it. "What are you doing messing with Keir? I mean, he's a good kid and all, but he's hardly your speed."

"I'm not messing with Keir. He's my best friend."

"He has other ideas about your relationship."

The heat from Charlie's breath tickled my cheek. "How do you know?"

He fell back against his seat. "Here you go again,

77

playing dumb like a fox."

"If you think Keir's into me, then why are you hitting on me?"

Charlie's eyes twinkled, and he smiled something filthy in French. "I see you have a hard time believing I care about the kid, New Jersey. But *me and you* have nothing to do with him. What's that saying?" He cocked his head. "All's fair in love and war?"

"I'm sure Keir would agree with that." My voice oozed sarcasm.

"The real question here is why are you flipping your wig over him?" Charlie stroked the back of my neck.

I fought off his black magic spell and straightened my spine. "Why don't you tell me, Mr. Know-it-all?"

"Because I want to hear you say it." He held his gaze steadfast and rolled his hand.

He was trying to rattle me, but I could be as tough as him. "You'll make me break your little heart."

Charlie roared with laughter. "Go on. I can take it."

"If you're sure?"

He smirked.

I was determined not to let him get the better of me again. "Keir is smart, and he's giving, and he's kind. Everything you're not."

"Bam! Pow! That hurt." Charlie rubbed his cheek mockingly as if I'd slapped him.

I smiled. "There'll be no more talk of you and me, then?"

He shrugged. "Okay, no problem."

Ouch. That did hurt.

"I do have one little question."

I clucked my tongue. "Go ahead, ask."

"I'm Keir's blood, so no matter what happens, I'll always be in his life. If you think you're going to keep him in yours as *best friend*, you're wrong. He might be a wimp, but he's still a guy. As for me, I don't stay on hold with a lady for long. So, tell me, who do you want to spend your quality time with?"

I hadn't expected that. And I wasn't sure I wanted to respond. The old me, the good girl from New Jersey, wouldn't have choked. She would have told Charlie to take a hike. But the new me didn't want to let him go.

What was it about this strange boy with greased hair that attracted me so?

"What's the matter, New Jersey? Cat got your tongue?"

My face flushed. "Why don't you quit asking me ridiculous questions and do something that you're good at?"

"What's that?"

"Drive, Teddy Boy."

One of Charlie's brows tipped upward in a cocky salute. His knuckles whitened as he gripped the T-shifter, while rivers of veins formed on his muscular forearm. With a look of steely determination etched on his face, he slammed the shifter into first gear and jammed the accelerator pedal to the floor. The car rocketed forward. My head slammed against the seatback, and I dug my nails into the black tuck and roll upholstery.

"You scared, New Jersey?" Charlie asked, his eyes aflame.

"No," I said as the blood left my face.

"Then hang on, baby, 'cause you're about to go for the ride of your life."

Charlie slammed the shifter back to two. The live oaks blurred into a solid wall as The Ghost swallowed the pavement in front of us. Adrenaline rushed through my body, and I closed my eyes, hoping to stop an encroaching case of motion sickness. All the while, a grainy movie played in my head.

The doors rattled, and the seat trembled below me. The car dipped, screeched against the ground, and sprung upward. I covered my ears, and we took flight. In the next second, I was upside down, right side up, upside down again.

Shards of glass gouged my skin, and the sharp snap of my bones cracking hijacked my senses. Just when I thought I'd be sent to hell for all my sins, we came to a spine-jarring halt. My head hit the pillar post, and the rusty taste of blood filled my mouth, followed by pain that burned every ounce of my body, layer by layer, right down to the marrow.

Then something warm and gooey flooded my seat. Charlie's head lay in my lap, blood pouring from a gash in his skull. I screamed, but no sound came out. My mind, unable to tolerate any more, combusted into a million tiny pieces, and my world went black.

My eyes shot open. I had to stop Charlie before he killed us both. "Slow down."

He ignored me, his face taut and focused on the road.

Instinct told me to speak calmly and not to panic. "Please, Charlie? You're scaring me."

His expression softened ever so slightly.

"Please," I tried again.

Charlie eased off the gas and coasted down to a reasonable rate of speed. I melted into my seat.

"The power in this car gives me a hard-on," he crowed.

My gaze fell to his lap. An unexpected shimmer of excitement jolted from my head to my toes when I saw he was telling the truth.

"So, New Jersey," he said. "You like the kind of ride I can give you?"

I imagined my face cherry red as Shorty's hotrod. "It's okay."

"Just okay?" Charlie punched the gas.

I caught myself on the dash. "Stop it."

He pumped the accelerator pedal, dancing the car down the road. The front end dipped and rose. A nanosecond later, the rear tires followed in the same motion. The same motion I'd felt in the strange vision I'd had moments earlier, only less intense.

"What was that?"

"That was the infamous Thunder Road Bump."

"The what?"

"I'm surprised you haven't heard about it. That bump's put a lot of worthy cars—and some worthy souls—into the graveyard."

I swallowed. "How do you mean?"

"The fastest anyone has been able to take on the Bump, and not total their car, is eighty miles an hour. I'm aiming for one-hundred and twenty."

"Why would you risk totaling your car, or even worse, killing yourself to break a record that no one cares about?"

Charlie cranked the wheel hard to the left. I anchored myself to the armrest, and the rest of the world followed us in a haze. When we quit spinning, we were speeding in the opposite direction. The corners of his mouth twitched up into a wicked grin.

"Can't you drive like a normal person?" I pulled my seatbelt tighter.

"Maybe for a kiss."

"I can't kiss anyone with my skull plastered to the back of the seat."

"Then it's a good thing I like you." He slowed the car down to a crawl.

"He likes me. He really likes me. Lucky me."

"Why don't you stop stalling? Kiss me. You know you want to," he said, tapping his finger on his lips.

Pillowy and rose water pink, they were sort of tempting. Oh, no way. What was I thinking? If I couldn't convince myself whatever we had going between us was wrong, maybe I could convince him.

"I don't want your cooties."

"Hmm. I suspected you'd chicken out."

He fiddled with the radio, settling on an oldies station. Charlie bobbed his head in time with the music. "They don't make tunes like they used to."

"They certainly don't," I said. "Rockabilly died years ago."

"The things you say, girl. It will never die. Seek, and you will find."

At the edge of the range of the headlamps, the menacing ripple appeared in the stream of the perfectly flat pavement. We rolled over the Bump again—a mere annoyance at our rate of speed.

"Look here, New Jersey. Maybe the record ain't on the books nowhere, but anyone who is anyone in this town knows the Thunder Road Bump is legendary. Once I make that jump, I'll be a legend, too."

I sighed. If Charlie believed driving one-hundred-

and-twenty miles per hour over a bump would make him famous, who was I to argue? So many strange things had happened recently, Moncks Corner felt more like another planet.

By the time we made it back to the clearing, a crowd had gathered, and many new vehicles lined the opposite side of the road. Mixed in the middle of a convoy of monster pick-up trucks, sat an old car with fins that ran to the end of the trunk. Charlie swung The Ghost around and parked it.

"See that?" He pointed to the car.

I nodded.

"That's Paul's rod. It's a worthy ride, but his rich daddy's money won't buy him victory. I'm going to whip him to a pulp tonight."

I paused, deliberating his words. "How can you be so sure?"

"Because the boy ain't got no rhythm."

"Rhythm? What does that have to do with driving a car?"

"It has nothing to do with driving, baby, but everything to do with winning. He's not in sync with the motor. The boy don't have it. When it's time to change gears, he screws the pooch." He jerked his hand back, pantomiming a shift. "In a race, syncing with the engine is everything."

"You make driving a car sound like playing a musical instrument."

"It is when you do it right." Charlie sucked in a breath and patted the steering wheel. "New Jersey, it's been fun, but I've got to go. I'll catch up with you later."

He winked at me and then climbed out of the car.

As he strutted across the road, a heavy feeling settled in my chest. I shook my head. How had I gone from confused about Charlie to obsessed in less than an hour? I was a dope. That's how.

Melody appeared from out of nowhere and scuffed after him. She stopped in front of The Ghost for a second to sneer at me. I sent I-hate-you-vibes in her direction. Though I'd never intended it to happen, we'd become rivals.

The car door opening startled me. Keir stood in my view.

"So did Charlie scare you?"

"Not at all. He drove like a perfect gentleman," I said, hoping to avoid an I-told-you-so.

He tilted his head and frowned a little. "I'm not sure I believe you."

He gave me his hand, urging me out of The Ghost. I grabbed on tight, hoping my incredulous infatuation with his brother might vanish through osmosis.

We joined the rest of the gang while Charlie and Paul hashed out the details of the race. A tense coupled of minutes passed before the rivals shook hands. Charlie returned, his expression determined.

"Okay, guys, the winner's pot is a grand. You'll all get a cut. So, let's do this thing right." He reached in his pocket, pulled out a wad of bills, and shoved them at Slick. "Give this to Paul's girl."

Slick regarded the contents. "Hey, you promised I could do the honors."

Charlie raked a hand through his hair, his nose pointed at the sky. "Paul's girl gets to hold the money because Emmy's flagging the race."

Me? Flagging? I dug my nails into Keir's arm. He

smiled as if he was proud that I'd been chosen.

Slick's brows rose. "Oh. I get it. One girl from their side and one from ours. Makes sense."

At least someone understood what Charlie said.

Charlie shoved him. "Now, get moving before I go ape on you."

Slick headed across the road with the money. Charlie threw open the trunk of The Ghost.

"Heads up, New Jersey."

A flashlight came sailing in my direction. I caught it mid-air.

"What am I going to do with this?"

He rolled his eyes. "Come here, and I'll show you."

"But I-I…" I lost my voice.

Charlie tugged me to the centerline of the road, stood behind me, and placed a hand on my waist. My skin flushed with warmth at his touch. While Keir's brother worship had obviously blinded him, Melody shot deserved daggers at me with her gaze.

I tried to listen as Charlie fed me the instructions, but his breath tickled my cheek, and his words faded to blips of sound in space and time. Next thing I knew, Paul and Charlie were pulling their cars forward, their engines vibrating the pavement below my feet. My legs went all rubbery.

The race that seemed only a dream thus far was on.

Chuy and a guy from Paul's posse got down on their knees and examined the front bumpers. They instructed both drivers to inch forward or back until it was decided the cars were aligned. My body trembled as I raised the flashlight in front of me as Charlie had instructed. I counted to three, closed my eyes, and switched on the light.

The cars screamed by in a tornado of dust and debris. By the time I turned around, the taillights had disappeared into the tunnel of trees. Moments later, the insane growling of the motors died, then a neverending silence.

Finally, Shorty emerged from the tree-line and shouted, "We won."

Keir threw his arms around me and lifted me off the ground.

Slick pumped his fists. "Charlie is the man!"

Jason, Layla, and Melody hugged each other, jumping and screaming.

Chuy dashed across the road to Paul's girlfriend with his hand out. She slapped the money in his palm.

He waved it in the air, yelling, "*Adelante,* Charlie!

Paul's crowd stood motionless; their silence was as loud as the gang's jubilation. The Ghost emerged from under the tunnel of trees and rumbled toward us with Paul's car trailing behind. Charlie cruised past at a crawl, waving like he'd won a million bucks.

The boys surrounded The Ghost. They pulled Charlie from the car and hoisted him on their shoulders. All this fuss over a ten-second race. Still, I couldn't stop the bubble of pride from bursting inside me. We had won. And this time, I was a part of it all.

****

After the race, we met up in the parking lot of Jake's Garage. Charlie divvied the money amongst the gang members and Keir. He pivoted around, handed me a few crisp bills, and stuffed the rest in his pocket. Melody threw an arm over Layla's shoulder and held her palm out.

"Did you forget about us?"

Charlie's eyes narrowed. "You know ladies don't get a cut."

"Emmy looks like a lady to me," Melody whined.

There was a heavy silence. "She flagged the race, airhead."

"I wanted to, but you wouldn't let me." She blew a puff of cigarette smoke in Charlie's face.

I'd seen Melody do a lot of aggravating things, but that was just wrong. The veins in Charlie's neck throbbed, and he smacked the cigarette out of her hand. Melody stepped backward, leaving a wide-eyed Layla standing alone in front of him. Charlie spun around and kicked the tire of The Ghost. A stream of profanity spewed from his mouth.

Keir placed a protective arm over my shoulder. "Come on. We're out of here."

Melody's chin dropped, and she flashed a watery smile as she edged toward the front doors of the shop. I hesitated.

"He won't hurt her," Keir said. "Let's go."

****

We rode in silence while I stewed. How did a night that started so good end so miserably? More disturbing, how could I have felt an attraction to such a brute? Charlie had gone too far.

And what was fast becoming a happenstance, the farther I was from him, the less I liked him. Nearly home, my attraction to him had dropped toward nonexistent.

"Sorry you had to see that," Keir said.

"It's not your fault. Your brother's a jerk."

He sighed. "He's not. He's under pressure."

"So is everyone else in the world. It doesn't excuse his behavior."

We rolled into my driveway, and Keir cut the engine.

"Listen, I promised Charlie that I wouldn't tell anyone, but hell. Last night, Melody told Charlie she was pregnant."

My throat went dry. "Omigod."

"Melody's been drinking and smoking the whole time. The cigarette must have been the last straw. He says he doesn't love her, but this morning he asked her to marry him. He planned to give her a ring tonight."

Of course, Charlie was angry. Any guy would be if he caught his pregnant girlfriend drinking and smoking. But that didn't excuse his behavior, or even worse, his flirting with me. Charlie was going to be a father. It was time he acted like one. From here on out, I'd do my best to avoid him. I would pretend he didn't exist.

I'd do it for Keir's sake, for the baby's sake, and maybe even for my own.

Chapter 11
The Dare

I'd vowed to avoid Charlie and avoid him, I had. Lucky for me, a girl in my art class moved, and I took her seat on the opposite side of the room. On my fifth Charlie-free day, I believed I'd broken his spell once and for all.

In between classes, the hallways echoed with the buzz of indistinct voices. If I believed in ghosts—which I didn't—I would have presumed the spirit of every student who had ever attended Moncks Corner High had come back to cheer me on in my effort.

Then I heard it, the thump, thump, thump of heavy footsteps. Charlie and the boys marched toward me in V-formation, all sporting greasy hair and dressed in jeans and black leather jackets. Students scrambled out of their path, nearly pinning themselves to the lockers to keep from being trampled. Charlie glanced at me and raised an eyebrow in a movement so slight, surely only I had noticed it. The leather-clad procession continued full speed ahead, ignoring the glares and derogatory comments from the other students.

Me? I followed in the gang's wake, unable or unwilling to resist the invisible tether Charlie had cast between himself and me with just a blink of an eye. My resolve to be free of him morphed into the thrill of joining the *verboten* procession.

As we rounded the corner, I spied Jade, mouth agape, with one hand on her hip. I tromped over to her and looped my arm through hers. After all, there was safety in numbers. At least that's what I told myself.

Jade stumbled along beside me. "What are you doing?"

"We're going to lunch."

"If my boyfriend catches me following The Back Lot Gang, he'll kill me."

"Do you always do what he says?"

"Oh, Emmy. You're going to get me into so much trouble."

I laughed despite the overwhelming premonition that the trouble would not be hers alone. When we reached the double doors to the cafeteria, the boys opened up formation. Jade tugged me toward the lunch line, prompting Charlie to follow. I shuffled through, tray in hand, with Jade glued to my side, clearly disturbed at being in the proximity of Charlie Fields.

When we stopped to pay, Charlie took out his wallet and tossed down a couple of bills. "The ladies' lunches are on me."

Jade winced.

I turned to him. "What a surprise. I never had you pegged as a gentleman."

"Now, why would you say that? It ain't the first time I've sprung for your lunch."

Jade's eyes widened. An image of Charlie and myself sharing a cola at The Olde Soda Shop in the center of town popped into my mind. I'd never been anywhere alone with him, but the memory seemed crystal clear. My flip-flopping emotions were no longer my only problem. The strange visions I had when he was around were growing more frequent and stranger.

"What are you talking about?" I stammered. "I...you...never..." Charlie skimmed past before I could call him out. "He's lying, you know."

Jade zoned in on the popular kids' table. "Um, I hate to leave y'all, but I promised Ashanti I'd meet her for lunch today."

I nodded, releasing her from any self-imposed obligation, and she happily took off. Remaining my friend, however fair weather, had knocked her popularity rating down a notch or two. She tried to act like it didn't bother her, but I could tell that it did.

Charlie motioned for me to come to The Back Lot Gang's table. It was one thing to follow him down the hall, but the thought of sitting with him in front of a quarter of the student body brought on a bout of nervous anxiety. I shook my head. He shot a wry grin and mouthed, "please." I was getting sucked back in, but since I seemed to have been cursed with an enigmatic need to understand him, I went.

Everyone in the cafeteria watched as I weaved through the tables past my regular spot and toward Charlie Fields. From the center of the room, Ashanti angled herself to get a better look, glaring like a hawk. Next to her, Jade sat plastic-faced, staring in the opposite direction. Charlie nodded to an empty spot across from him at the table. Melody gave me the evil eye. I sat anyway.

Keir flew out of nowhere and crashed down next to me. "I heard a rumor, and I want to know if it's true."

"Shoot," Charlie said, pointing a finger gun at him.

"What do you and Paul have brewing?"

Charlie scanned the faces at the table. "All right,

which one of you guys is the sewer?"

Melody colored and focused on her pizza, tearing it into tiny bits. Charlie rubbed his nose on her cheek and sniffed.

"Do I smell a rat here?"

"Of course not, Charlie," she squeaked.

"It doesn't matter how I found out," Keir said. "I want to know what's going on."

Charlie slicked the sides of his hair. "Since when'd you become my daddy?"

"I may not be your daddy, but you could sure use one."

Charlie snickered, but humor never met his eyes. "You don't need to worry your pretty little head off, bro. I can take care of myself. But since you got your spy-wear on, I'll clue you in." He rested his forearms on the edge of the table and leaned forward. "Middleton has dared me to take on the Bump. He's putting up the title of his rod as the prize. It's a cool ride, and the jerk is practically giving it away. It'll be easy. Like taking money from the collection plate when the priest ain't looking."

The Bump? That big dip in the road? The one we rode over the other night?

"When is this supposed to happen?" Keir asked.

"Tonight, nine o'clock. It'll be fun." Charlie winked at me.

Karl frowned. "We're supposed to eat dinner at Emmy's house with Mama. Don't you remember?"

"Not until her shift's over. I'll make the jump, collect my prize, and we can all be back before midnight." Charlie took a large gulp of his soda and belched.

"Man, Charlie." Keir groaned. "What if you total The Ghost or get hurt or something?"

"I'm not going to total nothing."

Chuy slapped him on the back. "If anyone can bust the record, Charlie can."

"Yeah," Jason said. "Charlie's 'da man. Middleton's going to be wearing the word *sucker* all over his ride-less forehead."

Keir threw his hands up, motioning them to stop. "How fast?"

"The wager is for eighty miles per hour. But I figure I can get The Ghost up to a hundred-twenty no problem. Might as well set a record while I'm at it."

The gang broke into hoots of encouragement.

Chuy pounded his fists on the table, chanting, "Charlie, Charlie, Charlie."

The rest of the table joined in. Everyone but Keir and me.

The students in the cafeteria gawked. Some of their faces twisted in disgust, while others laughed at us as if we were a bunch of freaks. I rested my forehead in my hand, using it as a shield.

Ms. Jones, the new Home Economics teacher, rushed over. "Boys! Boys! Quiet down, this instant."

Charlie's head dropped and rose as he traced the line of her slight figure. "Enough already. The lunch warden speaks."

Ms. Jones lifted her glasses, wearing them like a headband. "Charlie, if you don't want detention, you better watch your mouth."

"You know, you're beautiful when you're angry." Charlie wiggled his eyebrows.

Her cheeks turned cotton candy pink. "That's not

an appropriate way to speak to a teacher."

Charlie ran his tongue over his lips. "I'm sorry, Miss Jones. I'll behave. I promise."

The anger melted off her face. "Okay, Charlie, I know you will."

Chuy's jaw dropped.

"What are you staring at?" Ms. Jones snapped.

"Jeez, nothing," he muttered.

Ms. Jones clapped her hands, commanding attention. "All of you. Get busy eating. The bell's about to ring." She smiled at Charlie once more before flitting away.

Melody scowled at her, and pangs of jealousy spasmed in my chest. Charlie's aura emitted some powerful magic. The gang and their girlfriends worshiped him. So did Keir. Even poor Ms. Jones wasn't immune to his charms.

But most importantly, no matter how hard I tried, I couldn't stop worshipping him either.

****

When the final bell rang, the halls transformed into a passageway to Friday-night-freedom, abound with slamming lockers and exultant voices. Charlie caught me by the elbow and dragged me into the recessed doorway of an empty classroom.

"I need to talk to you."

My breath hitched. "I don't think this is a good idea."

"Listen, New Jersey. I owe you an apology. I haven't always been on my best behavior around you, but I'll try harder. Keir really likes you. And as much as it kills me, he's better for you, so I'm going to back off." He paused, twisting the ring he wore on his middle finger. "If anything were to happen to me. Like I'm not around anymore—"

I shook my head. "Don't make that jump on Thunder Road if you think you're going to die."

He brushed my cheek. "Calm down. I meant if I were to split town or something."

"Oh." I exhaled.

He smiled. "Can I finish?"

"Yes," I whispered.

"If I have to leave, I want you to look after Keir. Don't let him do anything stupid. Make sure he stays in school and graduates. Make sure he enlists in the Navy. Don't let him give up his dream."

It sounded as if he were saying goodbye, and I didn't want to hear it. "What makes you think I have that kind of power over him?"

"Keir would do anything for you. He told me so."

"Why are *you* telling *me* this?"

Charlie focused on something behind me. "Oh hell, here comes Melody. I've got to go. If she sees me talking to you, she'll rag on me till I want to punch her, and it ain't right to hit girls. She doesn't like you, you know."

"No kidding?"

He chuckled. "Got to go."

Just as quickly as he had appeared, Charlie Fields was gone.

He'd never cowed to Melody in the past. Something was wrong. Maybe he planned to run away so he wouldn't have to get married. Melody would surely get tired of waiting. She wasn't the type to be without a boyfriend for long. And if he ran away, he wouldn't be gone forever. And if I waited long enough, maybe he could still be mine. If I wanted.

What was I thinking? Melody was having his baby. I had no chance of happiness with him. Not when our coupling would only bring pain to all involved.

Why couldn't I banish him from my thoughts? Why did I let him suck me back in? Then it dawned on me. There was only one explanation. I was as bad as he was, and all our negative energy was drawing us together. Maybe I couldn't help Charlie, but I could help myself. I could change. I still had a chance for redemption. And I would find a way.

I had to.

Chapter 12
Wrong is Right

Night time arrived fast. Too fast. Keir and I told Sunshine we would pick up Charlie, then headed to Jake's Garage instead. I had my reservations about supporting this foolishness. But Charlie was taking on the infamous Thunder Road Bump, and I needed to be there. Why I wasn't sure, but soon enough, the future would be revealed.

When we arrived, rockabilly music bounced off the walls in the shop. Charlie and Melody danced in the center of the floor while the gang cheered them on. Charlie twisted her under his arm, and in a move that seemed to defy gravity, he rolled her over his back. Melody bounced down on her toes, not missing a beat. Pregnancy hadn't affected her athletic ability one bit.

Charlie noticed us, spun Melody into Chuy's arms, and headed over. He gave Keir a one-armed hug and me a smoldering gaze. Then he shuffled us into the lobby and shut the shop door behind him.

"Hey little bro, can you do me a favor?"

Keir cocked his head. "Depends on what it is."

Charlie plucked his wallet from his back pocket and handed him a fifty-dollar bill along with his I.D. "I want you to pick me up a carton of cigarettes."

Keir ran his finger along the edge of Charlie's driver's license and frowned. He hated Charlie's smoking habit as much as I did.

"I don't look anything like you. Send Slick. He's eighteen."

"Slick's working on The Ghost. Just flash my I.D. No one will ask any questions. Come on, man. I have to drive tonight. Don't stress me out."

Charlie's ulterior motive shined through, at least to me. Keir's blindness to it aggravated me, but in all fairness, he wasn't privy to all sides of Charlie, or me for that matter. I could only hope that maybe this time he would catch on.

Keir took the money. "All right, but this is the last time. You understand me?"

The underlying meaning in his words made me want to cry. I remained dry-eyed, too selfish to let the tears roll.

Charlie slapped his back. "Thanks, bro; you're the best."

"Yeah, yeah, go tell it to someone else." Keir turned to me. "Do you want to ride along, Em?"

The overhead lights flickered. Perhaps an omen I was about to do the right thing, or more like err to wrong.

"Not to buy cigarettes. Those things are going to kill you, Charlie."

He rolled his eyes.

Keir glanced at the money in his hand. "I'll be back in a flash."

And then he was gone.

Charlie ducked into Jake's office and returned with a beer. He stood so close to me, the toes of our shoes touched. While my head told me not to be alone with him, my heart disagreed. Where was Melody when I needed her? Any other time she'd welcome a reason to punch my lights out, and this time I would deserve every blow.

Charlie swigged on the bottle, then offered it to me.

"No, I can't. I promised my mom I wouldn't drink." Sunshine and I never had that conversation. She believed in free will, but Charlie didn't know that.

He stroked my cheek with his oil-stained knuckle, and my apprehension, my guilt, my sense of right, all disappeared. I accepted the beer and took a sip.

"Let's talk in private."

He pointed to Jake's office. I nodded and followed Charlie Fields into the darkened room. He closed the door behind us and switched on a small desk lamp. The dim light cast smoky shadows on his face.

"I know I promised to stay away from you. But I can't do it."

My chest rose and fell rapidly as I struggled to breathe. His gaze dropped to my breasts. Self-conscious, I stepped backward and tripped on a throw rug. Charlie dove forward, steadied me, and then in a fleet-footed move, pinned me against the wall blowing the sickly-sweet smell of whiskey in my face.

"You've been drinking."

"Yeah, so what of it?" He sounded agitated.

"Just saying, that's all."

"Well, don't. We have more important things to talk about than my drinking. I tried to tell you the other day."

He must be talking about when we were under the door's recess leading into the science room. Melody had interrupted us. I bowed my head.

"I remember."

He gnawed on his lower lip. "I won't lie to you. The stunt on Thunder Road is going to be tough."

"Charlie, I don't think—"

"Let me finish," he whispered into my hair.

"Okay," I squeaked.

He pulled a butane lighter from his pocket and snapped open the lid. The blue flame flickered, lighting the space between us. He balled his hand.

"See this ring?"

I examined the gold ring with the unusual crimson gemstone, then ran my finger over the etched heart with angel wings topped by a king's crown. "It's beautiful."

"It was my grandfather's. If something happens to me, make sure Keir gets it."

"If you think this jump is that dangerous, don't do it."

Charlie shook his head. "It's cool. I'm ninety-nine percent sure everything will be fine."

I didn't believe him. He was keeping something from me. "Then why have you been drinking?"

"Call it liquid courage."

"Didn't you tell me one of the rules of racing is not to drink and drive?"

"I hate rules." He pulled out the half-empty bottle from his back pocket and unscrewed the lid with his teeth. He spit it on the floor and swigged.

"Give me that." I made a grab for the bottle.

Before I could take it from his hand, Charlie had me in his arms, his hot whiskey breath tickling my lips. "How about a good luck kiss?"

My knees buckled, and I clung to him for support. "Charlie, we can't. We shouldn't. What about Keir? What about Melody? What will people think?"

"New Jersey, you care about other people, and that's good, but I've been waiting for a girl like you for a long time. I'm going to find a way for you and me to be together forever. And no one will get hurt. I promise."

He kissed my forehead, allowing his lips to momentarily linger before releasing me and backing away, the bottle of whiskey dangling between his first two fingers. His dark unwavering gaze held me captive as he reached behind his back and opened the door.

Without breaking his stare, he pressed the bottle to his lips, threw back his head, and poured the remainder of the amber contents down his throat. Then he wiped his mouth on the back of his hand and tossed the empty bottle into a trash can.

Before the ping from the glass against the metal quit ringing, Charlie Fields was gone.

Chapter 13
The Smell of Cinnamon and Motor Oil

At 8:45 p.m., we set out for Thunder Road. Keir clutched the steering wheel, tailgating The Ghost so close, the nose of our rod obscured the view of the rear bumper. Charlie drove one-handed with Melody in the crook of his arm, looking like an oversized appendage. Behind us, Chuy, Slick, the pink-haired girl, and the faux redhead rode with Shorty in his Ghost wannabe ride. Jason and raccoon-eyed Layla pulled up the rear, in Jason's grandmother's old sedan, because his rod lay on blocks in his yard with a blown-out transmission.

By the time our convoy reached the clearing, a crowd of about thirty had gathered on Thunder Road. Paul Middleton, wearing a cowboy hat, towered a good head above the rest. He'd beat us there, perhaps inspired by the thought of Charlie's car ending up in the graveyard once and for all. We parked in the same order where we arrived, in spaces left open for us near the tunnel of trees. Just beyond, the Bump lay in wait.

Keir and I got out and aligned with the gang. We all followed Charlie down the embankment onto the field. Paul and Charlie shook hands and moved into a private huddle. Their voices rose high enough for all to hear.

"Shorty," Charlie shouted. "Bring me the radar gun."

Shorty hustled to his car and came back with a device that looked like a hand-held scanner. He offered it to Paul.

Paul lifted the gun and pointed at something in the distance. "This thing is older than dirt. How do I know that it's accurate? Cause if it ain't, the bet is off."

Was the great Paul Middleton, captain of the football team back-pedaling? I hoped so.

"Quit wasting time," Charlie said. "If you don't want to use it, just clock me. Speed equals distance divided by time. It's simple."

The ease with which Charlie pulled the formula from his head surprised me. I didn't think he listened in school.

Paul waved his wrist in front of Charlie's face. "You want me to time you with a wristwatch? I got too much riding on this bet."

The side of Charlie's mouth quirked up. "Then ride with me, and you can watch the speedometer yourself."

"You think I'm stupid, don't you?"

Charlie twisted a single strand of hair that hung in the middle of his forehead. "Maybe not stupid, but since you're too big a pussy to ride in the car with me, you'll have to take my word for it."

"Just because you're a crazy son-of-a-bitch, doesn't mean I have to be. That wasn't part of the bargain, man."

Paul's girlfriend, Cherie, walked over and hooked her arm through his. She eyed Charlie from head to toe, not bothering to hide her disgust. Charlie picked at a piece of pink fringe hanging from her jacket and tugged.

"How about you let this little honey ride with me."

Cherie wrinkled her nose and leaned away from him.

Paul shoved Charlie. "Get your filthy hands off my girl."

Charlie threw back his head and laughed. "I didn't know you liked girls."

Paul puffed out his chest and stepped forward, his hands balled in white-knuckled fists. Keir stiffened, and I latched on to his arm. A confrontation might not be such a bad thing. If they fought and Charlie got hurt, Paul would have no choice but to cancel the crazy bet.

"I'll ride with him," Chuy shouted, plowing his way through the crowd.

"Hell, since when did a Mexican ever tell the truth?" Paul sneered.

Chuy's eyes grew fiery. He lunged at Paul's throat. Charlie caught hold of him by the waist and tossed him to the side. Slick caught him and stopped him from tumbling to the ground. Charlie jabbed Paul in the chest.

"You're not good enough to speak to him. So shut the hell up."

"Forget it, boss," Chuy shouted. "He ain't worth it."

Charlie didn't budge. His steady stare intensified to rage. "Apologize to him."

Paul's moon-lit face glistened with dewy sweat. "I was kidding."

"Apologize," Charlie spat through gritted teeth.

The rest of us stood still as stones. Watching. Waiting for Charlie to pounce. Several tension-filled beats passed before Paul's defiant stance shrank, and he muttered, "Sorry."

Charlie breathed. "Okay. Let's get this deal settled. Fast. My patience is wearing real thin."

Paul took a few cautious steps backward. "Give me a second. I've got an idea." He signaled his gang, and they formed a huddle. When the group dispersed, Paul's wary expression had been replaced with a smirk.

"How about you let one of your ladies ride along. How about that one over there? She looks honest enough." He stretched his long arm out and pointed.

The crowd opened ranks and formed a half-circle. Me? I choked on pure air. Paul couldn't be sure I'd be honest. He wanted out of the bet.

Charlie scrutinized me. A gamut of emotions scrolled across his face—first indecision, followed by a hint of sadness, and finally, resolve. He nodded.

"Okay."

Keir stepped in front of me. "I won't let Emmy get in that car."

Charlie's eyes narrowed. He moved toward Keir, his fists clenched. Charlie Fields was in his second standoff of the night, and this one was with his brother. Someone shoulder-checked me from behind. The pain from the blow shot all the way to the tips of my fingers. Melody zipped past and threw herself into Charlie's arms. She scowled at me.

"I'll ride with you, babe."

Part of me wanted to punch her in the nose for ramming into me. Another part of me wanted to rip her hair out in a jealous rage. But then there was the sane part of me, the part that wanted to kiss the ground she walked on for volunteering to ride in the car with a lunatic hell-bent on risking his life to break a record no one would ever care about.

Charlie lit a cigarette. "Okay. You can ride along if that's what you want."

Amidst the cloud of stinky smoke, she kissed his cheek. Watching the two of them made me realize I had always been Charlie Field's second choice, and it hurt.

"Listen up," Keir said. "I don't think it's a good idea to have any of the girls in the car. I'll ride along."

"Get bent. This ain't your call," Charlie snapped.

Melody propped her fist on her hip. "Yeah, Keir, back off."

He shook his head. "Have it your way, Mel."

Charlie turned to Paul. "So, are we cool?"

Paul kicked the ground, and a puff of sandy dirt sprinkled over the toe of his boot. "Okay. Let her ride, but I'm not stupid. We're timing you too. Remember, you have to take the Bump at eighty miles per hour. If it's too close to call or you wreck your car, you owe me five grand. And if by some crazy chance, you're able to drive out of here, the title to my rod is yours."

"I'll be doing one-hundred-twenty, sucker. Be prepared to hitch a ride home," Charlie said.

Melody latched on to his belt loop, and the two headed for The Ghost. The crowd disbanded, and a group of Paul's friends hopped into a pick-up truck, filling both the cab and the bed. They took off toward the tunnel of trees.

Charlie turned to Keir. "Little bro, I owe you an apology for getting hostile on you."

"Forget it. You're under pressure. I get that."

Charlie took off his leather jacket and tossed it to him. "Hang onto this for me, would you?"

Keir cocked his head. "Why?"

"I can't drive with it on."

Keir nodded and slipped the jacket on over his hoodie. "Be careful. Will you?"

Charlie waved him off. "Don't worry. Everything's cool."

The mighty Ghost roared to life, growling and rumbling like a caged jungle cat desperate to be set free. As the rest of the crowd migrated to the tunnel of trees where the Bump lay waiting, I was struck by a sense of déjà vu.

I'd been here before; only I'd been the passenger in the car, not Melody. My heart thrummed in my chest. Everything was all wrong. Charlie was making a mistake letting her ride along. I had to warn him. I darted to The Ghost and pounded on the window.

"Charlie, I'm supposed to ride with you."

He shook his head. "Not this time, New Jersey."

"This time? What do you mean, not this time?"

"Emmy," Keir shouted, "Get out of the road."

"Give me a second," I yelled back.

Charlie beat the steering wheel like a bongo drum, pounding out a beat to a tune only he could hear.

"Get lost, Emmy." Melody scoffed.

"Charlie, what did you mean by *this time*?"

"Move out of the way, New Jersey. I've got to go."

In the distance, bodies scurried off the road. Charlie gripped the wheel with one hand, while his other dropped onto the shifter. He revved the engine and pressed the gas pedal twice. With a jerk of his shoulder, the rear wheels screamed, and The Ghost shot forward. Clouds of burning rubber scorched my eyes and lungs. My adrenaline spiked, and I darted after it, the muscles in my thighs screaming as my feet hit the pavement in long hard strides. Despite my efforts, the car moved farther and farther away and entered the tunnel of trees.

In the next instant, an ear-splitting metallic noise pealed out through the night, followed by sparks that shot out everywhere like firecrackers on the Fourth of July. The car sprang off the ground.

Time stood still as I waited for The Ghost to crash down. But it rose higher and higher as if some unearthly demon lifted it into the sky. Two beats later, it disappeared from view. There was a thunderous crash, so loud it reverberated in a place with no valley or no hills. Scraps of metal shot through the trees and clanked and clattered to the ground.

I ran faster, through the mist, the dust, and the smoke, through bits and pieces of debris falling around me. I weaved unyielding through the bystanders, many screaming and falling to their knees. I leaped down the easement and landed hard but recovered my footing and dashed to the wooded area. Someone shouted at me to stop, but I continued to the place where the terrible noise still resonated.

Fifteen feet above, obscured behind a sweet-smelling haze, The Ghost lay wedged in the arms of a giant oak tree. Someone's footsteps thudded behind me, and light shot up into the trees, exposing the once-mighty car. It lay askew and teetering haphazardly on a sturdy limb. What was left of the engine compartment curled around the shattered windshield in a tangled ball of steel.

I cupped my hands around my mouth and screamed, "Someone call 911." Then, I gaped at the mangled car, looking for signs of life. "Charlie? Melody? Are you okay?"

No one answered. Charlie and Melody were only eighteen years old. They were still kids, and kids didn't die. Therefore, they could not be dead. I would not allow it.

"Charlie? Answer me!"

Noise creaked from above, and the driver's door popped open. I took a breath. Any minute now, Charlie would hop down out of the tree and laugh at me for being such a basket case. I balled my fists until my nails dug into my palms.

"Charlie?"

He didn't answer. He sat upright, unbroken, his head resting against the back of the seat. Someone behind me sighed with relief. The door creaked farther and thumped against a tree limb. Charlie fell sideways, and his body hung half in, half out, still and limp as if he had no skeleton. Drops of blood from a wound in his head pattered like raindrops on the dried leaves. His fist unfolded, and something dropped at my feet.

I fell to my knees and read the ground like a blind person, sifting through the loose dirt and fallen leaves, ignoring the blood dripping all around me, on me. My fingers met with something round, something hard. Charlie's ring. I slipped it over my middle finger, the same one he had worn it on.

His voice played in my head. *If anything happens to me, give this ring to Keir."*

Reality hit me hard. Charlie knew this would happen. He'd warned me, and I didn't catch on. Maybe if I hadn't resisted him. Maybe if I told him, I loved him. Maybe if I'd gotten in the car, I could have talked him out of making the jump, and none of this would have happened. Charlie was hurt or maybe dead, and it was my fault. I didn't stop it.

I clutched my fist to my heart and rocked back and forth. This wasn't happening. I was in the middle of a nightmare and would wake up at any moment. There was too much screaming. Some idiot kept the horror show going with their blood-curdling wails. I covered my ears.

Someone grabbed me from behind. I clawed at the person that held me, digging until flesh hung from beneath my fingernails, but he wouldn't let go. He shook me. He shook me hard until my neck felt it would snap in two.

"Emmy, stop! You're scaring me," a familiar male voice said.

Slowly, carefully, he urged my clutched fists from my chest and pulled me to sitting. He walked his arms around my waist. I buried my face in his jacket and inhaled the familiar scent of cinnamon and motor oil.

Charlie.

He was here, alive, watching me suffer! I pushed him away and drew back my hand to slap him. Then I hesitated and blinked to clear my vision.

My target was Keir, wearing Charlie's jacket.

The world fell silent. Everything stopped, including my breath. As I stared into his eyes, unable to utter a sound, I realized that the torturous wails, the ones that held me in the nightmare, the ones that wouldn't quit, the ones that nearly split my eardrums, had been my own.

Chapter 14
A Common Enemy

Sirens and spiraling lights created a trippy psychedelic aura, adding to the surreal experience. As the wailing whirred down to nothing, slamming doors and stomping feet replaced it. Emergency workers, lots of them, tramped past Keir and me to gawk at The Ghost hovering above.

Through it all, my panic had crashed into utter numbness. Just because Melody and Charlie didn't answer, it didn't mean they were gone. They were hurt, not dead. That's what I told myself, over and over.

"Can you hear me, son?" a fireman yelled at Charlie.

No response.

"Are you alone?

Still nothing.

A second fireman kneeled in front of Keir and me. "I've never seen anything like this. Were you two in that car?"

Tears streamed down Keir's cheeks, leaving rivers of dirt streaks. He shook his head. "My brother and his girlfriend are up there. Please help them."

The Ghost shifted, and everyone below it skittered off to the sides. The fireman pulled a radio from his belt.

"We're going to need more backup and a crane."

He turned back to Keir and me. "Are you hurt? Can you walk?"

We both nodded.

"You need to move out of here. Now."

Keir wiped his nose on his sleeve and helped me to my feet. A sickly sting burned in my stomach. I didn't want to leave Charlie.

"Hurry up," the fireman said, steering us away from the site.

We stumbled through the sea of first responders, side-stepping burning embers in the brush. We made our way back to the road through the acrid fumes, now lit with emergency vehicles. Police officers corralled the boys and what was left of the bystanders onto the side of the road. Any other time, law enforcement presence would have sent the gang flying for cover, but loyalty to Charlie always came first. Notably missing from the crowd was Paul Middleton. Coward.

A cop waved at us. "Hey, you two, over here with everyone else."

We obeyed his orders and joined our friends.

"Has anyone called my mom?" Keir asked no one in particular.

Layla stepped forward. Tears glistened on her heart-shaped face.

"She's on her way. What about Charlie and Melody? Are they…?"

The boys stepped closer. Keir's face crumpled, and he leaned against me.

"I couldn't see Melody. But Charlie doesn't look so good."

Layla dove on us and clung to our necks. Seconds later, our friends swarmed us. We huddled together, clinging onto each other, seeking refuge from an enemy we never thought would find us. Death.

A horn blared in a string of continuous beeps. The Dub sped up the road and abruptly halted a short distance away. The doors flew open. Sunshine, Sid, and Keir's mother, Elise, bolted toward us. Sunshine shoved through the crowd and swallowed me in her arms.

"Emerald! Are you all right?"

I clung to her. "Yes, Mom."

Elise, still in her waitress uniform, raced up behind us. "Where's Charlie?"

No one spoke.

She grabbed Keir and shook him. "I'm tired of you boys keeping secrets from me. I swear, you better tell me where he is."

Keir hesitated, then pointed toward the heavily lit woods. High above the ground, in the eye of a spotlight, glints of blue paint glistened through the tangled and broken branches of the giant oak. Sid hacked on air. Sunshine clutched me tighter.

"Omigod!"

Elise tore down the embankment. A cop darted after her and caught her around the waist.

"Let me go. My baby's in there!"

He guided her back to the road. "I'm sorry, ma'am, I can't let you any closer. The emergency team is working hard to get those kids down from that tree. We need everyone to stay clear."

Elise strained against the cop's hold. "Charlie, Momma's here. I'm coming!"

"Is there anything I can do?" Sid asked the cop.

He tipped his head toward Keir's mother. "Take care of her."

Sid laid his bearlike hand gently on her shoulder. "Elise, they're trying to save your son. You don't want to slow them down, do you?"

She burst into gut-wrenching sobs. The cop released her, and she collapsed into Sid's arms. Sunshine took off her suede jacket and draped it over Elise's shoulders. Then she and Sid coaxed her back to the side of the road where we had all settled on the ground, sitting cross-legged in a silent vigil. Sometime later, maybe an hour, maybe a lifetime, a large black car arrived and parked behind our microbus. A man in an overcoat and shiny black shoes stalked past us into the woods.

"Who's that?" someone whispered.

Chuy rested his head on my shoulder. "It can't be good."

I reached my arm around him and squeezed. "Charlie's tough, and Melody is mean as nails. They're going to be okay. We just have to wait for the firemen to get them down."

Chuy let out a ragged breath, buried his face in his knees, and sobbed. I rubbed his back, trying in vain to console the inconsolable.

A cop appeared from behind the trees. We all rose.

"I want to see my son." Elise's voice rang clear through the night.

The cop froze, his face stony. Tension grew between them and spread out like mutant kudzu coiling its wiry stems around us.

"Where is he?" This time her voice was shrill and demanding.

The cop removed his hat. "I'm sorry, ma'am, but he didn't make it. Neither of them did."

Agonized wails sounded around me. I jolted to my feet, but a sharp pain broke me in two. I heaved until my ribs ached. My eyes bled tears faster and thicker than Charlie's gaping wound.

Charlie and Melody had entered a vortex of nonexistence. And the real tragedy was that no one in the world but the few of us on Thunder Road knew that the universe would never be the same.

I had to get away. I had to find someplace safe where kids didn't die. And people like me made the right choices and didn't hurt others.

First one step. Then another. Each one was harder than the last. It hurt, but it was imperative I get somewhere different from the place I stood. Only a few feet farther from the pain, my knees buckled. The earth tilted, then spun on its axis, and the ground flew up to meet me.

****

I awoke, choking on the taste of ammonia and bleach. A man in a white shirt held a small cylinder under my nose. I swatted his hand away. Behind him stood Sunshine and Sid with their mouths open in giant O's.

"She's coming to," the man said.

Medical cabinets lined the walls of a tiny room. I struggled to sit, but the man-in-white held me firm to—the gurney? I searched my mind for answers, but white space had replaced my memory.

"Where am I?"

"You're in an ambulance." The man spoke softly as if he were talking to a wounded animal. "I'll let you sit upright after we check your vitals."

He pressed a button on the blue bulb he held in his

hand. The blood pressure cuff tightened around my arm.

"What's wrong with me?"

Sunshine brushed a strand of hair out of my eyes. "Honey, you passed out and bumped your head."

"Why?" I dreaded the answer, for reasons I sensed but couldn't recollect.

Sunshine pursed her lips. "Don't you remember what happened?"

I squished my eyes together and concentrated. The white space segued into a stream of events. The sound of the crash. A crumpled image of The Ghost. Charlie hanging from the tree, blood leaking from a gash in his head. The policeman removing his hat.

"He's dead," I whispered.

Sid brushed a tear from his eye. Sunshine covered her mouth and muffled a sob. I grasped the metal bars on the side of the gurney.

"Where's Keir?"

Sunshine rubbed my shoulder. "He's taking care of his mother."

The emergency medical tech removed the cuff from my arm. "Her vital signs are normal, but she needs to go to the hospital for overnight observation."

I shot upright. "I don't want to go. People die in hospitals. I don't want to die. I want to go home."

"Emerald, calm down, please." Sunshine hugged me.

"I mean it, Mom. Get me out of here."

She turned to the EMT. "Would that be all right?"

He ran his hand lightly over a spot on the side of my head. I shied from his touch. He held my chin and shined a light in my eyes.

"She has a large contusion, but she doesn't appear to have a concussion. I can't force you to bring her to the hospital, but you'll have to sign a release. And if you take her home, you'll need to watch her closely for the next twenty-four hours. If she becomes confused or her pupils become dilated, bring her straight to the emergency room."

"I can do that," Sunshine said. "What do you think, Sid?"

"Let's take her home."

Outside, the stars twinkled, and the moon shot a path of blue light across Thunder Road. Apart from a couple of cop cars, there was nothing to connote two kids and an unborn baby had died on this very road a few hours ago.

A lone policeman patrolling the area rushed me. "I'd like to ask you a few questions if I could, miss."

My heart sank into my stomach, leaving emptiness in its place. I burst out crying. Sid stepped in between us.

"My daughter was an innocent bystander. You heard the witnesses. You can call the house tomorrow, but you need to leave her alone tonight."

The cop handed him a card. "Just make sure she's available for questioning tomorrow."

Sid had called me his daughter and stuck up for me as if I really were. A day ago, I'd have been livid if he even suggested such a thing. Not tonight. Not now. From this point forward, I vowed not to waste any more time on this earth being an ungrateful brat. I hugged him with all the strength I could muster. He scooped me up in his arms and cradled me like a baby. I snuggled against his barrel chest and inhaled the scent of

Sunshine's lavender soap mingled with man smell.

Then I closed my eyes and let him carry me away. Away from the cop. Away from Thunder Road. Away from the tree with the unbending arms where Charlie and Melody died. I held on tight and didn't let go.

Because this night, there was no place else I'd rather be.

Chapter 15
Death Be With You

Four days later, Charles Lewis Fields the Fourth was laid to rest between two strangers in a tiny cemetery in Moncks Corner. The small group of mourners gathered at our house afterward to celebrate Charlie's short life, dining on the food left over from the family dinner that never was.

****

The morning after the funeral, everything hurt—my neck, my back, my stomach, my brain. It had been five days since Charlie and Melody died, and I'd yet to catch my breath. I had no firsthand experience with death. Until now. And death sucked.

I forced myself to get out of bed. The blood-spattered clothes I'd worn still lay balled in a pile. I'd refused to let anyone touch them, but it was time. Their presence had become an unbearable reminder.

As I picked them up, a tiny bit of gold pinged on the floor. The ring. Charlie's ring. In all the chaos, I'd forgotten about it. I hooked it with my forefinger and cleaned away the dirt with the bottom of my T-shirt. The scent of cinnamon and motor oil came out of nowhere and filled my senses until I tasted it in the back of my throat. Warm breath tickled my neck.

If anything happens to me, make sure Keir gets my ring.

Susan Antony

Charlie Fields. I spun around. After three deep breaths, it was apparent my sick and disillusioned brain was playing a trick on me—a cruel, evil trick. Charlie was really dead. All that remained of him was his ring. I hugged it to my chest. The selfish part of me wanted to hide it under my pillow and keep it forever, so a piece of him would always be with me. After all, I was the one who found it.

But the sense of right I'd inherited from my father wouldn't allow it. The ring belonged to Keir. Charlie wanted him to have it. Who was I to deny his final wish?

I threw on some clothes and hurried to the kitchen. Sunshine and Sid were at the table. In front of them sat a large platter of scrambled eggs and a bowl of fresh fruit.

"Grab a plate, Emerald," Sunshine said.

The thought of food gagged me. "Thanks, but I'm not hungry."

"If you don't eat something, you'll make yourself sick."

"I'll eat later. I promised Keir I'd come over this morning, and I overslept."

Sid slid his chair back from the table. "Listen, if you're on your way to see Keir, I have something I want you to give him." He left the kitchen.

I looked at Sunshine, and she shrugged.

Sid returned moments later with a fist full of money. "I tried to give this to Elise, but she refused to take it. I know they spent every last dime the two of them had to pay the funeral costs. I want to help."

My jaw dropped. "Sid, are you sure you can afford it?"

"Hell, there's more where that came from. I have a pile of money hidden under the mattress."

This time Sunshine's jaw dropped. "I've been sleeping on a small fortune and didn't even know it?"

"Damn it." Sid snapped his fingers. "I gave away my hiding spot. Now, I'm going to have to come up with another place to stash my dough."

I hugged Sid's thick, hairy neck. "Thank you."

Sunshine smiled. "This is why I love him."

Sid's cheeks colored strawberry, clashing with his orange beard. "Aw, geez folks, it ain't no big deal."

I thought to apologize outright for judging him without really knowing him, but the huge grin on his face suggested he probably already knew how I felt. "Mom, would you mind if I borrowed The Dub?"

Sunshine elbowed Sid. Sid dug into his pocket and pulled out a single key on a braided, black leather ring.

"No need to borrow your mom's car. I finished yours up yesterday."

He flipped the key, and I caught it with one hand.

"Thanks, Sid. You're the best."

For a moment, the pain consuming me disappeared.

****

Outside, the warm wind whipped around the house and blasted me with gritty dust reminiscent of the handful of dirt we'd dropped on Charlie's grave. The thought of him alone, lying in the hard, cold ground triggered the waterworks again. Through blurred vision, I made my way to my car and took off for Keir's house.

After a short drive I hardly recollected making, I parked in front of his family's trailer. Plucking a tissue from the box on the floorboard, I dried my cheeks and blew my nose. I had to be strong for Keir's sake. I strolled up the walk, past the gardens filled with sagging brown clumps where flowers once bloomed. Death was everywhere.

The tin door shuddered under my knuckles as I knocked. Keir greeted me with a weak hug. He looked as if he hadn't slept for days. From the door, I spied Elise in her lounge chair, staring at a blank TV screen.

"How is she?" I mouthed.

Keir's face twisted, and he motioned for me to step inside. I tiptoed into the living room. Elise glanced at me and turned her attention back to the television. I bent and kissed her on the cheek. Her eyelids fluttered once, but she didn't break her stare.

"Mom?" Keir said. "Emmy and I are going to my room for a while. Do you need anything?"

She didn't answer. Keir led me down the narrow narrow hallway.

The door to Charlie's room was wide open. His work boots and leather jacket were laid out on the floor in front of his closet door like a memorial display on a grave. When we reached Keir's room, he closed the door behind us. It was just him and me, and a poster on the wall of Albert Einstein with his runaway hair. Keir threw himself on top of the rumpled sheets. I sat beside him.

"How are you doing?"

"I'd be better if I wasn't so worried about Mama." He turned to me, his expression unexpectedly angry. "The doctor gave her some pills to calm her down, and she's gulping them by the handful. I'm afraid if I fall asleep, I'll wake up and find her dead, too."

I squeezed his hand. "Sunshine says everyone deals with grief differently."

"Yeah? Well, I'm grieving, and I need a mother, not a drug addict."

"I'm sorry, but I don't know what to do."

"Just the fact you're here helps. I know Charlie wasn't one of your favorite people, but you were always nice to him. That meant a lot to me."

If he knew I was torn between Charlie and him, he'd be crushed. I could never hurt him that way. A tear rolled down my cheek. But this one didn't belong to Charlie. This one belonged to Keir, the sweetest guy I'd ever known.

Charlie was gone. I loved them both in different ways, and now the terrible choice of who to pick had been made for me by a much greater power. I shifted to quell my angst. The bulk in my pocket reminded me of Sid's gift. I jumped up.

Keir startled at my movement. "What's up?"

I pulled the wad of cash from my pocket and dropped it on his stomach. His eyebrows rose, creating horizontal wrinkles on his forehead.

"What is this for?"

"To help with expenses."

"I can't take your money, Em."

"It's not mine. It's from Sid."

Keir rose to sit. His lips moved as he silently counted the bills. "This is three thousand dollars." He rolled the money into a ball and shoved it back at me.

I pushed his hand aside. "Sid insisted. If I try to give it back, he'll be insulted. You need to keep it."

"Sid," he whispered, stuffing the wad inside his pillowcase. "Tell him thank you for me. And tell him I'm coming over the first chance I get to thank him in person."

"I will, but, um, Keir, I have something else for you."

Keir leaned away from me. "I'm not sure I can take any more of your surprises."

I uncurled my fist.

His eyes widened. "That's Charlie's ring. The one that belonged to his father. How did you get it?"

"I found it on the ground the night of the accident. I forgot about it until this morning."

Keir took the ring and ran his finger over the etched stone. He slipped it on his middle finger and flexed his hand. He smiled, and his gaze captured mine. I'd known him for years but never noticed how crystal blue his eyes were.

"Keir," Elise shouted from the other room. "Where are you?" Her voice sounded frantic, similar to the night Charlie died.

Keir leaped to his feet. "I'm sorry, Em. I've got to go to her. If I leave her too long, she panics."

"I understand. I can come back tomorrow."

"Promise me you will, Em. Without you, my life would totally suck."

Chapter 16
The Swamp Fox Trail

The next morning as I started for school, Keir's rod slid to a halt, blocking the driveway. A puff of street dust fogged the otherwise clear sky. I marched across the lawn, my backpack bouncing off my hip, and I plopped into the passenger seat. His tanned legs, covered in curly, sun-bleached hair, caught me by surprise.

"What are you doing here? Is something wrong?"

"I came to get you."

"I thought you were taking a week or two off to take care of your mom. And what's with the board shorts?"

"One of Mama's friends came to give me a break. I have a surprise for you." He leaned over and glanced at my side of the floorboard. "Good, you're wearing sneakers."

I lifted a foot. "What do my shoes have to do with anything?"

He grinned. "You're cutting school today."

As if I couldn't get myself in enough trouble on my own. Now I had Keir creating it for me. I frowned, and his broad smile melted into disappointment as he read my expression.

"Come on, Em. You said you were tired of always being a good kid. Remember? Besides, it's too nice outside to waste the day sitting behind a pressed-wood desk. I have a place I want to show you. Grab your swimsuit."

Frantic butterflies did a number on my stomach. "What about work? Iola's counting on me."

He flipped the AC vent back and forth. "You have the day off. I cleared it with her yesterday. She feels sorry for me, you know."

He'd never been a scammer. Charlie's death had messed him up more than I thought.

"She went along with your hair-brained scheme? Without asking me?"

"You're not the only one to fall victim to my charms." He wiggled his eyebrows.

Me, a victim of charm? More like a victim of machismo. Keir leaned closer, resting his forehead against mine.

"Please? I really need a friend right now."

Dad would kill me if he found out, but he was thousands of miles away, and if I had to lay a bet, Sunshine would never tell him. How had I made it to senior year without cutting a single day anyway? Keir was my best friend, and he needed help.

"Okay. I'll go with you. But give me a second." I leaped out of the car, leaving the door open, and rushed inside the house.

"Emerald? Is that you?" Sunshine called from her bedroom.

"Yeah. I forgot something."

I dashed to my room and dug out my black bikini from the bottom drawer of my dresser. I stuffed it under my shirt and bolted back to the car. Keir stared at my bulging belly.

"What do you have under your shirt?" he asked.

"My swimsuit."

"Well, give it here, and I'll put it in my backpack."

I handed it to him. There was no backing out now. The only consolation I had was that I'd shaved my legs the night before.

"What are you waiting for? Get in."

"I can't. If Sunshine sees my car, she'll know I'm not at school. Let's park it at Georgy G's for the day?"

"It's a deal."

We dumped my car in the back lot behind the building, and, after a few turns, we were on Highway 52, heading west. The scenery soon changed from small towns to forests, farmlands, and an occasional billboard. We passed a slow-rolling truck towing a boat. I wondered if we were traveling to the same destination. Several miles later, Keir pulled off the road into a gravel parking lot. A small wooden sign reading "Swamp Fox Passage" marked the entry.

"There isn't another car in sight," I said. "Where are we going?"

"Do you really want me to tell you? You'll ruin my surprise."

He grabbed the back of my neck and squeezed. My flesh prickled where his fingers had been. I rubbed the sensation away. If I gave in to it, he might end up dead, too.

I rifled in the back seat and tossed him his backpack. "Let's go, then."

I followed him to the highway. A couple of cars whizzed by in a long suck like a riptide. When the road cleared, we sprinted across and sidled the grassy easement, stopping when we came to a sign reading

"Francis Marion Hiking Trails."

Keir pointed to a wooded area. "That's the Palmetto Trail. It runs along Lake Moultrie and Lake Marion for forty-seven miles."

"I can't hike for forty-seven miles. Even if my legs hold up, Sunshine will kill me if I don't come home tonight."

He burst out laughing. "We're not hiking the entire trail. We're going roughly an hour in."

He led me onto the pine needle-covered pathway leading into the tea green forest. We strode in silence, our arms bumping every so often.

A warm breeze rustled the treetops. Squirrels scampered through the underbrush, seeking refuge from the thump of our footsteps. Off to the left, a little creek whispered to me. I turned to look, and I tripped over a root. Keir caught me around the waist and spun me around until I faced him.

"Thanks." I took a conscious step back.

The corners of his mouth dipped for a second, then he turned and walked ahead. "We better keep moving. We've got a way to go."

He slowed when we reached a 'T' in the trail and weaved left. A man walking his dogs in the opposite direction passed by, and we waved hello. A little while later, we crossed a small paved road and picked up the trail on the other side. It led us to a rickety bridge with a post in the center to deter anyone not on foot.

We stopped for a moment to admire the creek below. Tadpoles and lizards darted about in the slow current. On the other side, the trail opened up to a field. Yellow flowers dotted the dusty, green southern terrain. At the tree line to our left, an eagle swooped down, plucked a squirrel from the ground, and flew off into the turquoise sky.

"Did you see that? Poor little thing," I said.

Keir shrugged. "It's nature, Em. There are predators, and there are victims. That's what keeps the cycle of life going."

I frowned, realizing he was right but not wanting him to be. I wanted him to don a superhero's cape and snatch the squirrel from the eagle's beak, cursing at all the injustice in the world.

"Race you." Keir took off running.

"No fair. You cheated!" I scrambled after him.

He stopped short at some railroad tracks.

I barreled into him, bumping us forward. "No one leaves me in the dust and gets away with it."

He mussed my hair. "Be careful now. I don't want you to get your foot stuck."

Keir held my elbow and guided me across the rails. He pointed to a small hill on the horizon. "Wait until you see what's on the other side."

We climbed to the top. I froze, dazzled by the sun's scorching path on the blue-green waters, contained by an endless wall of large rocks. A bicycle rider sped by on the sand-packed road skirting the edge.

"We've reached Lake Moultrie," Keir said. "It was man-made back in the nineteen-forties. The road leads all the way around the dike system."

"I know. We studied about it. I've never been to the lake this way, though."

I trotted down the hill to the water, prompting Keir to follow. A rock caught my attention. I dug it free. An intricate picture of angel wings atop a dagger was painted on the flat side.

Keir perched his foot on an adjacent rock. "You like that?"

"The artist is clearly talented, though I despise it when people feel the egocentric need to deface landscapes with their mark."

"That's my brother's handy work. We used to come here together sometimes."

He seemed miles away, like my dad after Sunshine left.

"Is that why this place is so special to you?" I handed Keir the rock.

He tossed it on the road.

"Why did you do that?"

I retrieved the rock and put it back in its place on the riverbank. Keir stalked off. I'd made him mad. Why I didn't know. But Charlie had just died. I loved him, but so did Keir, and I was here for Keir. I caught up to him.

"I'm sorry. I didn't mean to upset you."

"You didn't. It's just I came here to forget. Could we not talk about him?"

I nodded and kicked the ground with my sneaker. Dust covered the rubber toe.

"We've still got a way to go," Keir said. "Are you thirsty?"

I surveyed the area. No bathrooms. Sucking down water had its pitfalls in primitive conditions like these.

"No, I'm okay."

A good hike later, my legs ached, and my tongue stuck to the roof of my mouth, calling to mind the water I rejected earlier. Apart from the faint pulse of the lake against the shore, nothing had changed. We were still engulfed in overgrown pines, foliage, and vines. A fishy odor wafted in the air. Keir parted some branches and gestured from me to pass through.

In front of me lay a tiny beach, only slightly bigger than a king-sized bed. The yellow sand curved like a half-moon and met the water's edge, giving way to verdant, muddy ledges on either side. Apart from a tent clearing behind us and a nearby well pump, no signs of civilization existed, not even a footprint.

Twenty-five feet ahead stood a bald cypress anchored in the lake by a heavy dome-shaped root system. Its narrow trunk stretched up toward the sky. The top branches were spindly and covered in a smattering of green leaves. Gray moss hung from the lower limbs and blew like tattered dishrags in the wind. I removed my shoes and dipped my toes in the water.

Keir stripped off his shirt, revealing his lean but muscular torso, smooth except for a scanty dark blondish-brown hair below his belly button. He knelt and dug inside his backpack and placed two bottles of water in the sand. Then he pulled out a towel, and my bikini fell out.

"Why don't you put it on?"

My head ricocheted from side to side. "Where?"

He pointed at a nest of trees that lined the shore. "Over there."

My pulse raced. "Someone might see me."

"There's no one out here but us."

I stared at him wide-eyed while my feet grew roots deeper than the bald cypress in the lake.

"Give me a second."

He disappeared under one of the tree limbs and strategically draped the towels around the shrubbery. Seconds later, he returned with a smirk.

"Not even the squirrels will see you now."

I clutched my bikini to my chest, unstuck my feet, and ducked behind the towels, my composure but a fragile shell around me. Peeking over the top of the makeshift dressing room, I spread the bushes a bit. Keir had turned his back.

I removed my bra, slipping off one strap at a time, never removing my shirt. I put my bikini top on in the same way. In a move worthy of a runway model changing between walks, I dropped my jeans and underwear and shimmied my bathing suit bottoms up over my hips. I gathered my belongings and joined Keir on the tiny beach. Then spread out the towels, balling my clothes at the head of one of them to use as a pillow.

Keir reached in his pocket and pulled out Charlie's ring. He twirled it around before slipping it on his middle finger.

"I was going to bury it here, but I can't bring myself to part with it."

"I don't think Charlie would want you to, either. He told me he wanted you to have it."

Keir pulled a face. He hesitated as if he had wanted to know more but then passed me a peanut butter and honey sandwich. We sat in silence, eating. I thought of happier times to keep the tears welling in my eyes from spilling over. After I managed to force down my food, I flopped back onto my towel and shielded my eyes from the sun's glare with the crook of my arm. Keir popped a potato chip into my mouth, then settled beside me, his head propped up on his fist, watching me chew. The air between us buzzed with electricity. I shot up.

"Want to go swimming?"

"If you do."

He sounded disappointed but jumped up first and pulled me to my feet. We waded waist-deep into the murky water, the coolness snapping me out of my funk. The mud from the lake slithered between my toes. The current shifted, and something slimy wrapped around my ankle. I leaped in the air. Then lost my footing and grabbed onto Keir. We both went tumbling into the lake. I flipped like a fish, desperately avoiding the creepy unknowns on the mucky bottom. Keir found his footing first and guffawed so hard he doubled over.

"Ew, ew, ew! Help me up! I'm being attacked by fish guts!"

He caught me under the arms and pulled me to my feet. I scrambled to the shore with Keir at my heels, still howling with laughter.

"What's so funny?" I asked, brushing debris of unknown origin off my shoulder.

He looked at me with sparkling eyes, struggling to contain his laughter. "Nothing."

Water dripped off his thick eyelashes, and I plucked a leaf from his hair. "You should have warned me the bottom of the lake here was that gross."

"Let me make it up to you." He stroked my cheek and pressed his lips to mine.

My skin burst into a flaming wave of pleasure. His kiss deepened, and he pried my lips apart with his tongue. If I let this go further, our relationship would never be the same. It couldn't be. Panic set in, and I pushed him away.

"What are you doing? You're going to ruin everything."

"Come on, Em. How can one kiss do that?"

I spewed the first thing that came to mind. "I'm

eighteen, and you are seventeen. It's not legal."

"That's ridiculous. It's only a kiss, and I'll be eighteen in a few months anyway."

"You didn't ask first. You're not supposed to kiss a girl without asking." My voice was loud and shrill. The last thing I wanted to do was hurt him, but Charlie had just died, and confusion got the best of me. "Is this why you brought me here?"

"No, of course not. You're right. I should have asked. I don't know what came over me. You are my best friend, and you deserve someone better than me." His physique shrank, and his voice cracked in defeat.

He was the one who deserved better.

"Keir, once we go there, we can never go back."

"I know that. I'm sorry. Do you want to go home?"

The sun was high in the sky, and water sloshed gently against the shore. The clouds on the horizon rolled lazily by on the tips of the breeze. I really didn't want to leave.

"Lets' enjoy the rest of the day. It's okay."

He shook his head. "No, it's not. I take you to a place Charlie used to love, and I start acting like him. What's wrong with me?"

He was beating himself up when it should have been me doing the self-loathing. I had to find a way to comfort him.

"There is nothing wrong with you. You're a good person, a kind person, and I really, really like you."

He faced me, and I hugged him.

"Em, I really, really like you too. You can still trust me. I promise you. I will never do anything to hurt you. Ever."

And I believed him.

Chapter 17
Changes

Charlie had been gone for just over a week. Suddenly the weather turned unseasonably cold and wet. I zipped my rain jacket to the neck and snatched my keys off the rainbow-colored gecko hook that hung by the kitchen door. Sunshine swiped a plate with a sudsy sponge and held it under the running faucet.

"I thought you'd be riding with Keir on his first day back? He could use the moral support."

I stared at the floor. I should have known her intuition would kick in. It was impossible to hide anything from my mother. Still, I didn't want to admit to her, or anyone, that Keir's new priority seemed to be Charlie's gang. It hurt too much.

"He wants to ride with the boys, and I don't feel like sitting on someone's lap."

Sunshine stared me down. "Did you two fight?"

I shook my head. Since the day at the lake, Keir had come up with a pile of excuses not to see me. He had to shuttle his mother to her doctor appointments. His teacher dropped off a ton of makeup work. The boys needed him. The list was endless. I didn't want to believe it, but I feared he was punishing me for putting on the brakes. I took a slow, calming breath.

"No. Everything is fine, Sunshine. As fine as it can be under the circumstances."

Her brows knitted together, wrinkling the bridge of her nose. "Okay then, but drive carefully, please? I don't know what I would do if anything happened to you."

I hugged her. "I will. I promise."

At school, I parked in my spot on the back of the lot, near the empty space that once belonged to The Ghost. Keir's rod was nowhere in sight, so I headed inside alone. As soon as I entered the building, Ashanti, Melissa, and Laura swarmed me.

Melissa squeezed my shoulder. "Hey, Emmy, where's Keir? Word is he's coming back today."

"He's on his way." I tugged at my jacket collar, swung around, and stepped on Ashanti's toe. "Oh, I'm sorry."

"Don't worry about it." She forced a smile. "I texted you. Why didn't you text me back? If I didn't know better, I'd think you've been avoiding me."

She was right. I had been. She never cared about Charlie when he was alive. I sure as hell wasn't going to give her anything to gossip about now that he was gone. The image of him hanging lifeless, blood pouring from his skull, flashed through my mind. I had to get away.

"Leave her alone," Jade demanded from behind the many people who had gathered around me. "Can't you see you're upsetting her?"

No one moved, but I wasn't surprised. They'd been probing me for gory details since Charlie's death. Now they wanted the scoop on Keir. I'd make a blubbering fool of myself before I spilled a word.

The front doors flew open, and a gust of wind blew into the hallway. Keir, clad in Charlie's leather jacket, stood in the passageway with Chuy and Slick on either side of him, each with a firm hand on his shoulders. Then Shorty, Jason, and Layla entered behind them. Students slowed as they trolled past and stared. With Keir at the helm, they barreled through the crowd, edging my fair-weather friends to the side.

"Everything okay, Emmy?" Keir asked.

"Uh, yeah," I croaked, still stunned by his over-the-top entrance.

Keir removed the backpack from my shoulder and passed it to Slick. Then he dipped down, and with his fingerless-gloved hands, he hoisted me over his shoulder. Had he gone mad?

"Stop it! Put me down!" I pounded on his back.

"Quit struggling, or I'll drop you."

Students scattered as he steam-rolled down the hallway, with me hanging on for my life.

"What are you doing?" I squawked.

"I'm taking you to your locker."

"Are you crazy?"

"Crazy in love with you."

"This is not the right way to show it."

"See this girl? She's mine," he announced to everyone in earshot, then said to me through the corner of his mouth, "Is that right enough for you?"

"Keir, people are staring," I hissed.

"You won't listen to me any other way."

A group of students laughed, and I buried my face into the back of his jacket. The smell of cinnamon and ashes assaulted my senses. I jerked my head back.

"Why are you wearing Charlie's clothes?"

"I figured if he wanted me to have his ring, he'd want me to have his clothes too."

"Is that so?"

When I gave Keir the ring, it brought tears to his eyes. Now he seemed almost indifferent.

"Put me down."

"All in good time, my little pretty. All in good time."

Now he was quoting the Wicked Witch of the West. What had gotten into him?

We reached my locker, and he worked the combination on the lock with me still on his shoulder.

"Enough is enough. I want down now. My ribs hurt."

He bent at the knees and eased me to the floor. I straightened my clothes and turned to open the locker. The door stuck.

Keir brushed my cheek with his finger. "Let me get that."

With a bang of his fist, the door sprung open.

All week I'd stewed in sadness and self-doubt because he was too busy to see me, and now this. I tossed my jacket into the small space.

"Here you go, ma'am." Slick came up from behind and handed me my backpack.

"Thanks," I said flatly, pulling the books I wouldn't need until later and throwing them into my locker.

Keir walked me to my homeroom with the Back Lot Gang members following behind us like overprotective thugs.

"Chuy," he said. "Take the boys and go find something to do."

At Keir's command, the gang scattered, and he backed me against the wall, stopping millimeters before his body met mine.

"Meet me in the cafeteria for lunch." His voice was foreign, deep and raspy, from somewhere in the back of his throat. My knees weakened, and I braced against the wall for support.

"Okay," I answered before I could stop myself.

Then as quickly as he'd arrived, he wheeled around and took off down the hall.

****

Keir sat in his usual place at the Gamers' lunch table. Though now, The Back Lot Gang members hovered around him like personal bodyguards. His friends stared at their plates, obviously uncomfortable with being surrounded. I pushed between the gang, a little harder than necessary, and squeezed onto the bench beside Keir.

"Hey, beautiful," he said, in an unlike-Keir manner.

I ignored him.

Nero, sitting opposite of us, brushed his long brown bangs out of his eyes. "Hey, Emmy."

I nodded cordially.

Nero's gaze shifted to Keir and back. "You like his new look?"

"Real funny, jerkwad," Keir said.

Nero's hands flew up in front of him. "No, really, man. I'm not joking around. Actually, you look kind of cool."

Keir's eyes widened. "Thanks. The clothes are Charlie's."

Nero's face fell. "Yeah. I've meant to tell you how sorry I am about your brother."

Keir waved him off. "Stuff happens, man."

Stuff happens. Anger shot from my pupils, ricocheted off Keir, and struck me in the heart.

"What's wrong with you? Your brother just died."

The entire table stared at me as if I'd committed murder. Keir rubbed the crimson stone on Charlie's ring he wore on his middle finger.

"He's gone, and nothing's going to bring him back. I've got to move on with my life. We all do. You need to get over it."

I barked out a laugh. "I'm not ready to *get over it.*"

Keir pounded his fist on the table so hard he garnered the attention of the surrounding tables two deep. "Jesus, woman, shut up! You're bringing me down."

Grief-stricken or not, no one treated me like that. I would not allow it.

"You're an idiot."

His face slackened, but I didn't wait for a response. I jumped to my feet and ran from the cafeteria into the nearest restroom. Locked safely inside a stall, I sat on the toilet and allowed my anger to spill out my eyes.

****

Already weepy from the lunchroom episode and Keir's bad behavior, it was nearly impossible to concentrate on my artwork. Charlie's empty seat only made matters worse. A tear trickled down my cheek and plopped in the middle of my chalk sunset. The oranges, reds, and browns blurred into a starburst of color.

I pushed my pastels to the side and replayed the cafeteria incident in my mind. Keir had never been intentionally mean—at least up until now. His actions reminded me of the way I'd seen Charlie treat Melody the night of the big race with Paul Middleton. Only I wasn't pregnant or drinking alcohol.

When the final bell rang, I gathered my belongings and hustled to the back lot. Keir lounged against my car, elbow on the roof, head braced against his fist. My cheeks stung as the blood rushed to my feet.

"Hey, beautiful. What's up?"

"Back off, Keir."

The corners of his mouth tipped up, hinting at a smile. "Don't be mad. You know I didn't mean it."

"Get lost. Your stupid charm isn't going to work."

"Come on, Em."

"Tell me, Keir, what makes you think you have the right to boss me around?" He opened his mouth to speak, but I gave him the hand. "And where do you get off acting all tough? Less than a week ago, you were a gamer just like the friends you and your goons were intimidating today."

Keir squeezed his head between the heels of his hands and then threw them out as if pantomiming a bursting bomb. "I know, and I'm so sorry. I don't know what's got into me. Since Charlie died, I don't know who I am anymore."

I cautiously stepped forward, unsure which of his emotions would crop up next. A tear leaked down his cheek, and my steely resolve melted like an iceberg targeted by global warming.

"Please, Em, I don't know what I'd do if I didn't have you in my life."

The ulcer-sharp pain I'd been enduring throughout the day disappeared.

"I understand your connection to Charlie's gang, but they're acting as if you're their leader. And I don't like it."

"You've got to understand. Charlie was a father figure to the boys. And now they're turning to me for guidance. If I don't step in, Jason might kill himself, and Chuy might get the tar kicked out of him. And there's no telling what Slick might do. I need to take care of them. Charlie would have wanted it that way. Can't you put up with it for a little longer?"

Keir as leader of The Back Lot Gang? It didn't add up. The whole shebang seemed more about him and less about the gang. But if that was what he needed to get over his grief, perhaps I could put up with him, at least for a little while. I'd promised Charlie to watch out for him. I only hoped I could.

"Okay, Keir, have it your way. Dress up and play the leader of the pack if that's what you think you need to do. But if you want me to stick around, I have a few conditions."

"Anything you want. Just spill it."

"Never disrespect me in front of anyone ever again."

"You got it." He bowed his head, clearly ashamed.

"And don't do anything to mess up your chances of joining the Navy. You've always been a smart, motivated guy, not some dumb thug."

"I'll do whatever it takes to keep you in my life. Will you forgive me?"

"Well, maybe," I whispered.

Keir winced. "Em, there's something else I need to tell you."

By the tone of his voice, I could tell I wouldn't like it. "What?"

"Don't panic. It's no big deal. Jake offered me

Charlie's old job, that's all."

"What about Georgy G's? I thought you liked it there."

"It was all right for a while. But Jake's pays better. With Charlie gone, I have to help out more at home."

I'd forgotten Elise needed his help. "Of course, you have to take the job. I'll miss working with you."

"Yeah, that'll be a bummer, but you can always stop by the shop on your way home. Or better yet, just quit. Then you can come to Jake's and hang out with me after school."

I shook my head. "I need to earn extra cash for college next year."

"Keir!"

The boys frisked across the parking lot, spinning and play fighting. Chuy slapped Keir on the back.

"Hey man, ready to go?"

"Yeah, sure," he said before turning his attention back to me. "I'll call you later."

And without a second glance, he took off with the gang. Keir had become a different person since Charlie's death. It was as if he was trying to assume his brother's persona. Maybe it was his way of coping. Maybe he'd return to normal once he got over his grief.

I sure hoped so because it was getting really hard to like the hybrid he'd become.

Chapter 18
Twisted Life

Miss Iola waved as I walked into Georgy's.

"Sorry, I'm late. Got held up at school." I flipped on the *Available* sign and settled behind my register.

"Don't worry about it. Ya can't be perfect all the time."

I smiled and then scrubbed at the spots on my conveyor belt with a rag. I sensed Miss Iola's stare boring a hole in the back of my head, but I pretended not to notice. Idle chat didn't interest me. I was too miserable.

"How's Keir doin'?" she asked.

She wasn't put off easily. She'd keep pricking and prying in her sweet country way until she got an answer.

"He had a real hard time for the first week, but he seems better now."

That was an understatement. For most of the day, he'd hardly seemed affected at all.

"I'm just sick over what happened to poor Charlie." Miss Iola placed her hand over her heart. "He had a rough time growing up, then to meet an untimely death." She dabbed at a tear in the corner of her eye and leaned closer. "I know people 'round here say he hasn't any kin on his daddy's side to speak of, but I don't believe it to be true. I met his granddaddy or great-granddaddy or something like that once. 'Least, I believed him to be. They had the same name and all."

Blood pounded between my ears. "You knew Charlie's grandfather?"

"It was a long time ago. I haven't seen him since the early sixties."

"Where is he now?"

"Lord only knows. I was near your age the last time we crossed paths."

Not wanting to miss a word, I left my post and rested my elbows on the back of Iola's workstation. "Where'd you meet him?"

"I was living in Irmo at the time."

"Charlie's family is from Irmo?"

"No, child. I come down to visit my cousin, Judy, in Moncks Corner."

"So Charlie's family is from here?"

"Nope, Judy said they were city folk who moved to Charleston from somewhere up north. I'll never forget the day he drove into town in a big blue car. It looked something similar to the one *our* Charlie drives. Well, like he used to drive anyway, bless his heart." Miss Iola drew a cross on her chest with her finger.

My brain rendered me speechless while I processed that Charlie's grandfather drove a car just like The Ghost. Miss Iola settled back into her station and rearranged the plastic bag holder. I took it as a subtle hint to urge her on. Miss Iola followed homespun rules when discussing what she called "idle gossip"—meaning she'd be glad to do it if the recipient took the responsibility by begging.

"Go on, Miss Iola. Tell me more about him, please?"

A big smile spread across her face, and her eyes widened. "Well, Charlie's grandfather reminded me of Marlin Brando in *The Wild Ones*."

Miss Iola's excitement indicated Brando must have been good looking at some point, but all I could think of was the mob boss in *The Godfather*.

"I've never seen that movie."

"Let me tell you. Charlie strut into The Olde Soda Shop wearing a black leather jacket, tight blue jeans, and slicked-back hair looking like he owned the place." She stopped to fan herself. "I couldn't imagine why a boy from Charleston would come all the way to Moncks Corner just to drink a soda, but he did, every night for the good part of my stay."

A couple walked in through the automatic doors and past our registers.

Miss Iola straightened. "Hey y'all, welcome to Big George's Groceries."

The customers waved and pushed their cart toward the vegetable section. I chewed my nail until they passed.

"What else do you know about his grandfather?"

She shook her head. "I don't know if I should keep speaking on the subject. You know that old saying, darling. Curiosity killed the cat."

"Yeah, but satisfaction brought him back," I retorted.

Miss Iola laughed. "Some things are better off forgotten."

She couldn't stop now, while every ounce of me burned to know more. "You can't leave me hanging. It's not fair."

She stared at the ceiling and fingered her chin.

"Well, since you insist." She leaned in. "The moment I laid eyes on that boy, I could see he was trouble. He was wound up tighter than an eight-day clock, chasing all the girls and right behind their boyfriend's backs. It's a wonder nobody shot him."

Miss Iola's Charlie sounded so much like my Charlie. "He chased after other guys' girlfriends?"

"And the girls without boyfriends, too. I'd have never given him the time of day if he hadn't lured me out to the parking lot with the promise of a non-filter cigarette."

I raised my eyebrows. "Cigarettes. Gross. I didn't know you smoked."

Miss Iola frowned. "I don't, now. And don't look at me that way. Smoking wasn't a big deal back in those days." She pulled at the corners of her Georgy G shirt and smoothed it out. "Besides, before I had a chance to take my first puff, he tried to steal a kiss."

I giggled.

Miss Iola turned a vivid scarlet. "I know it seems funny now, but I was a purty thing back then."

"I'm sorry. I wasn't laughing at you. It's just he sounds so much like...never mind. What happened next?"

"I'm not sure it's healthy gossiping about kin of the dead."

"You don't believe Charlie can hear you, do you, Miss Iola?"

She bit her lip. "Well, I reckon not. Where was I?"

"You were telling me about him trying to kiss you."

"Oh yeah, that's right." She fluffed her hair. "Well, I almost caved and let him do it, but just before his lips

Susan Antony

met mine, I thought better of it and ran back inside."

Old Miss Whitley rammed her cart into the side of Iola's workstation. "Are you going to stand there yapping all day, or are you going to ring up my groceries?"

"Oh, I'm so sorry, Miss Whitley. Let me help you." She ran around the side and loaded the purchases onto the conveyor belt.

"Y'all done moved the shelves around again," she huffed. "And I can't find the jars of my favorite store-brand baby peas. Where's that boy?" She tapped her foot.

"Keir don't work here no more," Miss Iola said. "So you'll have to wait until I can find them myself."

"Kids today don't have an ounce of responsibility," Miss Whitley grumbled.

Miss Iola held her finger to her lips. "Shhh! Don't talk that way about him. His brother just died."

Discussing a piece of Charlie's life had brightened my spirits. It hurt too much to talk about his death.

"I'll get the peas," I said.

"Thank you, sugar," Miss Iola said.

I hurried off to aisle three, where they'd hid the peas. Miss Iola told me the more the customers had to look, the more they'd see other items to buy. It didn't seem like an honest practice, but who was I to judge. By the time I returned, five people were lined up at Miss Iola's register. I plopped the can on the belt and hurried back to my workstation.

"I'll help the next customer here."

Patrons came in a heavy stream for the rest of the night. It was as if the whole town went grocery shopping at the same time, on the same night. In

148

between cordial register conversations, Miss Iola's story swirled in my mind. Had she actually known Charlie's great-grandfather, or had her memory become fuzzy over time?

Charlie was no longer with us, but attempting to unravel his twisted life made it feel as if he were alive again.

At least for a moment.

Chapter 19
Grease

A few days later, I was still no closer to figuring out the mystery of Charlie's life or the reason for Keir's out-of-character behavior. Work kept me busy. Since Keir took Charlie's job at Jake's and his leadership of the boys, our time spent together had become next to nil. By his choice, not mine.

I drove to school and headed in alone once again. A few paces into the hallway, someone grabbed me around the waist from behind.

I took a deep breath as I ran my fingers over the dusting of blond hair on the hands that bound me. "Keir Harper, you nearly scared me to death."

He nuzzled his nose in my hair and kissed the back of my neck. "That's because you're not living right, baby."

I wormed out of his arms, then stepped back. My silky-haired friend sported a head full of grease. The gang engulfed us like a wrought iron fence, the gaps filled in by a number of Keir's gamer and brainiac friends, all looking like Back Lot Gang clones.

I tugged on the curl hanging in the middle of Keir's forehead and examined my oily fingers. "What have you done to your hair?"

"Watch it. You'll mess it up." He gestured to the two-inch high mound of golden grease. "How do I look?"

I studied him until the right words came to me. "Don't you think it's a little big?"

"What do you mean?" His face was smattered with disbelief.

I tried unsuccessfully to suppress a smile. "It looks like Charlie's hair on steroids."

"Come a little closer, and I'll show you something big." Keir wiggled the top of his zipper.

The guys roared with laughter. I'd had enough of his antics. The time had come to put him in his place.

"I would, but I forgot my microscope."

A maniacal grin stretched across his face, and he wrestled me into a headlock, holding my face a bit too close to his groin. I dug my fingernails into the thick muscles in the back of his thighs. He didn't flinch.

The boys circled us, chanting, "Come on, Keir, give her a full-frontal boogie."

"Show her who's daddy."

Keir tickled my side.

I pinched him harder. "What's wrong with you? Let go of me, you big jerk. You have exactly two seconds before I punch you in the—"

The noisy hallway lapsed into silence. A pair of black loafers adorned with silver buckles stomped into my line of view.

"Mr. Harper, what is going on here?"

I recognized Principal Tanner's voice at once and hazarded to guess he wasn't happy. Keir released me, and I straightened, keeping my gaze on the pink laces on my hiking boots.

"We were just messing around. Tell him, Em." Keir nudged me.

My mouth went dry. I was mad, but I wasn't a snitch.

"Is that right, Miss Russo?" Principal Tanner asked.

I smoothed my tussled hair. "Yes, sir."

"If Mr. Harper has threatened you or hurt you in any way, I need you to speak up." He pursed his lips.

"Mr. Harper, I mean, Keir is my friend," I said, even though lately he'd been hell-bent on revolting me.

Tanner's gaze shifted beyond me and moved from left to right. "What the heck are you boys doing with grease in your hair? And what's with the matching outfits?"

No one answered. His mouth twisted, and the lines in his face deepened. A crowd had coagulated nearby.

Tanner whipped around and gave them a hard stare. "Get to class."

The clot of students burst apart, tripping over each other in their haste. He turned back to us, and his six-foot-plus frame seemed to grow.

"Nero, what's the reason for the sudden change in your appearance?"

"It's the new fashion, sir." Nero's shoulders jiggled.

A few random snickers followed.

"For your information, this fashion isn't new. It's old," Tanner said. "You look like a bunch of hoods. It was one thing when there were five of you skipping around, acting like James Dean wannabes, but now you're a mob. Let me remind you that the school has zero-tolerance for gang activity. If you boys give me one reason to believe that you're engaging in any type of criminal behavior, you will all be expelled. And I don't want to see any more girls in headlocks or physical aggression against anyone, consensual or not. Do I make myself clear?"

After a considerable amount of muttering and grumbling, Derrick, whose black-rimmed glasses and pimply complexion didn't look so nerdy anymore, goose-stepped forward and saluted.

"Yes sir, *Herr* Principal."

Tanner yanked him by the arm so hard the two nearly collided. "You're coming with me to the office. The rest of you, on to your homerooms."

"Come on, guys." Keir motioned for everyone to follow.

"Wait a minute," Tanner hollered. He rapidly closed the gap between Keir and himself, towing Derrick along with him. "Mr. Harper, I want to see you in my office at the end of the day, no later than five minutes after the final bell. Do I make myself clear?"

Keir shrugged as if being in trouble were second nature to him.

Tanner stared hard at me. "I hope you know what you're doing?"

He paused for a moment before dragging Derrick toward the office. I elbowed Keir.

"Now look what you've done. Not only are you and Derrick in trouble, the principal thinks I'm stupid."

"Don't worry about it. He's got nothing on me."

Maybe he didn't, but I couldn't help worrying. Not so much what the principal thought of me or any trouble I may be in, but about Keir. He'd always been sweet and kind, a model student. For some reason, his undying need to impress the gang had taken precedence over everything: his school standing, his drive to succeed, and me.

While the day started out whack, when I entered the cafeteria for lunch, I discovered the level had risen to new heights. Girls clambered about The Back Lot Gang's tables, which had multiplied to three. And they weren't just the rockabilly girls that the gang attracted. There were jockettes, redneck girls, and even a cheerleader or two. Apparently, a lot more than Keir's hair had changed. I hurried through the lunch line, fearing if I didn't claim my spot, it would be gobbled up by one of the gang's groupies.

"Excuse me," I said to a blonde with a beauty-parlor blowout, sitting between Keir and Chuy.

With a glare and a huff, she rose and moved to another table. I wedged myself in her place.

Keir snagged a roll off my plate and took a bite. "Look at all the girls, would you?" he said between chews. "When Charlie was alive, most of them didn't give us the time of day. Now they think we're cool."

"Don't talk with your mouth full," I said, planning a blunt force attack with my plastic tray if the blonde dared to put her painted claws anywhere near Keir again.

At least imagining her with a goose egg on her forehead and lettuce hanging from her hair gave me reason to smile. I'd never been jealous over Keir in the past, but he'd never showed an interest in other girls when I was around. The situation had forced the realization upon me.

I liked Keir more than I cared to admit.

"Mind if I eat your fries?" he asked.

The unexpected estrogen rush at the table had done a number on my appetite. I pushed my plate toward him and took a sip of my cola instead. Chuy swiveled around to ogle a passing brunette and bumped into my arm. Soda splashed over the sides of the can and dribbled down my chin. I wiped it off with my forearm and jabbed him with my elbow on the backstroke.

"If you keep craning your neck, you'll make it stiff."

Chuy hooked his arm over my shoulder and leaned across me. "Hey, Keir, Emmy's acting all psycho again. She'll scare the girls away."

Keir belted out a laugh.

I pushed Chuy. "You're invading my personal space."

His eyes twinkled. "See? She's mean, man. None of the other ladies want to come near. They're afraid Emmy will kick their butts. Would you mind if I sat with some of the new guys?"

"Go ahead, Romeo," Keir said, "But don't forget where your loyalties lie."

"No sir, boss-man; that'll never happen." Chuy grabbed his tray and squeezed in next to one of the cheerleaders at the table beside us.

"Those girls aren't really afraid of me, are they?" I asked, hoping Keir wouldn't think I was taking myself too seriously.

He shot me a sideways glance. "Sure, they are."

"Why? I'm hardly an Amazon."

Keir stopped eating. "You belong to me. Anyone who messes with you messes with me." He brushed my cheek with his knuckle. "You're the top lady, bae."

I paused, allowing my mind to process what he'd said. "First of all, I don't *belong* to anyone, and I certainly didn't sign up to be anyone's lady."

"You don't have to, Em. Everyone knows I'm into you. It is what it is. So, get used to it."

Boy, his grieving process was starting to weird me out. Still, as much as I didn't want it to, having the power his status allotted me felt good. Sort of.

When the final bell rang, the boys and I met up on the back of the lot to wait for Keir, all of us anxious about the outcome of his meeting with Principal Tanner. Gray clouds loomed around the half-mast sun, and the temperature dropped rapidly. Very odd for early fall.

Chuy rubbed my back. "Don't worry 'bout Keir. Tanner's just trying to scare him."

Don't worry? That was easy for him to say. I wasn't used to being on the wrong side of right where school was concerned, and neither was Keir. Shorty hopped onto the fender of his car. It dipped under his weight.

"If Keir don't get out here soon, we won't have time to drop the engine he bought in my rod."

Surely, I'd misunderstood? Keir would never spend money on someone else's ride. His mom needed his help.

"Did you just say that Keir bought you an engine?"

"Yep. He's da man, Emmy. I could never come up with that kind of cash."

Chuy punched him in the arm. "Maybe you should get a job, *cabrón*."

Shorty raised a leg and pushed Chuy back with the toe of his boot. "Hell, it's all I can do to keep up with my school work now. Two years as a senior is enough."

After I pieced together a few disconnected thoughts, the realization gobsmacked me. Sid had given

Keir three-thousand dollars. Had he spent that money on Shorty's car? He wouldn't. Unless there was some sort of emergency?

"Hey, Shorty, why do you need to replace your engine?"

"Keir said if we make my rod just like The Ghost, we won't miss Charlie so much. It will sort of be like he's here."

That was the craziest logic I'd ever heard. Why would anyone want to replicate the killer Ghost?

Nero pointed. "Hold up, people. Here comes trouble."

All heads turned to follow the line of his outstretched arm. Paul Middleton's girlfriend, Cherie, and two of her brunette friends pranced across the parking lot in our direction. Could things get any worse?

"That's my kind of trouble," Chuy said. "The kind with large capital T's." He cupped his hands below his chest and bounced them.

"Hey, y'all." Cherie flipped her long, blonde hair over her shoulder and smiled at Chuy. He blushed and dropped his juggling hands to his sides. She gestured to the line of vehicles on the back row.

"Which one of these is yours?"

"None of them, baby. I haven't found the car of my dreams yet, but I may have just found my dream girl."

Cherie shifted her weight to one foot and propped her fist on her hip. "If I was your girl, how would we get around? By bicycle, with me on the handlebars?"

Chuy grinned. "We'd always have a place in the back of my pal Shorty's rod." He rubbed the fender of the soon to be Ghost Two.

She shifted her weight to the other foot. "With him gawking at us from the rearview mirror?"

Cherie's friends giggled. Chuy inched closer to her and tugged on the edges of her jacket, opening it slightly. "Well, if a girl like you needed a ride, I'd beg, borrow, or steal."

"Really?" She twirled her hair around her finger.

I thought of something Sunshine always said. *Every time something happens to tip the earth, the earth fights to right itself.* This moment, in which Chuy believed he could covet Paul Middleton's girlfriend without grave repercussions, was one of those inevitable happenstances.

Paul stormed across the parking lot. He bore a scowl that could be seen from three rows away.

"Cherie, what are you doing with those losers?"

As if she'd been stricken with sudden palsy, Cherie's flirty expression fell. Her brunette posse assigned themselves to her sides, standing slightly behind her.

Paul stumbled to a stop, short of breath, his cheeks blotchy.

Chuy spit on the ground, narrowly missing the toe of Paul's boot. They scowled at each other.

"Who you calling loser, loser?"

Paul yanked Cherie by the arm. She stared at his fingers, biting into her flesh, and frowned.

"I was only talking. Right, y'all?"

While the brunettes nodded like bobbleheads, the veins in Paul's hand pulsed as he squeezed her arm harder. I didn't particularly like Cherie, but Paul's abuse inflamed me.

"Leave her alone."

Paul glared at me, and Cherie jerked loose from his grasp.

Chuy threw his body weight into Paul's midsection and knocked him to the ground. Paul's head hit the pavement with a *thunk*. He lay still for a moment, appearing dazed. Then he flipped over and pushed himself up. Chuy jumped on his back and hooked his arms around his neck in a stranglehold. Paul staggered to his feet despite the extra weight on his back.

A flash of silver appeared in Chuy's hand. There was an audible click and then a switchblade poked against Paul's neck.

"Don't you ever touch her like that again. *"Comprende, güey?"*

One of the girls screamed. Jason covered her mouth. "Quiet, you'll spook him."

Paul's eyes bulged. "Are you going to stand there and let this crazy son of a bitch kill me?"

"Keep talking, *pendejo*. Give me a reason to slit your throat." Chuy ran the knife teasingly across Paul's jugular.

The whole rivalry thing had gone too far. I had to stop them before something terrible happened.

"Chuy, he's not worth it. Put down the knife, please?"

"Stay out of this, Emmy. This isn't a lady's business." He pressed the blade into the fleshy skin under Paul's chin.

I flinched and grabbed my neck as if the knife was at my own throat. "Don't ruin your life over him."

Chuy's hand shook. The blade pressed deeper into Paul's neck. I searched the faces of the gang members seeking connection.

"Do something, will you?"

They stood unmoving; their faces blanched as if Paul were already dead.

"What's going on?"

Keir's voice. He ran at us fast.

"A little scuffle," Slick hollered back, his gaze never leaving the action.

Keir skidded to a stop. He paused, focused on the blade, then presented his hand. "Chuy, give me the knife."

"I don't want to. This scum got rough with the girl." He tipped his head at Cherie. "Someone needs to teach him some manners."

"You're right, someone does, but not here. Not this way. Not now." Keir stepped closer. "Put down the knife before you get yourself into trouble I can't fix."

Chuy shook his head. "I'm not their punching bag no more."

His arm twitched, and the knife indented the skin just below Paul's jugular vein. Paul whimpered.

Keir stepped closer. "Drop the blade."

Chuy gritted his teeth. The veins in his neck throbbed. Blood pumped in my brain just as hard. The unbearable ache of Charlie's loss coveted me, and tears streamed down my cheeks. One wrong move and another life would be snuffed out. I could not allow it.

"Please, stop. We've had enough death. Charlie wouldn't want this."

Chuy's head jerked toward me, his face marred with pain. "Charlie."

"She's right, brother," Keir said, in a voice just shy of tender.

Chuy's eyes watered, and his wrist went limp. The

knife slipped from his hand and clanked on the ground. Keir kicked it out of the way and yanked Chuy off Paul. Slick and Jason jumped in and held Paul's arms behind his back. Chuy collapsed into Keir's arms, sobbing.

"I'm sorry, boss. I didn't mean to."

Keir held on to him for three beats and then shoved him to the side. His blue eyes darkened and narrowed into slits. He grabbed a handful of Paul's shirt.

"This is your last warning. Mess with Chuy again, and I'll let him cut you like a friggin' pig."

Paul wrestled against the hold Jason and Slick had on him. "Tell him to keep away from Cherie."

Keir laughed. "Slavery was abolished in 1865. She's allowed to think for herself." He turned to her. "What do you want to do? Or do you know?"

Cherie grabbed two fistfuls of her hair and held them tight at her neck. "I know one thing. I don't want to be part of this idiocy."

"Then leave." Keir pointed to the road. "Or go with him." He jerked a thumb in Paul's direction.

Cherie's lower lip trembled. She spun around and double-stepped toward the road, the brunettes following close behind.

Keir turned to Paul. "She doesn't seem too into you right now."

"Listen, Harper. Don't you or any of your slimy-haired friends ever look at her again. You understand me?"

Keir's mouth rose into a half-smile. "Maybe if you learned to swim right, she wouldn't come wading in our pool."

Paul's face blazed. "I'd kick your ass right here if it weren't for the herd of greaseballs backing you up."

An aura of hatred stretched between them and grew like a living, breathing thing. One by one, it spread to the boys, and they surrounded Paul.

I picked up the knife and hid it behind my back. "Keir, stop this before we're all thrown in jail."

He turned to me, hatred still beaming in his eyes.

"You'll ruin your life. Think about your mom. She needs you."

Keir closed his eyes. His lips moved as if he were conversing with himself. An eternity, or maybe a minute passed before he jerked to attention. His gaze locked on Paul.

"Meet me at the clearing on Thunder Road tonight. We'll make it a fair fight—just me and you."

I'd never known Keir to fight, though lately, I was finding out lots of things I didn't know about him.

Paul let out a one-syllable laugh. "Like I can trust you."

"Right. I get it. You're scared," Keir countered.

Paul blinked a few times, smirked, and shook his head. "I'll be there."

"Good." Keir smoothed the sides of his slick hair. "Bring all your buddies if you want. We'll have a field demonstration. One of yours to one of mine."

This was beyond comprehension. Keir had arranged a massive gang fight, like the one in *The Outsiders*. What was wrong with him?

Paul shuffled his feet and wiggled against the stronghold Jason and Slick had on him. "All right," he finally said, "We'll be there. But call off your goons."

Keir nodded, and they let him go. The gang hooted and cheered as Paul hustled to his pick-up truck.

I stood absolutely still, wallowing in dread. Full-blown madness was happening all around me, and I couldn't stop it.

I didn't know how.

Chapter 20
Revenge of the Rockabillies

At nine-forty-five p.m., we gathered at the clearing on Thunder Road. Keir marched in front of us, in full oration mode, his breath forming a cloud of fog above his head.

"I know most of you have never been in a fight, so I'm going to give it to you straight. Those guys are deer hunters. They are familiar with the scent of fear and will seek it out. Whatever you do, don't let them see you're afraid or you're done for."

A breeze cut through the crisp night. I zipped my jacket up to my chin and shoved my hands into my pockets. Though I suspected my chattering teeth were more a symptom of the angst I harbored than the record-breaking cold Southern temperature. Where had Keir gained this knowledge of fighting? In the six years I'd known him, the only time I'd seen him raise a fist to anyone was a few hours ago.

Brandon O'Malley, a skinny guy with red hair and freckles, raised his hand, pulled it down, and then raised it again. "Ah, excuse me?"

"What?" Keir grunted.

"How do I hide fear when some dude two times my size is about to punch my lights out?"

"How?" He threw his hands out, palms facing skyward. "It's easy. Channel your anger. Go ape on them, dude. There's nothing more terrifying than a madman."

I smiled at the irony of Keir's words. He had been anything but sane lately.

"That's easier said than done," Brandon muttered.

"Listen," Keir said. "I've had enough of this sissy bunk, so reel it in. Aren't you tired of people calling you weirdoes, geeks, and greaseballs?"

"Damn right, we are," Chuy shouted.

Cries of unity followed, and with each one, victory spread farther across Keir's face. He fist-pumped the air. "That's what I'm talking about, boys."

More cheers sounded, but I didn't join in. Fighting never really settled anything. The fact this rivalry still existed after Charlie died was proof of that.

Keir motioned the mob quiet. "We're going to win tonight, and not only for ourselves, but for all the poor saps who were too chicken to join with us. We'll face off with these bullies. When word gets out that we slaughtered the lot of them, no one will ever mess with any of you again."

The cheering reached a crescendo while the gang darted about, high-fiving and play fighting. All the glee dropped like a dead weight on my chest because there would be no real winners. The only thing that could come from this event was more hatred.

Keir came over and placed a hand on my shoulder. "Take Layla and Kat and wait in the car. Paul and his crew will be here soon."

I nodded and sought out the girls, more than happy to leave the soon-to-be battle arena. Keir had promised he would never put me in danger, but my confidence level in his judgment had plummeted. Even as the incredulity of my decision to stay here on Thunder Road pounded at the backdoor of my mind, my heart wouldn't let me leave. I cared too much about him.

At my urging, Layla and Kat settled into the back seat of the 'stang. I took the front. The two of them chatted and laughed while I remained focused on the road, awaiting the arrival of the challengers. Someone jostled my shoulder.

"Don't look so worried," Layla said. "The guys are going to stomp them tonight."

I faked a smile and then turned away, unable to agree but also not ready to share my overwhelming apprehension with the senior members of the gang's *property*.

Headlamps glinted off the rearview mirror. A single set of lights blended into many. I rolled down the window to shout a warning. Keir headed to the road. Pickup truck after pickup truck pulled up and parked on the opposite side.

Paul climbed out of a testicle-bearing redneck machine with his fists clenched to his sides. Only in the South.

Keir motioned him away from the crowd. The two exchanged a few words and took off for the clearing, with the rest of Paul's group trotting behind them. The Back Lot Gang lined up, their black figures bathed in bluish moonlight, while the opposition positioned themselves directly across.

Keir and Paul met in the middle. They bounced on their toes and circled, stretching their necks from side to side the way fighters do. A few revolutions later, Paul swung. Keir bobbed right, narrowly escaping a blow to the head. He returned the punch and landed a fist square on Paul's jaw. Paul's head snapped back, but he didn't fall. Both sides charged, and the field became a dusty mass of flying appendages.

I scanned the melee for Keir and caught sight of him just as he knocked Paul to the ground with a right hook. Shouts and moans and smacking of fists against flesh by multiple rivals followed, and Keir disappeared from my view again.

I jumped from the car and watched the tangled web, but the fighting's intensity made it nearly impossible to determine who was whom. I shuddered at each blow, no matter which side dished it out.

On the outskirts, closest to me, a gorilla-sized brute hooked his arm around the neck of a guy half of his size. He drew back his fist and pounded the smaller guy mercilessly in the head, nearly pulverizing him.

I inched closer, my heartbeat racing. Chuy hung limp and lifeless in the crook of the gorilla-boy's arm. I wholly expect the big guy to toss him to the side. Instead, he slammed his fist into Chuy's head once more. Keir's friend, my friend, my fellow gang member's body bounced from the impact. Rage spread through my veins, choking out every sane thought I had left in my head. I wanted blood.

A cry exploded from my mouth, and I charged, leaping over the embankment and dashing into the field. I jumped onto the brute's back, locked my arms around his neck, and used my body weight to choke him. He gagged and pawed at my arms with his meaty fingers. Chuy crumpled to the ground, blood trickling from the corner of his mouth.

My mount stumbled backward and spun in a circle. I wrenched my arms tighter and wrapped my legs around his waist. He grabbed my wrists and cinched me higher on his back. My neck jerked, and he pulled out a clump of my hair. I wailed.

"Don't worry, Emmy. I'll save you!" Layla hoofed down the embankment and kicked him in the shins with the pointy toe of her pump.

He let go of my hair and took a swipe at her. She darted behind him and kicked him from behind. Then she circled him and shot a foot at his groin. He caught her heel and tossed her backward. She landed on her tailbone and cried in pain.

Chuy stirred and opened his eyes. He crawled to his knees, but Gorilla-boy kicked him in the ribs and bore down on my arms until they popped loose from his neck. He hoisted me over his back and into the air. Time froze as I hung like a rag doll, waiting to be tossed to the ground. Somewhere between the suspension and the feeling of falling, I caught sight of Keir.

Terror flashed across his face. He shoved Paul into Jason's massacring fist, then ran like unleashed hell towards us. He crashed into my captor, and next thing I knew, I was safe on my feet.

"Layla, Emmy, get in the car now," he shouted.

Layla rolled to her knees and scrambled on all fours to the road.

"Now, Emmy. Run!"

With Keir's words still ringing in my ears, the guy nailed him with an uppercut. Keir rocked back on his heels, shook his head, and then spit out a mouthful of blood. I covered my eyes.

"Get out of here now," he howled.

The desperate tone of his voice jumpstarted my

senses, and I scampered off. Layla helped me up the embankment, and we clung to each other while Keir took a power-packed blow to the gut. He doubled over, gasping for air.

Chuy staggered to his feet again and reeled sideways.

"Somebody help!" I screamed in a voice loud enough to stop a freight train dead on the tracks.

No one seemed to hear me. No one but the brute. His lips curled up into a snarl. He drew back his fist. Layla and I screamed. Nero jetted up from behind, hands above his head, clamped in a tight ball, and smashed his fists into the side of the big guy's neck. He grunted once and toppled to the ground. Nero helped Keir to his feet. Keir took a deep breath, and the two ran back into the thick of the action side by side.

"Do you still think we're going to win?" I asked Layla, clutching her tighter.

"I don't know. When Charlie was alive, we always did." Her voice lacked the confidence it had earlier.

My rising anxiety reiterated something I had discovered a few days ago. I cared about Keir and this motley group of rockabilly greasers more than I wanted to admit. I cared because I was one of them.

Slick's pink-haired girlfriend, whom I now knew as Kat, got out of the car, popped a bubble, and parked her butt on the hood of the 'stang.

I frowned. "You better get down before Keir sees you."

She hopped off, and I turned back to the fight in time to hear Keir shout, "Come on, let's nail these losers!"

The former nerds, geeks, and weirdoes seemed to

grow taller. They unleashed a sadistic fury on their opponents. Paul's crew, bruised and bloody, fled the scene one by one. The few that remained were so hopelessly outnumbered they had no choice but to beat it to their trucks.

Riotous cheers rang out into the night. Injured yet smiling, gang members hobbled around the field, shouting praises to Keir. For the first time since we arrived on Thunder Road, I allowed myself a full smile.

"You did it, boys. You showed them who rules," Keir said, in a voice worthy of the demagogic idol he'd become. "Now it's on to Jake's to celebrate your victory."

Back at the garage, Layla, Kat, and I set up a makeshift hospital in the office with supplies borrowed from the shop medicine cabinet. We used a whole bottle of iodine, disinfecting busted knuckles, split lips, bloody scratches, and Slick's slightly ripped earlobe. Once everyone else had been patched up, Keir came into the office. He had a gash above his eye and a purple bruise forming on his cheek. Rust-colored blood streaked his face. He sat on the corner of the desk.

"Emmy can take care of me," he told Layla and Kat, unofficially dismissing them.

I cleaned Keir's face with an antiseptic swab and dabbed at his split eyebrow with iodine.

"Ow." He jerked his head back. "It's not bad enough I got slugged trying to rescue you, but now you're going to burn me with that junk too."

"Hold still. I've got to apply a butterfly bandage."

"I'll be all right."

He tried to stand, but I pushed him down.

"You better be still because if this doesn't work,

I'm driving you to the hospital for stitches."

"Okay, boss."

I attached half the bandage below the tear, pulled as tight as the latex would allow, and stuck the other end to his forehead. Keir winced.

"What the hell were you thinking, Emmy, jumping that guy?"

"I had to. He was killing Chuy."

"Now I've heard everything. From here on out, I don't care who's getting killed. Don't jump into a fight. I can't concentrate on what I'm doing if I have to worry about you."

The old me would have ripped him a new one in a skinny minute, but the new, gang-member-live-in-the-moment me chose to write his comment off as chivalry. I tilted his head from side to side and examined my handiwork.

"It looks pretty good if I do say so myself."

"Thanks, baby. I sure am lucky to have you." He snaked his hands into my back pockets and pulled me between his legs.

My insides went fuzzy warm. I'd never been this close to him.

"I know I've been a jerk lately, but filling in for Charlie hasn't been easy. It'll be over soon. I promise."

A bright light returned into my world. "You're leaving The Back Lot Gang?"

"Not yet. The boys still need me."

The light dimmed. "I was hoping after you won the fight, you'd go back to concentrating more on your grades and less about leading the gang."

"Please be patient for a little longer. You are the most important person to me, and I'd have never made it through Charlie's death if I didn't have you to help me."

I looked at him, really looked at him. Before me stood the person I'd always considered my best friend—the one with the crystal blue eyes. All my grief, all my worries, fell to the wayside like the battle scars of the night. He ran the pad of his thumb across my lips, then with feather-light contact, he kissed me. This time I didn't back away.

"Stay with me tonight," he whispered.

My body wanted to, but my mind screamed *no*. "I'm not ready for the whole night thing and all."

"We don't have to do anything you don't want to. I just want to be near you."

I'd been lying to myself for over a year, and it was time to face the truth.

I loved Keir. And I didn't want to leave either.

So I kicked my apprehension to the curb and agreed.

Chapter 21
The Disgruntled Teen

Keir left me alone in Jake's office to call Sunshine.

"Hello?" she croaked.

"Hey, Mom, it's Emerald." There was no harm in getting on her good side.

"Hey, honey. Is everything okay?" Her voice sounded winded, and Sid breathed in the background. I shook it off. "Layla asked me to spend the night. Do you mind?"

I hated to lie, but I didn't want to face the debate the absolute truth might trigger.

"Of course not. I'm glad you're spending time with a girlfriend for a change. Call me tomorrow when you're ready to come home. I'll pick you up."

I hesitated. That would be a problem, but one that could be dealt with in the morning. "Thanks, Mom."

Sliding lies past Sunshine had never been an easy task. Either I'd gotten better at it, or she'd been too busy doing things with Sid I didn't want to think about. Whatever the reason, tonight her radar wasn't tuned into my frequency.

I left the office, dancing to the beat of the strong rhythmed rockabilly music. In the lobby, behind the front entrance, stood Cherie and her brunette sidekicks, their noses pressed to the glass, making steam marks. A handful of the popular kids crowded in behind them.

Had The Back Lot Gang's strange new popularity gotten to them too?

It was too late to duck out of view, so I ticked the lock and opened the door wide enough to speak through the crack. "Can I help you?"

"Chuy invited us to the party," Cherie said.

"I don't think that's a good idea. If Paul finds out you're here, he'll be out for blood. Don't you think we've had enough fighting for one night?"

She wedged her foot in the opening and shoved her smartphone in my face. "It's freezing out here. Are you going to let us in, or do I have to text Chuy and tell him you're being a big 'B'?"

His invitation stared back at me in bold, black letters. I swung the door wide.

"Since you insist."

The girls spilled inside, giggling and yakking too loudly, the way flirty girls do when they're trying too hard to capture a boy's attention.

"So, like, where's the party?" Brunette number one asked.

"So, like, this way." I gestured to the shop door, and they tramped past.

Some of the gang members and rockabilly girls danced. Others bobbed their heads to the music. Chuy sat by himself on a workbench, holding a dry ice pack to his cheek. When he noticed the mob of estrogen and hairspray piling in, he smiled like a loon, then winced and pressed a finger to the cut on his lip.

Fate was sometimes cruel. Cherie had finally come just to see him, and he looked like he'd been trampled by a herd of buffalo. Her group rushed to him. Gang members appearing dazed and intrigued undulated over and formed a half-circle around the thunderhead cloud of girls. With my lips still buzzing from his kiss, I was relieved that Keir kept his nose under the hood of the soon to be Ghost Two.

Layla wasn't so lucky with her boyfriend. Jason ate up the attention along with the rest of the boys. She sat on an empty auto lift raised to chair level. I grabbed a deserted beer off a workbench and joined her.

She glared at the mob. "Who let the dogs in?"

"I did. Sorry."

She directed her narrowed eyes at me.

"Come on, Layla. You know Jason loves you," I said, despite the fact his actions said the opposite. At least at the moment.

"I suppose." She flashed a one-sided smile, pulled a blunt from her bra, and lit it.

The paper crackled as she drew the skunky-smelling smoke into her lungs.

"Aren't you even the least bit bugged by all the attention the boys are getting?"

"Not really. They're nice guys. They deserve to be liked."

"I know that. And you know that. But two months ago, those girls wouldn't have been caught dead anywhere around us. It was better when everyone hated us like they did before Charlie died. I swear if one of them so much as touches Jason, I'll rip her hair out, a handful at a time."

I laughed.

"I wouldn't be so smug if I were you. I heard through the grapevine that a couple of them are interested in Keir. Keep that in mind next time you apply an open-door policy."

My stomach burned. I'd just kissed him once, but the green-eyed monster bit me hard. Externally, I kept my cool. I wasn't ready to make my heart public property. "Keir can do what he wants. I don't have any claim on him."

"You don't fool me. I see the way you look at him."

I scowled at the girlnado surrounding the guys. "Okay. I'll admit I don't like them hanging around either. But Chuy invited them; what was I supposed to do?"

Layla exhaled a cloud of smoke. It hung heavy in the air between us.

"You should have doused them with a bucket of water and told them to get lost."

"I said I was sorry."

"Forget it. There's nothing you can do now." She examined the burning joint between her two fingers. "Want a hit, Russo?"

I nudged her hand away. "No, thanks. Marijuana doesn't do anything for me."

"I'll bet you've never tried it."

I flushed, suddenly and inexplicably embarrassed by my lack of experience. "I did. Once."

She shoved the burning cigarette at me. "No one gets high their first time. Give it another try."

Desiring to fit in for the second time in one night, I succumbed to peer pressure and sucked in a huge puff of smoke. Almost as quickly, I hacked it out. Layla patted my back while I fanned the smoke out of my face. After a couple of seconds, I caught my breath.

"Thanks, that was really good."

She shrugged and shuffled a stray bolt between her toes.

"Listen, Layla. I know you think of me as an outsider too, but I could sure use a friend around here. Especially one who isn't on a testosterone high."

"I think I can help you out," she said.

"Friends?"

She wiggled her pinkie. I hooked mine through hers, and we squeezed on it.

The blunt popped and fizzled, and I drew in another lung full of smoke. My head grew woozy, and a tingling sensation pulsed through me. The world grew smaller. It continued to shrink until it consisted of only Layla and the four walls around me. I'd hung out in the shop countless times and totally missed that the tire-changing machine looked like an evil robot with arms capable of crushing a mortal in two. Or that the cement floor bore an oil stain that looked like a black hole to the center of the earth.

Layla was talking, but her voice sounded muffled like she was ordering fast-food through a crackling speaker. She had two faces, one with a mouth moving and the other with lips pressed together. She nudged me, and I handed her the blunt. Her red lips curled around the brownish paper, leaving the end stained a magnificent shade of crimson.

"I'm really high," she said. "That weed must have been laced with something."

"Huh. What does that mean?"

"Mixed with something stronger."

That didn't sound good. And it wasn't. My tongue stuck to the roof of my mouth, and I'd knocked over the bottle of beer I'd brought with me. I tread lightly, one foot at a time, to the tiny refrigerator, hoping for a cola, but only found more beer. Dying of thirst, I popped open a bottle and took a large swallow.

The music changed from upbeat neo-rockabilly into a familiar slow bluesy number. The same song Charlie had played the time we danced. I leaned against the wall and closed my eyes. Then Charlie appeared.

"What's the matter, baby? You look all shook up."

"You came back," I said.

"Emmy." He brushed my hair behind my ear. "I never left."

He led me to the center of the shop and wrapped his arms around me, the exact way he had before. I buried my face in his chest and inhaled his cinnamon scent while we swayed to the bluesy wails of John Lee Hooker's guitar, Charlie's favorite. Then he kissed me. Shooting stars shot from my head to my toes as his tongue caressed the roof of my mouth.

I clung to him while my body rocketed to a place so pleasurable, I never wanted to return. "Oh, Charlie, I've missed you so much."

"You mean Keir, don't you, baby?"

I peeled back my head, and my heart lodged in my throat. What was *wrong* with me? I swallowed my unfaithfulness. It went down like dirt. "Sorry. I don't know why I said that."

"You sure? 'Cause I wouldn't want you to confuse me for my brother."

"I wouldn't. I could never."

I buried my head back into his cinnamon skin. I didn't want to hurt Keir. Not even if it meant I'd be tormented for the rest of my life.

When the music finally quit, the shop was empty except for the two of us. And Charlie's memory.

"I don't feel well," I said.

"We can sleep it off in Shorty's rod."

I tumbled into the backseat. As soon as I stretched out on the tuck and roll upholstery, I lost all focus on the world around me. Then I fell into blackness.

****

I awoke with my face stuck to vinyl. Keir was crushed behind me. His arm draped over my shoulder. I pressed on my temples with my fingers, attempting to force my memory to work.

The night before faded dimly into view. I stupidly drank a beer or two and smoked a blunt with Layla. I remembered feeling sick. Somehow Keir and I ended up in the backseat of The Ghost Two. At least we still had on our clothes.

I peeled his arm from around my shoulder and rolled onto the floorboard. Keir was using my hoodie as a pillow. I eased it out from under his head.

He flipped onto his back and glanced at his watch. "Damn, Jake will be here any minute. You got to get out of here. I'm supposed to work this morning."

"Jake's coming here? Now?" I shrieked.

"It's his shop, baby."

A short drive later, we turned onto the street leading to my house. We'd hardly spoken a word, but my head hurt too much to care. I insisted Keir pull over a block away since I was supposed to be with Layla. He gave me a quick kiss on the cheek, and I got out. Keir hung a U-turn and sped off in the opposite direction. I embarked upon my first walk of shame.

The porch to my house seemed miles away. By the time I reached the steps, sweat dripped from my temples. I clung to the railing and rested my head on my arm. The door creaked opened. I squinted through the glare of the sun. Sid stood over me, shaking his head. He offered me a hand. With his help, I conquered the three steps leading up to the porch.

"Just a warning, kid," he said. "Sunshine don't believe you were with Layla."

I groaned. "Is she mad?"

"You'll have to see for yourself. I've said too much already. You know how she can be if you get on her bad side." He held the door open and gestured for me to go in.

I adjusted my clothes, finger-combed my hair, and straightened my posture. After pasting on my best innocent face, I marched into the house. Sunshine sat in the rocker in the living room, reading a paperback novel. Her heels rose and fell as she rocked. She acted as if she didn't see me, but the twitch in her jaw indicated that she was well aware of my presence.

"Hi," I said.

Up and down she rocked, her gaze never leaving the book. "Just so you know, I never bought that bit about you staying over at Layla's house."

"Um, yeah. I'm sorry about that."

Her feet hit the ground, and she slammed the book shut. "I realize you're eighteen, and at your age, I was living with a man. I'm not mad at you for staying out all night—well, maybe just a little—but I'm furious you lied to me. I had a vision you'd call back and tell me the truth."

"I thought about it, but at the time, it seemed less complicated not to."

Sunshine's eyebrows rose, wrinkling her forehead. She dropped her book on the coffee table and moved to the couch. "Come here." She patted the cushion beside her. "It's time we had a mother-daughter talk."

I settled as far from her as I could, just in case the smell of the alcohol hadn't worn off.

"Emerald, you seem troubled lately. What's going on?"

I reached deep inside myself for the answer, hoping that by some slim chance she might actually be able to help me. "It's just that since Charlie died, nothing has been the same. Keir has changed. It's like he's morphing into his brother. And it gets worse. The kids at school who used to despise Charlie and his friends now think they're cool."

Her brows knitted together. "That's a bad thing?"

"No, I guess not, but it's a different thing." I couldn't tell her that Keir was now a gang leader and that I'd been involved in fights, drinking and drugs, and street races. Even Sunshine had her limits.

She leaned toward me and crossed one leg over the other. "I'm sure Keir will come to terms with his brother's death in time. Maybe until then, the two of you should take a little breather."

I rolled away from her. "Are you suggesting I not hang with him anymore?"

"You don't have to do anything you don't want to do. I like Keir a lot, and Sid misses him. How about this? Ask him to spend more time here with us, like he used to?"

Keir's loyalty had shifted entirely to The Back Lot Gang, but it couldn't hurt to ask.

"I will."

She patted my leg. Sunshine seemed satisfied, but there was still something I wanted to ask her.

"Mom? Do you think it's possible to love two

people at the same time?"

She relaxed into the sofa. "The heart has room for many loves, Emerald."

"Well, then how do you know if you've chosen the right one?"

"I guess you can never be absolutely sure. You have to look for compatibility with the individual. People grow and change, but their core values pretty much remain the same."

"I'm not sure I understand."

"The chemistry your father and I had was out of this world. But our values were very different. No matter how much we loved each other, we couldn't get past them."

"If your love was real, couldn't you have worked it out?"

She shook her head. "It isn't that simple. Values are ingrained. Your father was raised in a traditional family, and he married a free bird. He provided a gilded cage, but it was still a cage, filled with rules and many things I couldn't endure. I found myself yearning to be outside the golden bars."

Though many years had passed, their split was still painful for me. I rose, feeling I understood less now than ever.

"We're not done. Sit, please."

I plopped on the sofa. "What?"

"It seems to me that guzzling alcohol not only makes you sick, it makes you a liar. Drinking is obviously a poor choice for you, so I'm officially forbidding you to drink."

Damn. She knew. I dipped my head. I was in no position to argue. Besides, after last night I believed she might be right. "Yes. I agree. Can I go to bed now?"

"Go on. But I want you up in time for lunch."

"I've been up most of the night."

"Lunch."

I stomped out of the room like a disgruntled teenager would, even though my head hurt, I was thankful for my punishment.

Chapter 22
Starlight, Star Bright

The next day after work, I veered into the parking lot of Jake's Garage and went inside. The hood of The Ghost Two was open wide, its belly half-full of the engine. Keir and the boys stood at a workbench, examining the metal guts. No one stopped to say hello.

Keir lifted a contraption that looked like a thick broomstick covered with egg-shaped knobs and examined it for straightness, the way a person would a pool cue.

"What's that?" I asked.

"A racing cam," he mumbled.

"I thought you just replaced the engine?"

He rolled his eyes, not bothering to hide his growing impatience. "The car needs more power."

"Isn't it fast enough already?"

Keir suddenly focused on our conversation. "I want this car to be exactly like The Ghost, so when I take on the Bump next Friday night, I'll break the record."

Startled, I stepped back. "The Bump, Keir? Why would you even consider it?"

"For Charlie." He returned his attention to the camshaft.

A sinking feeling settled in my stomach. "Did you use the money Sid gave you for this car?"

"No," he said, averting his gaze.

My instincts told me he was lying, and I frowned. "Nobody on this planet gives a rat's behind about that record. Don't be stupid, Keir. Your brother died on Thunder Road, for God's sakes."

Keir placed the cam gently in the valley of the engine block. "You're right. My brother did die, and I won't let it be in vain."

I latched onto his arm, forcing him to look at me. "You won't win any award, and you won't go down in history. You'll kill yourself for absolutely nothing."

Keir shook loose from my grasp, leaned against the fender, and simpered. "For nothing? Everyone who is anyone knows about the Bump. Don't *you* be stupid, Emmy."

The boys turned their heads and zeroed in on me as if I were the checkered flag at the finish line. If they were waiting for a good fight, I wasn't about to disappoint them.

"You've changed. Up until now, I've gone along with everything you wanted because I thought I was helping you with your grief."

Keir's eyes shrunk to evil little slits. I continued anyway.

"I'll admit I've had some fun riding on your power trip, but if you take that car to Thunder Road…" I hesitated while I drummed up a worthy ultimatum— one he couldn't ignore. "I'll tell your mama."

The boys' take-aim postures slackened. They exploded into laughter, their loud guffaws echoing through the shop. Keir turned cherry-red. The veins in his neck bulged, and his breathing grew labored. One by one, the boy's ridiculous grins melted to grimaces.

Keir leaned toward me until our noses almost

touched. "I am the man. I am the leader of The Back Street Gang. Who are you to threaten me?"

Someone drew in a long breath. What was going on? This wasn't the guy I considered my best friend. This guy was a jackass. A jackass going crazy right before my eyes. Tears, hard-wired to my anger, clouded my vision.

"Fine. Go ahead and friggin' kill yourself. See if I care."

I ran from the madness of the shop and kept going until I was inside my Bug. My hand trembled as I worked the key into the ignition. I wrenched it forward only to be met by silence. I wrenched the key again and held it. A ratcheting noise that sounded like a chuckle clattered from the engine compartment in the rear.

Keir had made such a fool of me; even my own car was laughing at me behind my back. My hand curled in a fist, and I punched the windshield. Pain bit into my nerve endings and pulsed to the beat of my heart. A long string of profanity spewed out my mouth.

There was a rap on the window. Keir stood outside, hands cupped against the glass, peering in. I was so mad I hadn't seen him come out.

"Do you need help?" he asked.

"Not from you." I pushed the lock button down with my elbow.

He ran in front of the vehicle, then toward the passenger door. I reached across the seat and slammed down the lock button on that side, too.

"Come on, Em. Open up."

I shook my head.

His hard eyes softened until he looked like the old Keir, my Keir, the one with the crystal blue eyes. I wasn't giving in. Not this time. I'd had enough of his emotional ping-pong games. I collapsed over the steering wheel, hiding my face.

"Just go away, will you?"

"Come on. Don't be this way. I left my jacket inside. I'm freezing to death."

I peeked at him out the corner of my eye. Drizzle from the damp night wet his T-shirt, and my resolve softened. He was hell-bent on killing himself, and I had a dead battery. We both needed help. I lifted my head from my steering wheel pillow and leaned over to pop open the passenger door.

He dropped into the seat with a smile. "Man, it's cold for this time of year."

"After what just happened, all you can talk about is the freakin' weather. I should have left you outside to freeze," I said through gritted teeth.

Keir squeezed my knee. "I'm sorry. I was out of line. But you yelled at me first."

Now he was turning everything around to make it look like it was my fault. His time to return to normal had run out. "Get out of my car. Now."

"Let me explain. The boys won't respect a guy who lets his lady walk all over him. Don't you get it?"

"You never used to care what they thought of you. Or was that just a show you put on until you had me hooked?"

"Em." Keir reached over and caressed my neck.

"Don't touch me." I jerked out of his reach.

"How many times do I have to tell you? I'm only doing it for the boys, and they still need me."

"I need you too, and so does your mother. You can't expect me to keep my mouth shut like a good little girl while you go and kill yourself. Losing Charlie was hard enough. I refuse to lay back and watch you die, too."

"I'm not going to die. I can break that record. I'm a whole lot smarter than Charlie ever was. It's all mathematics, and I'm good at math. I can figure out a way to make that jump safely. I've got to. That record meant the world to my brother, and I want to make his dream come true. I'd really like your support, but unfortunately, this argument ain't negotiable."

Keir never used bad grammar, and his voice was all wrong. Charlie was good at math, too, even if he didn't try in school. If I hadn't been looking right at Keir, I'd have sworn it was Charlie talking.

"Are you going to forgive me, or what?" He nudged me with his elbow.

Part of me wanted to end our relationship on the spot, but another part of me, most likely the not-so-bright part, wanted to save Keir from himself. If I could put up with his antics for a few more days, I might be able to figure out a way to axe his plans on Thunder Road. In the meantime, since he was acting like Charlie, maybe treating him the way I would treat Charlie might work. I slipped my hands under my thighs and crossed my fingers.

"All right, Keir. I'll give you another chance. And I'll do you one better. I won't question your judgement anymore. From here on out, what you say goes."

His eyes widened. I hoped I hadn't laid it on too thick. He had to believe me for my plan to work. A smile tugged at the corner of his mouth.

"I friggin' love you, Em."

He hooked me around the neck and planted a kiss

on my lips. I kissed him back, searching for the old Keir. The gentle Keir. And just as I thought I'd found him, he pulled away.

His longing gaze flattened. "I've got to get back inside. Got work to do. I'll send Shorty and Slick out to help you jumpstart your car."

Before I could protest, he was gone.

I rubbed my chin, still raw with stubble burn. Something was terribly wrong. The old Keir would have fixed my car himself. He would never have wanted to jump the Thunder Road Bump. Charlie did crazy things like that. Maybe I was to blame for his behavior. Maybe he knew how much I cared for Charlie and took on his persona, thinking that's what I wanted.

I gazed at the blue-black heavens, seeking an answer. At the very same moment, through the drizzle and darkness, a shooting star trailed across the sky. I did something I hadn't done since I was five years old. I made a wish.

Starlight, star bright, let me have my wish tonight. Please, make Keir forget about Thunder Road. And please change him back to the way he was. If you guide him back to me, I'll never do anything that could hurt him ever again.

Chapter 23
Keir's Got A Secret

The next day when the final bell rang, I tossed my books into my locker and hustled to the back lot. I had to lure Keir away from the boys for my plan to work. First, I'd get him to his house, and then I'd confront him about Thunder Road in front of his mother.

Despite my mixed feelings, my heart sped up as he strutted toward me in a cocky gait reminiscent of his dead brother. Behind him, the gang fanned out into an askew triangle, flooding the parking lot in a sea of leather. Charlie never had such a following. I wanted to believe the sudden influx of gang members was solely due to Keir's leadership ability. But I had a growing suspicion that wherever Charlie was, in heaven, or in hell, in purgatory, or simply a sack of decaying flesh below the cold ground, he had some sort of hand in it.

Keir held my cheeks and kissed my lips. "Hey, baby, are you going to work?"

"Actually, no. I have a surprise for you."

"I hate surprises. Spill it." He squared his arms across his chest.

The gang mimicked his posture.

I took a deep breath. "I knew you were off today, so I called in sick. I thought maybe we could hang at your place for a while."

"Damn it, Em. Me and the boys got business."

He might have gang business, but I had a life to save, so I upped the ante.

I licked my lips and whispered in his ear, "Okay. I just thought you might enjoy some alone time with me, but if you have other plans, I can find something else to do."

He cleared his throat and smiled. "I can make some adjustments."

Of course, he could. Guys were so predictable.

He turned to the gang. "There's been a change of plans. Emmy and me's got something to do first. Go on ahead, and I'll catch up with you later."

Chuy cast a sly grin in my direction.

I glared at him. "Don't look at me that way. It's not what you think."

He winked. "Come on, guys, let's roll."

The back lot became a shaking, trembling, smoking, revolution of gunning engines.

Keir opened the door to the 'stang. "Hop in, baby."

There, in his gesture, appeared the first snag in my plan. I couldn't ride in his car. Once I ratted him out to his mom, I'd need my own ride.

I gestured toward my car. "I'll follow you."

His face twisted. "Leave it. I can drop you on my way to the shop."

"I can't."

"Why not?" His face tightened.

"Being your girlfriend has made me a target. The principal will have my car towed."

My excuse made so much sense even I believed it. He had to agree.

Keir pursed his lips. "You're probably right," he finally said. "Drive your car, but don't get lost."

"I wouldn't lose you for the world."

We made it to Keir's house without a hitch in my plan.

When we walked through the door, Elise's lounge chair was empty, so I made my way into the kitchen.

Keir followed and tossed his keys on the counter. "What are you looking for?"

"Your mom. I want to say hello."

"She's at work."

The tiny kitchen seemed to shrink as my well-cooked plan disintegrated into a half-baked idea. Claustrophobic and sweaty in the small space, I brushed past Keir and into the living room.

"I thought she was on sick leave."

"She's still a mess, but her head-doctor told her to go back to work. He thinks a normal routine will lift her spirits."

My spirits plummeted. How could I have been so stupid? I should have made sure Elise would be here before I even suggested going home with him. Now, I'd have to figure out another way to get the two of them together. Talking to her alone would never work. Elise always went on the defensive where her boys were concerned, and Keir had never given her a reason to question him. I had to catch him by surprise, or he would deny everything and get away with it.

Keir plundered a cabinet and retrieved a bag of chips. "I'm hoping that once I'm in the Navy, I can send Mama enough money that she won't have to slave at the diner any longer."

"You won't be able to send her a dime if you get killed on Thunder Road."

Keir's eyes dimmed to cloudy gray, a change so

subtle if I'd glanced away for so much as a second, I'd have missed it. "I thought we'd closed this discussion the other night, New Jersey."

My chest tightened to the point of physical pain. "What did you call me?"

"Nothing. Why?" He shrugged.

"You called me New Jersey. There's only one person who ever called me that. Charlie, is that you?"

Whoever he was grabbed me by the shoulders with a grip so strong I almost cried out. His eyes darkened to steel blue.

"Are you nuts?"

"Me? I'm fine. What in the hell is going on with you?" I tore myself from his clutches.

Perhaps he realized my fear because he looked at his hands as if they belonged to someone else. Then he led me by the elbow to the sofa.

"Sit down. Please?"

I stared at him a moment before sinking into the over-used cushions.

He sat beside me, with what seemed to be calculated caution. "You look pale. Do you want me to get you something to drink? Maybe a beer."

Did he think if he got me drunk, I'd forget what he said? "I don't want a beer. I want to know why you called me New Jersey."

His eyes faded back to their regular color. "Emmy, I never called you that. Have you been smoking pot with Layla again?"

I let my head roll back against the cushions. "Are you going to hold that over me for the rest of my life?"

"Of course not. It's just you're talking crazy and putting words into my mouth."

"I know what I heard."

My head crashed into my hands. The idea that Charlie was inside him somehow was ridiculous. Perhaps I was the one going insane, not him.

Keir rose then helped me to my feet. "Go lie down in my room. I'll get you a cola. I've heard low blood sugar can make a person delirious."

Maybe he was right. Maybe my blood sugar had gone wacko. I did feel dizzy.

When I reached his bedroom, I opened the door slowly, apprehensive of what I might find. His room was tidy as usual. Albert Einstein stared at me from the poster on the wall above the headboard of his bed. Nothing had changed.

Nothing but him.

I tottered to the bed, flattened out on the mattress, and I closed my eyes. Charlie's voice played in my head. *Don't worry. I'll find a way for us to be together forever.*

He can't be here. It's impossible. I squeezed my temples with the heels of my hands, trying to force him out. Even in death, he refused to leave me alone.

Keir entered the room, cola in hand, and settled on the edge of the bed. "Here. Drink this."

I propped myself up on my elbows and accepted the soda, savoring the syrupy sweet flavor.

"Better now?" he asked.

Confessing I'd been hearing Charlie's voice seemed doubly crazy, especially after accusing Keir of hosting his dead brother inside his body.

"Yeah," I lied.

Keir kissed my forehead, allowing his lips to linger. "Mmm…cinnamon and ashes. The one scent

I've never been able to resist."

My skin prickled like a thousand tiny cactus thorns went on the attack. Not only had Keir said Charlie's words again, but he had also spoken them in his exact tone of voice. I didn't have a blood sugar problem, and I wasn't losing my mind. It might be Keir's body sitting beside me, but it was *Charlie* working the controls. It had to be. There was no other explanation for everything that had happened. And for some reason, *Charlie* didn't want me to know he was present. Why?

Charlie took my hand and caressed my palm with his thumb. "So, baby, are you feeling good enough now to keep your promise?"

The promise was made to Keir, not him. And I'd never meant it in the first place. I stared at the black lines in his grease-stained hands, and in them, I discovered a road map of opportunity. Charlie Fields always liked a challenge.

"You're not rubbing those dirty paws all over my body. Take a shower first."

"A little grease never bothered you before."

"Well, it's bothering me now. Either shower or I go home."

He rose from the bed. "All right, you win. I'll shower. But why don't you join me?"

Charlie would not out-maneuver me. I wasn't giving in. Not today.

"I don't have my make-up bag. And without my conditioner, I'll wind up with a rat's nest." I grabbed a hunk of my long hair and stretched it outward, away from my head. "Sunshine will wonder why I'm coming home in such a mess."

His eyes flickered ever so slightly, changing from

Susan Antony

gray to blue. Keir again? Or maybe a hybrid of the two?

"Sorry, I don't know what I was thinking. Of course, you can't go home like that."

He turned robotically and stripped off all his clothes, absentmindedly letting them fall to the floor. Then without looking back, he walked out of the room. That was so not Keir. He was possessed. I had to tell someone, but who would believe me? Any normal person would think I was stark raving mad.

Proof. I needed proof.

At the sound of running water, I sprang to my feet and tiptoed into the hallway. The bathroom door was ajar. I leaped past it and slipped into Charlie's room—the room he used while he was still here in body. His bed lay unmade, the covers scattered as if someone had just crawled out of them. A wooden chair in the corner by the closet housed a mound of dirty clothes.

I picked up a T-shirt and sniffed it. It smelled of cinnamon, and memories flooded my mind. I shook my head to clear it. There was no time for sentiment. *Charlie* would be done showering any minute, and I needed answers. I tossed the T-shirt back on the pile and continued my impromptu search. I wasn't sure what I was looking for, but I'd never find it if I didn't try.

The top of his dresser was empty except for a picture of The Ghost and a child's model car. I eased open the top drawer. My face flamed as I rummaged through his underwear, looking for anything that might bring a clue as to what was going on. My fingertips met something flat and square. Tucked away in the back of the drawer, beneath a pair of checked boxers, was a picture of me. I'd taken that instant selfie and given it to

Keir right before I left last summer. Hardly proof.

But what was it doing in Charlie's drawer? I shoved it back into its hiding place and dug through the rest of the dresser. There was nothing besides clothing, so I turned my attention to the closet.

Save for two worn leather jackets and a dress shirt with the price tag still attached, the clothes rod was empty. On the floor, a pair of work boots and a pair of ratty sneakers lay next to a pile of drag racing magazines. I picked up the magazine on top and absentmindedly scrolled through the pages, then placed it back on the stack. Behind it, a horizontal cut, as if done with a jigsaw, marred the wall paneling.

I dropped to my knees and pushed the entire stack of magazines out of the way. Two more cuts continued vertically down the wall, forming a perfect rectangle. I wiggled the paneling until it popped out enough for me to stick my fingers behind and pry it loose.

Crammed in the small space was a vinyl folder. I finagled it out and tore open the zipper. A faded picture spilled onto the floor. A boy resembling Charlie leaned against a car with his arm around a teenaged girl. On second glance, I realized it was a picture of Elise when she was young. Written on the thick, white edge of the snapshot was the date. February 5, 1999.

The pipes in the walls thumped, and a graveyard-silence replaced the background noise of running water. For a moment, I froze, unable to breathe. What would *Charlie* do if he caught me snooping in his room? I shoved the picture back into the folder and hid the whole thing under my shirt. Then I wedged the rectangle of wallboard into the wall and moved the magazines to the exact place I'd found them.

I dashed to Keir's room and eased the door closed behind me. My heart pounded as I sought out a place to stash my find. My backpack lay on the floor by the bed. I snagged it and stuffed the stolen goods between my calculus and history books. Then I slipped my backpack over my shoulders, using myself as a barrier between whatever clues the folder contained and the entrance to the room. The bedroom door swung open. Keir or *Charlie*, whomever he was at the moment, stood in the doorway with a towel wrapped around his waist.

"Why are you breathing so hard?" he asked. "You look like you've just seen a ghost."

"Sunshine called. Sid's mother is sick. She wants me to come home right away."

My scalp tingled. If he caught me in this lie, I was doomed.

"Can't it wait until after we've…you know?" He tugged at the towel.

"No. Leave it on. I mean, I've got to go now."

"Give me a second. I'll go with you."

"You can't," I said, taking a step back.

He came at me, and I placed my hand on his chest, stopping him from closing the gap between us.

"Sunshine told me to come alone. Besides, the boys are waiting for you."

His eyebrows came together in a frown, framing his ever-changing eyes. He lifted my chin and kissed me hard on the mouth. Then pulled away just as quickly.

"All right, if that's what you want. But you owe me one."

"Soon. I promise." I brushed past him and fled his room, leaving no time for him to follow me.

When I reached my house, I headed straight for my room. Sid poked his head over the back of the couch.

"What you doing home, Emmy?"

Startled, I abruptly stopped. "Same thing as you. Playing hooky from work."

"Touché." He chuckled.

"Where's Mom?"

"She's out doing the Buddhist thing. She said she'd be home later tonight."

I dug in the drawer of a small credenza in the foyer. Unable to find what I wanted, I slammed it shut.

"Hey, Sid, do we have a magnifying glass somewhere? I need it for a science project. I felt bad about lying to him, but I couldn't tell him what I was really up to. Not yet.

"Yeah. Give me a sec."

He grunted as he lifted his large frame from the couch and then tramped down the hallway. The love-beads swayed and clicked together as he made his way into his and Sunshine's bedroom. He returned promptly with an ivory-handled magnifying glass.

"It was my grandfather's. It's old, so don't go cooking any eggs with it, okay?"

I gave the magnifying glass the once over. "It's beautiful, Sid. I'll take good care of it. I promise."

"I know you will, Emmy girl." He muffed my hair with one of his big paws. The old me would have been livid, but the new me, the more mature me, refrained from spouting off. Besides, Sid had grown on me, so I gave him a pass.

"I better get cracking, no pun intended. I have a big test tomorrow."

He laughed. "Sure thing, kiddo."

Moments later, locked in my room, I pulled the smuggled folder from my backpack. The zipper stuck, but I coaxed it open. A handful of old newspaper articles and pictures spilled onto my bed. I arranged them in chronological order, the articles by date, and the pictures by the style of fashion. Once I'd created a timeline of 1964, 1982, and 2000, I began to read.

Man and Woman Killed in Reckless Driving Incident

On September 18, an eighteen-year-old Charleston man and an eighteen-year-old Moncks Corner girl were killed in Moncks Corner on Thunder Road. Eyewitnesses said the two were traveling at an unsafe rate of speed when the vehicle careened off the road, rolled over multiple times, and slammed into a tree. The two were pronounced dead at the scene. Names are being withheld pending notification of family.

In the second article, an eighteen-year-old man and woman were killed in practically the same way. Only the year was 1982. The third article was nearly identical to the other two, but the man and woman died in 2000.

I grabbed a notebook from my backpack and scribbled down the dates. If my hunch was correct, all six of the victims had died on Thunder Road eighteen years apart. The news clipping shook in my hand. Charlie and Melody died in the same spot eighteen years after the last accident.

I used Sid's magnifying glass to examine the pictures. In the old black and white photos, a girl with dark hair, wearing saddle shoes and a circle skirt, leaned against a car that could have been twins with The Ghost. The boy wore rolled jeans, black boots, and a leather jacket, with hair styled the same way Charlie had worn his. Etched in pencil on the back, enclosed in a heart was: *Charlie and me forever. 1964.*

The second oldie pictured a group of guys looking like Back Lot Gang *doppelgangers*, surrounding the Charlie look-alike.

If the last two photos were only a coincidence, the two colored photos—I'd guessed to be from around 1982 and 2000—were definitely not. I held Sid's magnifying glass over one of the age-faded images. The man had his arm over the girl's shoulder. On his hand was a ring that appeared to have a reddish stone on the middle finger of his left hand.

My pulse raced as I scrutinized all four photos again, one right after the other. All three Charlie look-alikes had greased hair. A ring was visible on the middle finger of the Charlies in the color photos, though not in the black and whites. Was it possible the man in the 1964 photo had worn a ring also? Maybe the same ring Charlie asked me to give Keir?

I stacked the pictures to slip them back into the vinyl folder when in the corner, wedged in a seam, I found a fourth article. The word *Obituary*, in bold black letters, jumped out at me.

Charles Lewis Fields died at eighteen years of age. Though a recent Charleston resident, Fields was originally from Brooklyn, New York. Friends are invited to attend a memorial service for him on Saturday, Sept 26, at Redmond Funeral Home. Orphaned at a young age, Charles leaves behind his fiancée, eighteen-year-old Lana Mae Driggers of Moncks Corner.

The 1960's Charlie was from Brooklyn. The Charlie I knew claimed to be from up north even though Keir said his family lived in South Carolina his whole life. Also, according to Keir, Charlie asked Melody to marry him. If he did, she was *my* Charlie's fiancée.

But the obituary listed the fiancée of the 1960's Charlie as next of kin. If she was still alive today, and if I could find her, maybe she'd know if 1960's Charlie wore the same ring.

I dug out my laptop and searched for her surname. There were two full pages of Driggers in Moncks Corner alone, and none of them were named Lana Mae. She'd most likely married. I'd never be able to find her without calling every Driggers listed, and maybe not even then.

Then something Miss Iola told me popped into my mind. She said she met Charlie's great-grandfather. And if she had, then maybe, just maybe, she'd have met his 1960's fiancée, Lana Mae Driggers.

I pulled out my phone to call her but noticed the time. She was in the middle of a shift, and even worse, I'd called in sick. I had to go in person. That way, I could show her what I found, and maybe she wouldn't be mad.

After I grabbed a bite to eat, I still had a while to wait, so I cleaned my room to pass the time. Finally, 8:15 p.m. rolled around. I put the folder back into my backpack and sneaked past Sid, still snoozing on the couch. Outside, the sight of the starless sky sent shivers down my spine. I hurried across the gravel drive toward my car. When I turned the ignition, the car didn't make a sound. The battery was dead again. If I woke Sid, I'd have to explain what I was up to, so I stuffed my keys in my pocket and set off on foot.

I made it to Georgy G's, with only minutes to spare. Since I was supposed to be sick, I didn't dare go inside. I zipped my jacket up to my chin and skulked in the shadows of the building. Miss Iola finally emerged, with a multicolored scarf tied around her head. She started across the lot. I ran to catch up with her, swiftly gaining speed.

Just as she opened her car door, I shouted, "Miss Iola!"

She swung around, and her hand flew over her heart. Car keys dangled from her pinkie.

"Oh, Emmy, you scared me to death. What are you doing here? You're supposed to be ill."

"I know. I lied, and I'm sorry, but something terrible has happened to Keir."

She dropped her purse, and her keys, then grabbed my shoulders. "What's wrong? Is he sick? Is he hurt?"

"He's fine, well, sort of, but he may be in danger. I need your help."

"Keir? In danger? I don't understand."

I pried Miss Iola's fingers loose and bent to pick up her belongings. Headlights flashed across the parking lot. Every nerve in my body shattered. A compact car drove past and parked in a space close to the door. I exhaled.

"What's the matter, honey? You look like you just saw a ghost."

"That's the second time someone has said that to me today. Can we talk in your car? Please?" I handed Miss Iola her things.

"Sure, sugar, climb in." She clicked the lock switch.

Inside her faded blue sedan, my words couldn't

come out fast enough. I explained to her how Keir had been acting strange, spouting things off that only Charlie would have known. I showed her the contents of the vinyl folder, and she read all the articles. Her expression changed from sympathetic to skeptical, then finally to concern.

"I'm not sure I believe in spirits," she said, "But there does seem to be a lot of eerie coincidences between the four Charlies. Perhaps, Charlie Fields Senior passed his wild-hair gene to his heirs, that's all."

"That doesn't explain why Keir's acting like him."

"Ah, honey." She kneaded her muscles with one hand and rolled her neck. "Let's just say that if Keir is possessed by Charlie's spirit as you believe, how can we help him? I ain't no match for the supernatural, and neither are you."

"Keir rebuilt the engine in Shorty's car. Now it's just like The Ghost. He plans to take on the Bump on Thunder Road next Friday. The same Bump that killed all the Charlies."

"My lord, child! We have to stop him."

"I've tried, but he won't listen to me."

"Then call the police."

"If I foil Keir's plans, he'll just try it on another day. Besides, I don't have enough proof. No one will believe that Charlie is possessing him. Do you?"

Iola cupped her chin. "I will admit, honey, your story does sound far-fetched."

All the emotion that I'd been suppressing came flooding out in a stream of tears.

Iola wrapped her arm around my shoulder and squeezed me. "Now, don't you cry. Everything is going to be okay."

I'd heard those same words before, from Charlie the night he died. I cried harder.

"Please, honey, tell me what I can do to help." Miss Iola patted my back.

"Do you know Lana Mae Driggers?" I sniffled.

"The name sounds familiar, but I don't rightly recollect."

I dried my face with the back of my sleeve. "Do you think your cousin, the one you visited when you were in high school, might know her? Maybe if I could talk to her, I could find the proof I need to convince everyone."

"Tell you what. If you promise to stop crying, I'll call Judy first thing tomorrow morning."

I threw my arms around her. "Thank you so much."

She lifted my chin. "Emmy, you know I think the world of both you and Keir. Give it some time. Things will work out between you."

She thought I was having boyfriend trouble. She probably didn't believe a word I said and was only humoring me, but at least I'd convinced her to help. And that was enough for now.

"Thank you, Miss Iola. You'll call me as soon as you talk to her?"

"Certainly, sugar. You know, I will."

"I'd better get home now."

I cracked open the door. The chill from the night rushed in, and I shuddered.

"Let me drive you to your car."

"I walked."

"Then I'm driving you home."

"I don't want to cause you any trouble."

"Drivin' you home ain't no trouble at all, but the

callin' in sick thing, well that's another story. I almost worked myself to death today. You will be at work tomorrow, won't you?" she asked, with a hint of reprimand in her voice.

"Yes, ma'am," I answered in my most obedient tone.

Chapter 24
Leader of the Gang

The next morning, I arrived at school early to avoid Keir-Charlie. I wasn't ready to deal with him or the stupid, stupid promise I made.

On the way in, my phone buzzed in my pocket. Miss Iola's name popped into the caller I.D.

"Hello?"

"Hey, it's me. Can you talk?"

"Of course. What did you find out?'

"I've got some good news. It turns out my cousin Judy knows Lana Mae well. She lives up in Bonneau Beach, and she's agreed to meet with you directly after work tonight. I can take you there if you like."

"Thank you so much. You don't know how much this means to me."

"Think nothing of it, child. See you at work."

"Okay, bye." I clicked off my phone and stared at the dark screen.

Bursting with hope, I practically skipped the rest of the way across the parking lot. As I passed through the last row of cars, someone's hand clamped down on my arm and pulled me to a halt. I spun around and crashed into Keir. Or was it the body snatcher?

"Don't sneak up on me like that. You scared me to death?"

His grip tightened. "So, how's Sid's mother?"

"She's fine." I tried to wiggle free, but he held me in place, his gray eyes penetrating my soul.

"When you cut out on me yesterday, you told me she was sick."

I bit my lower lip. I'd been so distracted with the Lana Mae business, I'd forgotten all about my lie. "Oh, she was. The doctor thought something was wrong with her heart, but it ended up just being a bad case of indigestion."

I didn't know which was scarier, how easy lying came to me now, or if Keir-Charlie would believe me.

He deliberated for a moment before the suspicion melted off his face and his fingers uncurled from around my arm. I leered at him as I rubbed the spot where he'd latched on.

"Sorry," he said. "I didn't mean to grab you so tight, but I was mad."

"Mad at me? Why?" I asked, sounding a little too innocent for my liking.

"For avoiding me."

I pulled a smile from somewhere. "I'd never do that."

"Well, come here then." He locked me into a bear hug, surrounding me with his cinnamon scent. "I'm not going to let you go until you promise you'll come home with me today."

"I can't, babe. I've got to work." My voice trembled despite my best attempt to steady it.

He kissed me hard and fast, grazing the roof of my mouth with his tongue. "Then you'll just have to come to the shop after work."

I rested my hand on his chest to keep distance between us, no matter how slight. "I can't. I promised

Miss Iola I would go home with her after work and help her hang the new drapes she picked up at the discount store yesterday."

His hands flopped to his sides. "Tell her you can't make it."

"She's been so kind to me. I can't disappoint her." I drew gentle circles on his chest.

"Why don't her husband help her?"

The level of suspicion rising in his voice rattled me, but if I wanted to help Keir, I had to remain calm and come up with solid answers.

"He went out of town. He'll be back tomorrow, and Miss Iola wants to surprise him and have the room redecorated before he returns."

"Uh, huh. I'll bet she does."

"It's the truth. Call her." Gambling that he wouldn't take me up on it, I offered him my phone with Miss Iola's number selected on the menu.

He stared at the screen for a moment, then grabbed me by the wrist, spun me around, and smacked my butt.

"What was that for?" I rubbed the sore spot.

Sick amusement twinkled in his gray eyes. "Since when has making plans with some old lady more important than hooking up with me?"

Keir would never talk about Miss Iola that way. He thought the world of her. I was dealing with *Charlie*, and I had to treat him as such.

"No one is more important to me than you. You know that. What's one more day, when we have the rest of our lives to be together?"

"Okay, New Jersey, I'll let you off the hook, but remember, I need a girl who'll be around when I'm ready, not when she's ready."

I let the 'New Jersey' reference slide, elated *Charlie* was a bigger sucker than I thought. "Of course, you do. Next time I'll ask before I make plans." I backed up. "We better get to class. Mr. Chapman is itching to give someone detention. I'm sure he'd love it to be you and me."

"You're right, let's go."

Charlie flung his arm over my shoulder, and for the first time, I knowingly walked into school as the girlfriend of the gang leader.

****

When we finished our shifts at work, Miss Iola and I hopped in our cars and headed to Bonneau Beach. I stayed on her rear bumper nearly the whole way, determined not to get lost.

The ribbon of highway seemed to stretch on forever. Trees, farmhouses, and open fields appeared like silhouettes against the starry sky. Finally, Miss Iola turned off the main drag into a small neighborhood. She stopped in front of a doublewide trailer with flower boxes below the windows.

I parked behind her, we got out of our cars, and crossed under a vine-covered trellis and onto a stone walkway that led to a wooden deck surrounding the front door. Behind the trailer, the moon burnt a silvery path across Lake Moultrie's steely blue waters.

Miss Iola patted my back. "You ready, honey?"

"As I'll ever be,"

She rang the bell.

A small, unassuming woman greeted us. Through the wispy white hair and wrinkles, I searched for a hint of the girl in the picture I'd found in Charlie's closet. All that remained was a squint in the corners of her eyes when she smiled.

She opened the door wide. "You must be Iola and Emmy."

"Yes, ma'am," we said in unison.

"Well, I'm Lana Mae." Her gummy smile revealed tobacco-stained teeth. "I'm real sorry, but I'm going to ask you to whisper. My husband is in bed, and he'll be meaner than a bear if we wake him. He don't like it much when I talk about Charlie."

"Don't you worry none," Iola said. "We'll talk real quiet. Won't we, Emmy?" She jabbed me with her elbow.

"Of course," I practically mouthed.

"Y'all come in, now."

We crossed the threshold into a cozy living room crammed with an oversized couch and age-worn chairs with doilies pinned to the arms. Knickknacks covered every available surface, and above the door hung a plaque that read, *Bless this Home*.

Lana Mae grabbed a crocheted sweater off the back of a chair and slipped it over her shoulders. "We'll set out on the back porch. The view of the lake is beautiful at night. It won't be too terribly cold. I lit the gas heater before you come."

We followed her through sliding glass doors and onto a screened porch, then settled on the wrought iron furniture. Iola and I sat side by side on a bench seat, separated from Lana Mae by a rectangular table. Lana Mae lit a candle and placed a hurricane glass over the top of it. The flame flickered wildly, creating a small sphere of hazy light in the center of the table.

She cleared her throat. "So, tell me, why are you so interested in Charlie?"

Miss Iola squeezed my knee. "Go on, tell her, sugar."

Butterflies fluttered in my stomach. I took a deep breath and let it out through my nose. "I believe I met your great-grandson."

"I don't have any great-grandchildren. What makes you think your friend is kin to me?"

"He had something in his possession that led me to you."

Lana shifted. I pulled the vinyl folder from my backpack, dug inside, and handed Lana Mae the photo of Charlie and the girl dated 1964. She pinched her lips together and ran her fingers over the glossy finish as if she were caressing it.

"That was many moons ago." Her voice cracked. "But still, when I see him, it feels like yesterday. What's your friend's name? How'd he get hold of a picture of Charlie and me?"

"My friend's name was Charles Lewis Fields the Fourth."

Lana Mae bit her knuckle. "Where is he?"

"I'm sorry, but he passed."

She sunk in her chair, pulled a pack of cigarettes from the pocket of her housecoat, and popped one into her mouth. Her hands shook as she lit the end. Smoke billowed between her lips as she spoke.

"How'd he pass?"

"He was killed in a car accident," I said.

Lana Mae laid her cigarette in an ashtray on the table. She plucked a hanky from her bra strap and twisted it, whispering something that sounded like a prayer.

"Were you his girlfriend?"

"No, ma'am, not really."

"Was he a good boy?"

"The best," I said, despite the fact Charlie would cringe at being called that. He wasn't all bad either, but the real story was so complicated, it would have taken half the night to explain.

"Could you tell me a little about the Charlie who was your fiancé?"

She looked at me with flashbulb eyes. "How'd you know we were engaged?"

I passed her the newspaper obituary.

She glanced at it, then picked up her cigarette and took a drag. "You sure you want to hear about him? It ain't pretty."

"We sure do," Iola chirped, drowning out my 'Yes, ma'am.'

"Well, settle back in your seats, ladies. 'Cause this is a long story, and it don't have a happy ending."

I leaned forward, resting my elbows on my thighs. Miss Iola did the same.

"I met Charlie at the Olde Soda Shop in Moncks Corner. He was a cocky Yankee who moved to Charleston to live with an aunt after his parents died. Poor thing."

"My friend, Charlie mentioned his family was from New York," I said, recalling what he'd told me once.

Lana Mae's gaze shifted between Miss Iola and me. "Now, I don't want you to get the wrong idea about me. Wasn't like I couldn't have landed a good Southern boy. I wasn't one of those sexpot girls running around all harem-scarem. My daddy hardly let me do anything 'cept attend church socials. The night I met Charlie, Daddy thought I was at a slumber party at my friend

Lily's house. She was the preacher's daughter. I started off there all right, but when Lily's parents retired early, we snuck out. You know those preacher's daughters. People don't lie when they say most of them are barrels of fun."

Miss Iola and I laughed.

"I've certainly heard the same thing," Miss Iola said, "but I never knew one personally."

Lana Mae wrung her hanky in her hands. "If I hadn't been misbehaving, I probably would have never met him, much less become his girl. I never cared much for those hoodlum-types, but something set him apart from the rest."

"Was he a dreamboat?" Miss Iola asked.

Dreamboat? Hoodlum? Sexpot? Harem-scarem? Between the two of them, I was in senior-slang hell.

Lana Mae smiled. "Dreamboat wasn't the word for him. He wasn't bad looking, but a better word to describe him was magnetic. He was the kind of person you notice right off in a crowd. If I close my eyes, I can still picture him setten' up at the counter, sipping a cola through a straw. Though, knowing Charlie, it was most likely spiked with whiskey."

Miss Iola covered her mouth and snickered. My heart thumped. The Charlie I knew like whiskey, too.

Lana Mae adjusted her sweater, so it hung on her shoulder like a perfectly symmetrical cape. "I sure don't want you two to get the wrong impression of me."

"Honey," Miss Iola said, "Teenagers have been sneaking sips of whiskey for years; it ain't like we've never done it. Right, Emmy?" She smacked me in the arm.

"Oh, she's right, Miss Lana. Once, I drank so much

beer, I threw up on the floor.

Lana's nose wrinkled up. "My lord, child, no need to over-share."

I'd confessed too much. I prayed for the concrete floor to crack open and swallow me whole.

Iola gave me a look. "Go on with your story, Lana Mae."

Her brows scrunched together. "Where was I?"

"You were talking about Charlie at the counter sipping a cola," Iola said.

"Oh, yeah." A long cigarette ash tumbled into her lap, and she brushed it off. "The jukebox was playing, and kids was jiving in the middle of the floor. Charlie gazed at me like I was a sugar cube he wanted to melt in his mouth. Without looking away, he walked right over to the juke and yanked the plug. Then silence. You coulda heard a pin drop. Everyone stared at him. Some complained, but Charlie wasn't fazed, not one bit. He stuck the plug right back in the wall, plunked another dime into the machine, and pressed a button, and played a John Lee Hooker tune. One of those songs my Southern Baptist daddy would have never allowed me to play at home, Mr. Hooker being African-American and all."

"Was your dad a segregationist?" I asked.

When we'd learned about them in history class, it seemed like ages ago. Not so much anymore.

Lana Mae stared out at the lake. "No, I wouldn't say that."

"You're too young to understand," Miss Iola said, "Things were different here in those days."

Lana Mae dipped her head. "Yes. It was not one of our proudest moments here in the South. But I don't share Daddy's beliefs. Never did."

"I'm sorry. I didn't mean to imply anything," I said.

After a considerable pause, she stretched her housedress over her knees. "Charlie strolled toward me. He didn't stop until he had me backed against the wall. 'Miss Moncks Corner, may I have the pleasure of this dance?' he said. That boy sure had a fancy way of putting things."

My breath hitched, and I choked on air. *My* Charlie called me Miss New Jersey.

"Are you all right, honey? Is my smoke bothering you?" Lana Mae crushed the cigarette against the bottom of the ashtray.

Miss Iola patted my back. "She's fine, Lana Mae."

"I am. Go on," I rasped.

Lana Mae eyed me curiously. "Well, Charlie took my hand and hauled me to the center of the floor. First off, he was a perfect gentleman, but by the time the music stopped, he had me wrapped in his arms tighter than bark on a tree. I dare say that I didn't mind one bit. My, that boy smelled good." She closed her eyes and inhaled through her nose. "Just like cinnamon toast with a bit of motor oil seasoning."

My body trembled. *Her* Charlie was exactly like *my* Charlie.

Lana Mae held her hand over her heart. "He was my first love. I'll never forget him. I've always wondered what would have happened if..." She paused and shook her head. "I'm a silly old woman."

"You're not silly," I said, more desperate than ever to solve the mystery of Charlie's twisted life. I dug in the vinyl folder and handed her the picture of the boy and girl dated 1982. "Can you tell me who this is?"

Lana Mae shook her head, but the shock that overshadowed her face indicated she was lying.

"Please?" I begged. "I know this may not make much sense to you, but a friend of mine is in trouble. He could even die. Please tell me who the boy is."

Lana Mae took a deep breath. "I don't see how knowing who's in that picture is going to save your friend's life."

"I'm not sure it will, but I've got to try. I love him. The old him, at least. And he's in trouble. Please?"

She frowned. "All right. If it means that much to you. But I hope you've chosen your love wisely."

I held my right hand up. "I have. I swear."

A breeze from the lake flamed the hurricane lamp, casting an eerie aura on Lana Mae's face.

"The young man in the picture is my son, Charles Lewis Fields, Junior. Charlie is his father."

Miss Iola gasped.

"Please don't tell anyone," Lana Mae said. "No one but family knew his true birthright. The town folk believed my boy was a Driggers." She held two of the pictures side by side, the ones from 1964 and the late '90s, then placed them on the wrought iron table in front of her.

"I don't understand," I said.

Iola held her fingers to her lips. "Shhh, Emmy. There are some times when a lady should refrain from asking questions."

Lana Mae flagged her with her crumpled hanky. "It's all right, Iola. I've gone this far; I might as well tell y'all the rest."

"If you're sure, Lana Mae," Miss Iola said.

"I'm sure."

Miss Iola leaned forward even farther.

"When Charlie died, I was three months along with Charlie, Junior."

Miss Iola's jaw dropped, but when she noticed me staring at her, she snapped it closed. "Don't you worry 'bout a thing. Emmy and me could never think bad of you. Right, sugar?" She nudged me.

"Never," I said.

The space heater crackled and clattered. Lana Mae adjusted the dial until it stilled.

"Our wedding date had been set for a month after he died. I know that in this day and age lots of girls and even grown women get pregnant without the benefits of matrimony. But when I was a young'un, it weren't the case. My daddy shuffled me off to a home for unwed mothers under the guise I was studying in Europe. He insisted I give my baby up for adoption. After all was said and done, I was to return home and pretend nothing happened. I never dared question Daddy back then. Especially since I was only eighteen and had no man, but once I held that sweet baby in my arms, I couldn't go through with it. I'd lost Charlie. I couldn't lose our son, too."

Miss Iola shook her head. "That must have been horrible for you, having to choose between your love for your daddy and your love for your baby."

"T'was, but in this life, everyone has to eat a little dirt," she said.

Another breeze blew up from the lake. I drew my knees to my chest and hugged them, fighting a shiver.

"You cold?" Lana Mae asked.

I was freezing, but I'd catch pneumonia before I'd

interrupt her again. "I'm fine," I assured her.

Lana Mae lit another cigarette and shook out the match. "Daddy tried to force me to give Charlie, Junior away, but I threw a hissy fit and threatened to march down to the center of town and scream the truth for all to hear. Neither Daddy nor Mama could bear to live with that shame. So they concocted a story and told the town folk they'd adopted a baby. Charlie, Junior was raised as my brother."

"No one ever questioned it?" I asked.

"If anyone did, I never heard tell of it," she said, her tone defensive. "I met my husband soon after. He knew the truth. I told him. But that man loved me so much it didn't matter none to him. We married a year later."

"I'm so glad you found a good man, Lana Mae," Iola said, "But what did Charlie, Junior think of the whole thing?"

"We never told him about his real birthright, but he found out some way or another. At sixteen, he'd changed his surname from Driggers to Fields. Likely broke my daddy's heart. Being raised by a good and decent man like Daddy didn't change Charlie Junior's nature one bit. He was just like his real daddy. It was as if Charlie had returned from the grave and possessed him."

I'd discovered the identity of the people in the pictures and now was pretty sure that all three of the past Charlies had possessed their sons. But there was one crucial piece of information missing. Why Keir? He was not Charlie's heir. Dewy beads of sweat formed around my hairline despite the cold weather. I stared hard at Miss Lana Mae's. "Returned from the grave?

How do you mean?"

"Charlie, Junior took a liking to cars. A year or so later, just like his daddy, he developed this burning desire to take on that damn Bump on Thunder Road. The same one Charlie, Senior, bless his soul, never made. I begged him not to try, but he wouldn't pay me no mind. Perhaps I didn't try hard enough, but I never believed the good Lord would take a boy in the same way he took his daddy." She bowed her head. "But he did."

"I'm so sorry, Lana Mae," Miss Iola said.

The puzzle was nearly complete, but there was a jagged-edged piece missing. "Can I ask you one more question?"

"Go ahead," Lana Mae said wearily.

"Did Charlie, Senior wear a red-stoned ring?"

She lifted her chin. "Why, yes. How did you know that?"

"My friend Charlie wore a similar ring. Do you remember what it looked like?"

"Of course I do. It had a crown, with two wings etched right into the stone. Charlie loved that ring. He said he bought it off some carnival fortuneteller. She told him it had the power to grant eternal life, and Charlie believed that to be true. Darn lot a good it did him. I passed it on to Charlie, Junior on his sixteenth birthday. But it was lost somehow. I never knew what became of it."

Sheer panic pumped through my veins. My suspicions were true. The ring that held Charlie's spirit was on Keir's finger. Keir was going to die, and it was all my fault. I had to get the ring back before it was too late.

"Thank you, Miss Lana Mae," I said, unable to hide the quavering in my voice. "You have been more help than you'll ever know."

"Are you all right, child? You look pale as a ghost."

"I'm fine, but I need to go."

If I sat one moment longer, I'd lose it right on Lana Mae's porch. I collected Charlie's pictures, picked up my backpack, and fled to my car. I didn't stop until I was locked safely inside.

I stared out the window, looking at nothing as memories of the last half-year flooded back. Charlie playing with my hair and the strange visions in my head. Charlie holding me in his arms swaying to John Lee Hooker, the same way he had with Lana Mae and God knows who else before me.

And finally, the words he'd said the night of his death. *'I've been waiting for a girl like you all my life. Just give me some time. I'm going to figure out a way to make you mine once and for all.'*

I flipped on the dome light and dug out the yellowed newspaper clippings. Trembling, I re-read each article carefully. The girl who died with all three Charlies wasn't pregnant. Melody was. A terrible mistake had been made. She was the pregnant fiancée. She wasn't the one who was supposed to die with Charlie.

I was.

And now he was using Keir's body to be with me, and he would carry out his crazy death-wish on Thunder Road using it too. Charlie wasn't just a mean spirit. He was a stupid one.

How could I have let him con me into giving the

ring to Keir? If Keir died, I'd be an unwilling accomplice to his murder. My heart pounded rapid-fire. I would not allow Keir to die. Not while my heart was still beating. It was too late to save Charlie. He'd carelessly thrown away his life four times already and was eager to do it again. I couldn't save him. But Keir, I could save.

I turned to a sudden rap on the window. Miss Iola's face pressed to the glass.

"Emmy, where are you going?" Her voice sounded distant in the vacuum-packed silence of my car.

"Home," I shouted.

"Emmy, open the door." She pounded on the glass again.

I cranked the engine and slipped the car into first gear, my foot itching to release the clutch. "Move away, please. I've got to go."

Miss Iola seemed hurt by my harsh tone, but I didn't have time for regrets. My nerves were frail enough as it was. I shot her a warning look and revved the engine. She shook her head and backed off. I slammed the car into gear and pulled away.

Racing toward Keir.

Racing toward Charlie.

Racing toward what could be the end of us all.

Chapter 25
Spirits Among Us

When I returned home, Sid was sleeping on the couch with a motorcycle magazine draped across his chest. I tiptoed down the hall and stopped in front of the love den. Sunshine's back rose and fell in the throes of deep sleep.

I contemplated waking her to tell her of my discovery but decided against it. Why give her an excuse to drag me to one of her group analysis sessions or, even worse, a psychiatrist? I wouldn't blame her, though. A few months ago, had someone told me possession was possible, I'd have thought they were out of their skull.

Continuing down the hall, I entered my darkened room and turned on the small lamp on my bedside table. It cast an amber hue throughout the room. Not great, but much nicer than total darkness.

Something felt wrong. An eerie feeling as if I were being watched washed over me. The blinds were drawn, but I cinched the curtains across the windows just the same. Then I changed into a pair of old sweats and an oversized tee and climbed into bed, purposely leaving the light on. Now that I knew spirits walked amongst us on the earth, the dark took on a whole new meaning.

With the covers pulled to my chin, I allowed my head to sink into the feather pillow. Finding answers to the improbable was a lot more exhausting than I'd ever imagined. I needed sleep to be able to clearly sort through my thoughts. I counted backward from one hundred. Somewhere around sixty-four, I drifted off.

****

My alarm blared, yanking me out of a fitful sleep. The cool wood floor chilled my feet as I tiptoed to the bathroom, only to be greeted by black and white mosaic tile much colder than the wood. When would the unusually cold weather subside?

I showered quickly, towel-dried my hair, and tiptoed back to my room. Then I dressed in a pair of faded skinny jeans, a long-sleeved T-shirt, and a fur-lined hoodie. My backpack wasn't in its usual spot in the corner. Damn it. I'd left it in my car.

Sunshine was still in bed, and Sid was out cold on the couch. So I grabbed a bottle of orange juice and a granola bar, then headed outside.

The front seat of my car was empty. I opened the door and slid the seatback forward. My backpack wasn't on the floorboard. My breath quickened, and I scratched my neck below the collar. Where did I put it?

I ran back to my room and searched under the bed, in my closet, and underneath a pile of clothes in the corner, tossing them every which way. Everything I owned was inside. My laptop. My phone. My wallet. Charlie's blue vinyl jacket!

Maybe I'd left it at Lana Mae's house. I had to call Miss Iola.

With no landline in the house, I would need to wake Sunshine to ask for her cell. That would lead to a slew of questions, many of which I wasn't ready to answer. So I launched myself into my car and drove to

Georgy G's. With the sick feeling of dread weighing me down, I trekked to the end of the building where the payphone was attached to the wall. After dropping a few quarters into the slot, the dial tone hummed. I pecked out the number I'd memorized only a day ago.

"Hello," Iola answered in a scratchy voice.

"Miss Iola?"

"Yes."

"This is Emmy. Did I wake you?"

"I was about to get up anyway. Are you all right?"

I blew a strand of hair out my mouth. "Did I leave my backpack at Miss Lana Mae's house last night?"

White noise blared from the earpiece. I drummed my fingers on the metal case framing the phone.

"No, I distinctly remember seeing you take it with you when you left."

My adrenaline level surged. "It's gone, Miss Iola. I can't find it in my house or my car. Someone must have taken it."

"Are you sure? Why would anyone want your backpack?"

"All my electronics, my money, everything was in it." Tears clouded my vision.

"Oh, that's terrible. Do you want me to call the police?"

"No!" I shouted, startling myself. "Don't do that. Keir or one of the boys might be involved. I don't want to get them in trouble."

"Why would Keir steal your stuff, honey?" Miss Iola asked, her tone skeptical.

"He might have wanted Charlie's pictures. The ones I showed you last night."

Someone's footsteps thudded behind me. I spun

around. A guy in a baseball cap nodded and continued into the store. I collapsed against the cinder block wall. The metal cord from the phone acted as a lifeline, stopping me from slipping to the ground.

"You need to go home and have another look around. I'll call Lana Mae just to be sure you didn't leave it there. I doubt Keir would steal your stuff over a few old pictures."

Keir wouldn't, but *Charlie* would, and the only person I dared to tell didn't believe me. The reality of the situation slammed down on me like an anvil. My backpack wasn't at home, and it wasn't at Lana Mae's.

Charlie was onto me.

"You're right, Miss Iola. I'll go home and look again."

"That's a good idea, sugar. Drive carefully."

"I'll talk to you later." I hung up the phone before she said goodbye.

As I made my way back to my car, the gray clouds above parted, uncovering the threatening black patch. Perhaps an ominous warning of what was to come.

I had to go to school and face *Charlie*.

When I pulled into the school lot, Keir's 'stang was parked in the usual spot, but he wasn't in it. Only days ago, I'd have been anxious to see him, but today his absence brought only relief. I parked, and my door flew open. I yelped, and my hand flew over my mouth. Keir's blue eyes were now as dark gray as the stormy sky.

"You scared me to death."

He lifted his chin and looked down his nose at me. "I told you once before; you're not living right, Emmy."

I fanned the heat from my cheeks. "I didn't see you coming."

"You never called last night. I missed you. Did you get Iola's drapes hung?" His voice oozed sarcasm.

"Yeah. They look great," I said a bit too lightly.

"Let me help you out." He hooked my upper arm and pulled me to my feet.

"What are you doing?"

"What's the matter? Aren't you happy to see me?"

"Not when you treat me like a piece of property."

His eyes flickered a shade darker, almost brown. "Being my girlfriend makes you my property."

The time had come to proclaim my self-ownership to both the world and the spirit world. "Take your hands off me, you jerk. I know who you are."

"Little Miss New Jersey's gone crazy, hasn't she?"

"Don't try to change the subject. I said I know *who* you are. So why don't you admit it?"

He didn't respond. Instead, he spun around, snatched my backpack from his car, and shoved it into my hands. The blood drained from my head, and I staggered.

The twinkle in his dark, squinty eyes told me that rather than truth-or-dare, we were about to play a game of cat-and-mouse.

Charlie raked his hand through Keir's blond hair. "When you didn't call, I swung by your house. Your car wasn't there. So, I decided to wait." He jostled the strap of my backpack. "You left it in your car with the doors unlocked. You need to be more careful with the things you value."

The feeling of being watched last night hadn't been my imagination. He'd been spying on me. How much did he see? "I told you I was with Miss Iola."

"Were you?"

The stakes of the game were rising higher than the cards I had left in my hand. He was not going to confess his presence, and for Keir's sake, I dared not push him any further. It was time to fold.

"Listen, if you don't believe me, there's no point in talking anymore. I'm done with you." I stepped out of the wedge he'd created between himself and my car.

He grabbed my elbow. "I'm sorry, Em. Don't go. I'm a jerk. It's just I love you so much. I don't know what I'd do if I lost you to some other guy."

When I turned to protest, I noticed his eyes had changed back to crystal blue. "Keir, is that you?"

He scrunched his cheek. "Why would you ask me that? What's wrong with you? You've been so strange lately."

I latched on to his shoulders. "You've got to listen to me. You need to take off Charlie's ring right now. Your life might be in danger if you don't."

"Calm down. You're hurting me." He peeled my hands from his shoulders.

I made a grab for the red- stoned ring. He clamped his fist shut then held his hand teasingly above his head.

"Why are you freaking out. It's only a ring."

"It's more than that. Give me a minute, and I'll prove it to you."

I set my backpack on the hood of the car and rifled through my belongings. My computer, my phone, even my wallet was inside, but no vinyl jacket.

"Oh, no. It's gone."

Keir jumped back as if he believed I'd detonate. "What is?"

I'd never convince him that the ring held Charlie's spirit without any evidence. Even I'd have a hard time believing me. I'd have to get it off his finger another way.

"Never mind. You're right. It is only a ring. I don't know what's gotten into me lately. It must be hormonal."

"Well, I love you anyway."

He leaned over and pressed his lips to mine. He had a lemony scent mingled with boy smell, and I melted into the kiss. As his tongue probed deeper into my mouth, the lemon scent mutated into the overwhelming taste of cinnamon. I struggled to break free, but it only encouraged him to come at me harder. His lips covered mine, and the stubble of his chin burned my skin.

I couldn't breathe. Keir was gone, and *Charlie* was searching hungrily for something within me, possibly my soul. My knees buckled, but he held me firm and slowly removed his mouth from mine.

"That's more like it, New Jersey. That's how the leader of the gang's lady is supposed to act."

I stared into his hard, brown eyes. "I never auditioned for the part. I inherited the title by default. Don't you remember?"

"Well, don't get too confident. You still need a lot of fine-tuning."

Maybe there was still hope, but I had to get to him in a way he'd understand. What would a girl from the 1960s do if she wanted a guy's ring? I took his hand in mine and rubbed the red stone with my thumb.

"Seems to me that if I were really your lady, I'd be wearing this around my neck."

"I love you, Em, but you can't have the ring." His voice sounded sugary, a poor imitation of Keir's.

"Please," I tugged on the band. "I'll wear it around my neck, so everyone sees I'm yours."

He pulled away. "Hands off. You know how much Keir likes it."

"Why are you referring to yourself in the third person, as if you're some kind of god, *Keir*?"

"Because I am a god, and the sooner you realize it, the better off we'll be. Get it, New Jersey?"

Oh, I got it. Though, I wished I didn't. Keir was dying. *Charlie* was consuming him minute by minute, and I couldn't stop him. I didn't know how. I needed help.

Sunshine was versed in spiritual issues. Maybe the time had come to break my silence. Charlie may have won today, but he would not be the final victor. Not while I was still breathing.

I plastered on a smile. "Okay, I got it, babe."

"That's better." He draped his arm over my shoulder and urged me forward.

For the second time, I walked into school with the leader of the gang.

Chapter 26
Ferris Wheel of Reincarnation

The fire crackled, casting a warm glow in our tiny living room. Sid sat on the couch perusing a muscle car magazine while Sunshine meditated in the lotus position beside him. I planted myself in the rocking chair near the hearth, removed my shoes, and warmed my toes by the fire. Sid peeked over the top of his magazine.

I nodded toward Sunshine. "How long?" I mouthed.

He held up ten fingers and flashed them four times. Sunshine had been at it for forty minutes. Another ten or so minutes to go. I shifted positions, and the rails of the rocking chair creaked. I ground the balls of my feet into the floor to steady the chair. Disrupting Sunshine's zen wouldn't be good. I needed her mind to be sharp, even if that meant calf cramps.

The clock ticked forward at an agonizingly slow rate of speed. The flames on the fire died a bit. I gave up and let the rails of the rocker creak against the floor. Sid got a can of beer and polished it off. Finally, Sunshine stretched her arms above her head and blinked.

"Emerald, you're home." She untangled her legs. "Have you been here long?"

"Not too long."

Sunshine smiled briefly, and then her brows furrowed. "What's wrong? You look worried."

Her uncanny and sometimes annoying ability to see straight through me was hard at work.

"I need to talk to you." I glanced at Sid and then back at her. "Um. Can we go to my room?"

Sid tossed his magazine onto the coffee table and pushed himself off the couch. "I get it. Girl talk. You want me to leave."

"Thanks, Sid," I said.

He stretched and then patted his belly. "I guess I'll just go and get me something to eat."

"Remember your diet," Sunshine said. "The fresh vegetables are on the bottom shelf in the blue container."

Sid muttered something that sounded like 'damn diets' as he disappeared into the kitchen. The refrigerator door creaked open. A pop, followed by a fizzing noise, followed. Sunshine glanced at the empty can on the table.

"Was that another beer I heard?"

Sid leaned against the doorframe and burped behind his hand. "No, dear, it was one of your yummy veggie juices."

"Go ahead. Get fat as a pig. See if I care," she said.

Sid chuckled and disappeared into the kitchen.

"I swear, if I don't keep my eye on that man, his belly will grow so large, he won't be able to see his fly."

I rocked to my feet. "Leave him alone. It could be a lot worse, you know. He could be a big jerk. So what if he likes to drink a beer or two?"

The fire reflected in Sunshine's eyes. "My, my,

my, this is a change. Since when do you side with Sid?"

"I was wrong about him," I said softly. "He's okay, even if he does leave the toilet seat up."

"Come here." Sunshine held her arms out wide.

I sat on the couch next to her and rested my head on her shoulder. Enjoying the scent of lavender wafting off her skin, the same way it did when I was small.

"Now, what did you want to talk to me about?" she asked.

"I'm not sure where to begin." My voice sounded weak, defeated.

Sunshine shifted and pulled my head into her lap. She massaged my scalp.

"Relax a moment, and then when you're ready, ask me whatever you'd like."

I couldn't wait for a moment. "Do you think dead people can come back to life?"

Her hand stilled. "If you're asking if I believe in reincarnation, I do."

"How does it work, exactly?"

"If a person leaves the earth wanting something in this life, then he or she can get stuck on the Ferris wheel of reincarnation."

"I don't understand."

"During our time as humans, each one of us acquires a bundle of habits. They're made up of our desires, our goals, and our life experiences. If any of these earthly habits aren't satisfied while we're here, we will be born over and over again in different life forms until our habits are broken. Only then can you reach salvation."

It made sense, but it didn't apply to Keir and Charlie's situation. Not exactly.

"But can someone be reborn into an inanimate object such as a piece of jewelry?"

"No, honey. When someone is reincarnated, they are thought to be born into a new life form. Why would you think that possible?"

I rose to sit. "A friend of mine inherited a ring from a dead family member, and ever since then, that friend has been acting strange. Do you think a spirit could possess another through the ring?"

Sunshine sighed. "You're talking about Keir, right?"

I didn't answer. For reasons I didn't understand, I couldn't.

"Emerald, you and Keir both witnessed a horrible accident. You lost a friend and will probably be affected by it in one way or another for the rest of your life. Keir lost his brother. Think how hard this must be for him. Perhaps behaving like Charlie is a coping mechanism for him. If you give him time, he'll find his way back to himself again."

"So you don't think the ring could have anything to do with it, even though Keir didn't change until he put it on?"

"No, honey. I don't."

Charlie had stolen back the proof, and Sunshine, the most open-minded person in the whole world, didn't think my theory possible. A tear leaked from the corner of my eye.

"I don't think Keir will ever be the same. I'm afraid he might try something stupid and end up dead too."

Sunshine nestled me in an embrace. Now was the time to tell her that Keir planned to take on the Thunder

Road Bump, but the words eluded me.

She patted my back. "Emerald, you've been through so much in the last year—your father leaving for Iraq, the death of a friend. Perhaps it would be a good idea if I call and make you an appointment with Jenna."

I wriggled free and glared at her through my tear-blurred eyes. "You want me to see an analyst. You think I'm crazy, don't you?"

"No, honey, you're a young lady who has experienced a trauma in her life. Jenna can help you sort through your feelings. She can help you make sense of what's happening."

This was not a problem an analyst could solve. Keir needed me, and I wouldn't let some head doctor convince me otherwise. I had no choice but to delve into the spirit world on my own. I'd just have to find another way that didn't involve my parents or the police.

I faked a smile. "I don't need to talk to anyone. I had a bad day, that's all. In fact, I feel better already. You are absolutely right. Keir will snap out of it soon."

"Emerald, are you sure?"

I nodded, but I'd never been so unsure of anything in my life.

Chapter 27
Not a Motor Mount in Town

The next evening after work, I pulled into the parking lot at Jake's Garage. Another day had nearly passed, and I was no closer to getting the ring off Keir's finger and ending the death ride, but I refused to give up.

The shop lights burned dimly through the thick, rising fog. With my visibility level close to zero, I hurried inside, glad to be out of the hazy darkness. Keir and a good number of the boys were present, some lounging about, others hard at work under the hood on The Ghost Two.

"Hey," I called from across the room.

Keir ignored me. The others followed his lead. I fumed, though I wasn't mad. I couldn't blame Keir for *Charlie*'s rude behavior. My boyfriend's body housed a spirit who was old enough to be a grandfather. A spirit who in all his years on earth had remained a selfish teen who had no qualms about killing his heirs or his own brother to fulfill a foolish dream.

"Rev the engine," *Charlie* said in Keir's voice.

Shorty hit the gas. The engine roared like a herd of charging rhinos and then tumbled to an unsteady idle. Angry bursts of power echoed off the walls.

"One more time," *Charlie* ordered. "Stomp on the parking brake, put it in gear, and romp on the gas hard."

The engine screamed and twisted up on one side as if it were about to take flight. I covered my ears.

"All right. All right," *Charlie* shouted above the deafening noise. "Cut it off."

The engine thumped back into its cradle and sputtered once before coming to a rest.

Charlie kicked the ground and half-skipped, half-walked to the workbench, an orange shop rag swinging in his rear pocket. He pounded on the bench with his fist. "Damn. Damn. Damn."

Shorty climbed out of the vehicle. "What's the matter?"

Charlie faced him, his smoky eyes wild with rage. "The friggin' motor mount is broken. It's nearly ten o'clock, and every parts store in town is closed. We only have two days until I make the jump."

I mimicked the boys' solemn expressions, but inside, a ray of hope burned so bright it took all my strength to keep it from shining through. *Charlie* strode to The Ghost Two and pounded the fender. Shorty cringed and wiped the spot with a rag.

He continued his rant, stomping around the shop like a three-year-old, spewing curse words, kicking bolts and bits of metal on the floor. He froze for a second, then spun around. "We're cutting school tomorrow. Everybody. Slick, first thing in the morning, check out all the junkyards."

"Sure thing, boss."

"The rest of you guys meet me at the shop at eight. Emmy, you too. You're going to call every parts store in South Carolina."

I shook my head. "I'm not cutting school, and I'm not helping you either. I don't want your death on my conscience."

Charlie scowled at me. "You are either with us, or you're not. If you're not helping the cause, get out of here now." In a sweeping gesture, he pointed at the door. "And don't come back. Ever."

He had never threatened to ban me before. All the blood in my body swooshed to my feet. I looked around the room, seeking support from the guys. Shorty and Chuy took a sudden interest in something on the floor. Shock seared the faces of the rest of them. No one spoke a word on my behalf.

"That goes for everyone," *Charlie* said. "You're either in, or you're out. Got it?"

Calls of allegiance rang out.

"We're with you," Nero said.

"We'll be here," Chuy said, throwing an arm over Shorty's shoulder.

"Don't worry about anything, Keir. We won't let you down," Jason said.

Any hopes I had of finding an ally had been officially dashed. I stood silent and alone while the face of my former best friend and boyfriend glared at me. The shop wound down to a hush, save for random throat clearing and the subtle shifting of bodies. Behind *Charlie's* back, Chuy silently pleaded with me to get on board. I'd put up with a whole lot more than I could stand, but if I walked out, Keir was as good as dead. I had no choice but to pledge my allegiance with the gang. I could endure *Charlie's* bull for a few days more if it meant saving Keir's life.

"I'll be here," I said in a voice barely above a whisper.

The walls in the room seemed to expand as

everyone breathed out. *Charlie* rushed over, lifted me in the air by my underarms. He spun me in a circle, then lowered me into an embrace.

"That's what I'm talking about."

I remained stiff in Keir's hijacked arms while the shop exploded with hoots and whistles. Then, just as quickly, *Charlie* pushed me to the side and retrieved a half-gallon bottle of whiskey from his toolbox cabinet. He took a long swig and wiped a dribble of amber fluid from his chin before he passed it to me.

I looked at the large bottle in my hands. "I can't. I have to go home."

"Whatever." He snatched the bottle back and passed it to Slick, then backed me up against the Chevelle. His pelvis pressed into mine. "I was counting on you being here after the boys left."

The smell of whiskey on his breath along with his not-so-subtle request nearly turned my stomach. Still, I held a poker-face.

"You know Sunshine's practically psychic. If I worry her, she may try to read my mind. You wouldn't want her to find out your plans for Thunder Road, would you?"

Charlie's eyes narrowed. "You ain't gonna breathe a word. Got it?"

I couldn't hold my tongue a moment longer. I'd had enough of him and his rude macho behavior. "I'll do whatever I like."

Someone sucked in an audible breath. *Charlie's* mouth formed a hard line.

My insides turned to a big ball of mush, but I held my posture rigid. He remained motionless while anger and disbelief spiraled in his eyes. Beads of sweat formed on his forehead, and his body trembled. He wiped his brow, blinked a few times, and the angry gray color of his eyes exploded like dust into the crystal blue color I'd grown to love.

"Keir?"

"You need to go home." He spoke through his teeth in words that came out strained, almost forced. "Hurry up and leave."

I dove into his arms and buried my nose in his chest, inhaling his lemony scent. "Please, can we go outside to talk?"

His body stiffened, and the veins in his neck protruded. His eyes turned a fraction of a shade darker. "You've got to get out of here. Now. Before I change my mind."

Keir was present, and he was ordering me to go, most likely for a reason I didn't want to know the answer to. Without argument, I pushed out of his arms and rushed for the door. It was in front of me, only steps away, first ten, then five, then—

"Wait a minute," he called.

I flinched and slowly turned.

Keir's eyes were deep brown now, darker than I'd seen them since the real Charlie was alive. A grin crept up on one side of his mouth.

"Just get your sexy butt back here by morning."

I nodded once, then I pitched forward, stumbling over the threshold on my way out.

****

The next morning, still unsure how to derail *Charlie's* plans, I returned to the shop, albeit apprehensively. The only one there was Jake.

"Aren't you supposed to be in school?" he said.

I joined him underneath a car hoisted on a lift. "We're cutting today. Keir has something planned on Thunder Road Friday night, and the motor mount in Shorty's car broke. He wants me to call around town and find the part."

"Thunder Road? He got another race?"

"Yeah, something like that," I said, unsure whether telling Jake would help Keir or hurt him. If Charlie believed me to be a traitor, I'd never get the ring off his finger.

"Well, this is your lucky day." He wiped his hands on a rag and stuck it in his back pocket. "An old high school friend of mine, Rock Arnold, moved back into town a few weeks ago. He specializes in auto parts for classic vehicles. It'll cost a few pennies more, but he always comes through. Come to my office, and I'll get you his number."

It was times like these that made me think fate seriously hated me. I followed Jake into the dingy, wood-grained paneled room, bearing automotive certificates and awards on the wall, and a hint of his cheap cologne. He retrieved a personal phone book from the desk drawer and scribbled a name and number onto a sticky pad.

"Call him and tell him you're a friend of mine. He'll cut you a deal."

"Thanks," I muttered.

"What's wrong, Emmy? I thought you'd be jumping through the roof."

"I am; it's just I don't know if Thunder Road is a good idea." I thought to tell him everything, but the little devil on one shoulder knocked the angel off the other, insisting I remain loyal to the gang. The bell hanging on the front door jingled, limiting my choice even further.

"Anyone here?" a male voice called.

Jake squeezed my arm. "Got to go. My morning oil change arrived."

I folded the sticky note with the unlucky phone number and shoved it in my back pocket, then settled in behind the desk. The phone loomed on the right-hand corner, reminding me of the task I'd been assigned.

The bell on the door jingled a second time.

Keir or *Charlie* or whoever he was at the moment barreled into the office and slammed a paper in front of me. It was an endless list of phone numbers for parts stores and the info to get the exact motor mount he needed.

"Here. Get busy."

He marched out without a backward glance. Under other circumstances, I'd have chased after him and chewed him out. Today, I considered being ignored as a gift. I picked up the receiver and pecked out three numbers of the first phone number on the list, but a better idea came to me, and I hung up. Since no one was watching, there was no reason to call at all. Instead of searching for the part that would kill Keir, I would research possession using the Internet on my phone.

The first few sites I visited claimed possession wasn't possible through an inanimate object, but then I found a site that dealt with demonology and apparitions. That site listed a few plausible explanations as to what could have happened to Keir. The author, a professional ghost hunter, stated that it wasn't possible for demons to possess inanimate objects, but they could attach themselves to them, especially personal items lost or stolen from a cemetery. The author also suggested that all suspect items be researched for the place of origin to determine if those places were haunted or not.

Lana Mae said Charlie's ring came from a fortuneteller at a carnival decades ago. I'd never find the source in the limited time frame I had, if at all. And while the consensus of the rest stated that exorcism was the only way to remove a spirit possession, they also warned that it was too dangerous for an individual to challenge a demon unless they were clergy.

Even if I found a priest who didn't think I was completely insane, how could I arrange an exorcism before Friday night? I couldn't even get the stupid ring off Keir's finger!

Chuy poked his head in the door to check on my progress. I lied and told him I called the entire list and hadn't had any luck. He left to fill Keir—or maybe *Charlie*—in on the bad news. I braced myself for the outcome.

Seconds later, as I'd expected, he appeared, his eyes iron-gray. "What the hell are you saying? Nobody in town has a motor mount for a 454 engine?"

"I called the whole list." I held it up, showing him the phone numbers I'd crossed off as a precaution.

"Slick can't find a mount in the junkyards. You can't find one at any of the parts stores. This is totally insane."

Jake rushed in. "Hey! What's all the yelling about?"

I pled with my eyes, hoping he'd get the hint to not mention Rock's phone number.

Charlie threw his hands up. "No one in this podunk

town has a motor mount for The Ghost."

"Rock couldn't find one, Emmy?" Jake asked.

The neurons in my brain misfired, and I grabbed onto the desk to steady myself.

"Who's Rock?" *Charlie* said.

Jake's head swiveled between us. "He's a friend of mine. He specializes in parts for muscle cars."

Evidently, Jake had failed to decipher my panic. The only way I would get through this situation without being found out was on the wing-of-a-prayer. "I called him. He didn't have the part."

Jake looked at me, quizzically, and I bowed my head.

"Sorry, man," Jake said to *Charlie*. "I didn't mean to get your hopes up."

Charlie stared at me, his face all hard planes and angles.

Jake scratched his head. "I better get back to work. Good luck with your part hunting. But keep it down in here, okay?"

When *Charlie* didn't answer, Jake peered over his shoulder, looking at me questioningly. His concern had come too late. I made myself breathe before nodding. Jake shrugged and disappeared into the shop.

Once again, I was alone with *Charlie*.

He closed the door and locked it. Then he stepped directly behind me, leaned over, and rested his hands on the desk.

"Did you call the number Jake gave you this morning?"

I froze. "Yeah. Like I told you, Rock didn't have the part."

"Did you ask him to find one?"

I leaned away from him, twisting my neck, so he was in view from the corner of my eye. "It was the first call I made this morning. I didn't think finding a motor mount would be such a big deal, or I would have."

"Of course, you would." He kissed the top of my head and held out his hand. "Give me the number."

I shuffled the papers around on the desk. My phone slipped from between my knees and tumbled to the floor. I picked it up and examined the glass for cracks.

"I don't know what I did with it."

"Don't insult my intelligence." His tone was cold and demanding.

I reached in my back pocket and surrendered the wrinkled, sticky note.

"That's a good girl." He sat on the edge of the desk and picked up the receiver. His invasion into my personal space allowed me to hear the man's voice on the other side.

"Let me speak to Rock."

I held my pen between my teeth while I straightened the papers I'd left strewn about the desk. If Rock had that part, I was one dead girl.

"Hey, man, Jake gave me your number. I'm in dire need of a motor mount for a 454 engine, and he said you could help?" After a pause, the corner of *Charlie's* mouth turned down. "Cost is no problem." He straightened out the sticky I'd given him on the desk and grabbed the pen I'd been chewing from my mouth. He scribbled down an address. "Hold it. I'll have someone on the way in a sec."

Rock had the part. I wrung my hands while I waited for *Charlie* to—as he would say—go ape on me.

He slammed the receiver down and raised my chin

with two fingers until our gazes met. "Are you trying to sabotage my plans?"

"Of course not." I blushed. "I'll go get the mount for you right away."

"As if I'd send you. Next thing I know, you and the part will accidentally get lost." He held out his hand. "Give me your keys."

"But—"

"Just give them to me." He wiggled his fingers.

The ante on the cat and mouse game had been upped once again. Any fleeting moments of enjoyment I'd been getting out of it were gone. In its place, anxiety festered. I wanted to run away and never come back. But inside of the apparition that stood beside me, Keir existed, and I wouldn't give up. I pulled my keys from my pocket and surrendered them.

Charlie snatched them from my hand, crossed the room, and threw open the door. "Chuy, get in here."

"What's up?"

Charlie tossed him my keys. Then he dug in his wallet and pulled out two crisp hundred-dollar bills. He handed them to Chuy along with the crinkled, sticky note. "Take Emmy's car and go to this address. There's a motor mount waiting for you there."

"Sure thing, Keir. Be back in a flash." Without any questions, Chuy wheeled around and hurried out the front door.

Charlie directed his attention to me. "Get up."

Hesitantly, I rose. He pinned me against the door of Jake's private bathroom.

"I just want you to know that I'm going to make the jump on Friday, and you won't stop me."

He turned the knob and we stumbled inside.

"What are you doing?"

"We have some making up to do, New Jersey. A promise is a promise." He nuzzled my neck.

My stomach lodged in my throat, and I pushed him. "That promise was made to Keir, not you."

"Not only has Miss New Jersey gotten mighty brave all of a sudden, she's gone off the deep end."

"I've been putting up with you for too long. Let me go, or I'll scream." I tried to knee him in the groin, but he turned, and I hit his hip instead.

Charlie's face burned red. Sweat glistened on his temples. His jaw trembled, and veins popped out on his forehead. Then suddenly, he paled and went stone-faced. His eyes faded to blue.

"Keir?"

"I'm so sorry. I shouldn't have pushed you in here. I don't know what's wrong with me."

It was him. I held his cheeks and looked him square in his blue eyes.

"You have to take off the ring. Charlie's spirit has attached to it, and he possesses you through it."

"I can't. It'll make him mad." Keir's voice sounded far away, as if it came from beyond the stars. He must not have full control of his thoughts and actions. Or maybe Charlie was running interference.

"Who cares what he thinks? Take that off before it kills you."

His cheek spasmed, but his eyes remained brilliant blue. "I think you have an overactive imagination, but if it'll make you happy…" He pulled the ring off and stuffed it in his pocket.

My heart soared. "Let me keep it for you."

"Em, I took it off to make you happy, but I'm not

giving it away. It's all I have left of my brother."

What was the depth of Charlie's influence on him? Was he listening now? Did Keir know he was inside him? I'd had no experience dealing with spirits. I chose my words carefully so as not to cause alarm.

"Keep it in your pocket or, even better, your dresser drawer, but don't put it on again. Okay?"

"If it'll make you happy, consider it done."

"Oh, one more thing. Could you give me a ride? I have to go to work."

"Sure thing. Give me a moment."

Now, what was he up to?

"Wait, I've got an idea. You could come in with me. Miss Iola would love to see you." I was only guessing, but maybe a glimpse of his old life would help keep Charlie out of his brain.

"I can't. When we're done working on the car, I have to lock up the shop. I'll give you a lift and bring your car to you when you get off."

"I suppose, but after work, we have to talk. Just you and me."

"For sure, Em."

Getting Keir to take off the ring was a lot easier than I thought it would be. But I needed him to agree to one more thing. I hoped Charlie wasn't listening.

"Don't go anywhere near Thunder Road. Okay?"

"Of course not." He laced his fingers through mine, and as we walked to his car,

Charlie, the ring, and the Bump on Thunder Road all disappeared. I had Keir back.

Now I had to devise a plan to keep him here.

Chapter 28
The Ploy

At quitting time, I headed outside. The temperature had dropped to even a more unseasonably cold level. It wasn't long before my nose stung and my toes buzzed. And Keir was nowhere in sight. I texted him, and when he didn't respond, I speed-dialed his number. The call fed into his voicemail.

A wind picked up, and I trotted in place to keep my body temperature in check. Had Keir forgotten about me? I texted him again, then Chuy, and a few other of the gang members. After a minute or two with no responses, I called the shop, and I got the answering machine.

"Is anyone there? It's me, Emmy."

No one answered. I paced the walkway. What if Keir had a wreck on the way over? What if he was on the way to the hospital? *No.* That wasn't likely. He was an excellent driver, and if something had happened, one of the boys would have called by now. Besides, Jake's Garage was less than a mile away. I would have heard sirens. I stopped jogging.

What if Keir had put the ring back on?

I dialed Chuy's phone this time. He didn't answer. I can't say I was surprised. The little runt would cover for Keir at all costs. I called Sunshine, and when she didn't pick up, I phoned Sid.

"Hello?" he said in his gravelly voice.

"Finally, someone answers."

"Emmy, is that you? What's wrong?"

"Could you please come get me? I'm at Georgy G's."

He paused. "Where's your car?"

"It's a long story."

"Okay. I'll be right there."

"Thanks," I said, ending the call.

I paced the sidewalk, and with each slap of my foot against the cement, my blood boiled hotter. How dare Keir loan out my car and leave me without a ride! I stopped and braced myself against the wall to fight off a dizzy spell most likely brought on by my racing heart.

I still hadn't recovered when Sid rode up to the entrance on his motorcycle. The exhaust from the bike echoed off the brick wall.

I straddled the seat behind him. "Take me to Jake's."

He glanced over his shoulder. "You've got to tell me what's going on first?"

"I think my car is there. Let's go. Please?"

"Wait a minute." He unstrapped his black German War helmet from the handlebars and passed it to me. "Wear this."

I buckled the straps under my chin. Then I latched my thumbs through his belt buckle. He finagled my hands free and wrapped them around his waist.

"Hang on tight. If you fall off, Sunshine will kill me."

I rested my head against his back and squeezed. Sid released the kickstand, and we rode off into the night.

When we reached the shop, all the lights were off. Keir's 'stang was parked out front, but the boys' cars were conspicuously missing, and so was my little Bug. I hopped off Sid's bike and ran to the bay door of the shop. Standing on the tips of my toes, I peeked through the tarnished plastic window. A silver glow from the moon bled through a skylight, providing just enough light for me to see that the shop was deserted. The Ghost Two, which had been raised on the lift earlier, was gone.

After a bout of confusion settled, *Charlie's* words, the ones he'd said through Keir's stolen lips, replayed in my head. *I am going to make the jump, and I won't let you stop me.* And he wouldn't. I'd been played. Taking off the ring, lending out my car to Chuy, the ride to work had all been a ploy to get me out of the way.

"What's going on, Emmy?" Sid asked.

Tears rolled down my cheeks. "I'm not sure, but I think Keir may have gone to Thunder Road to take on the Bump."

"What?" Sid's face froze in opened-mouthed horror.

"I tried to talk him out of it, but he wouldn't listen."

Sid rushed to me and pulled me into his arms. Then, almost as quickly, he had me at arm's length, staring me down.

"Emmy, what are you kids up to?"

I couldn't tell him about Keir's unfortunate situation. But I could tell him enough that maybe he would help. I sniffed and wiped my nose on my sleeve.

"Keir's got this stupid idea that he's got to fulfill

Charlie's dream. He rebuilt Shorty's car, so it's as powerful as The Ghost. He's going to take on the Thunder Road Bump at one-hundred and twenty miles per hour. He wasn't supposed to do it until tomorrow, and I thought I could find a way to stop him before then, but it looks like I'm too late."

Sid slapped his hand on his forehead. "How long's he been planning this?"

I pressed my lips together and shook my head.

"Emmy," Sid warned, raising an index finger.

"For a few weeks," I finally blurted.

"What has gotten into that boy? He used to be so sensible. We've got to call the cops." Sid reached in his pocket and pulled out his cell phone.

I grabbed his wrist. "No. Can't we do this without them? I don't want to get him in trouble. It will ruin his chances of joining the Navy."

"The police ain't my best friends either, but the kid might die. I'm calling."

I gnawed off two nails while Sid talked on the phone. When he ended the call, he removed his leather jacket and handed it to me.

"Put this on."

He'd been nice enough to come out at night and get me. I didn't want to take his jacket, too.

"I can't. You'll freeze."

"Don't worry about me. My vest will do the trick." He patted his chest.

I slipped into his jacket, still warm with body heat. Only then did I realize I'd been shivering.

"Ready to go?"

I nodded and straddled the bike. With a quick jerk of his wrist, we took off. The wind whipped my hair, and my cheeks stung as we jetted down Highway 52. It seemed to take forever to get to Thunder Road. We leaned hard into the turn, and when we straightened upright again, Sid bore down on the throttle. The trees blurred into a single streak, like a racing stripe painted on the backdrop of the starry night.

As we neared the clearing, the glow of headlamps from multiple cars lit the road. My highjacked car was parked near the end of the line. Haloed in the center of the makeshift drag strip was The Ghost Two in all its cherry-red glory. We weren't too late. Maybe Sid could talk him out of it. Keir had always admired him, but would *Charlie*?

As Sid slowed, I vaulted off the back of the bike before he had a chance to come to a complete stop.

"Emmy, wait," he shouted.

I ignored him and sprinted onward. I was in an instant replay of a horror flick, and I wasn't going to watch this one play out to the end. I threw myself against the driver's door of The Ghost Two and beat on the glass. "*Charlie*, no!"

A glint from the ring on his middle finger caught my eye. He smirked at me and slammed the transmission into gear. The car shot forward, and I leaped clear of the spinning wheels. Gravel pelted me, and I choked on exhaust fumes as the car sped off down the road.

Undeterred, I zoned in on my target and ran after it, wholly believing I had the power to stop the inevitable. Surely, I could do as much. I loved Keir, and in every true romance, love conquers all. Right?

Before I even got close, The Ghost Two bucked and leaped up into the air. A stabbing pain immobilized

253

me. I waited for the car to disappear from view and end its journey with a thunderous crash in the arms of the oak tree.

But the car came down about twenty feet from where it first took flight. It skidded sideways on two wheels before rocketing off the side of the road. The chassis screeched as the car plowed into the field, mowing down thin pine trees before slamming to a halt. A header from the exhaust flew like a missile into the air and tumbled back to earth several yards away.

I darted past people staring in horror and ran down the embankment into the field, leaping over brush and fallen trees until I reached the car. Keir sat upright, not moving. I tugged at the door, but it was buckled over the girth of a tree. A few of the guys pushed me out of the way. I ran to the passenger side door and cracked it open far enough to slide in. Then I locked both doors.

"*Charlie*?"

Blood trickled down his face from a gash on his forehead. He didn't move.

"You have to hang on. I'll never forgive you if you kill Keir."

He didn't respond.

Why did I give Keir the stupid ring? If he died, it was my fault. I rested my head on his shoulder and sobbed. "I'm so sorry. I never meant to hurt you."

His thigh quivered. I pressed my ear to his heart. The rhythm of life played in even meter. I lifted my head.

"*Charlie*, can you hear me?"

Shouting figures frenetically circled the car.

"Emmy, get out," someone yelled.

I ignored them. I needed privacy. *Charlie* and I

needed privacy.

Sid smashed his face against the glass, his eyes wide. "Open up. Right now."

"No!"

I shimmied out of his leather jacket and let it fall to the floor. Then I stripped off my hoodie and gently blotted the blood from the gash in Keir's forehead. The police and EMS would be here any minute, and I needed to remove the ring before they arrived and hauled Keir off to the hospital.

Someone shone a flashlight in the window. "Is he okay?"

Multi-colored rays from Charlie's ring glinted like laser beams across the passenger compartment. I grabbed Keir's finger and twisted the ring. He coughed once and clamped his hand into a fist. Startled, I fell back into the lap of the seat.

Sid pounded on the roof. "Get out of the car, Emmy, or I'll bust the window. I swear, I will."

"I need a minute," I screamed before turning my attention back to the ring. I dug at Keir's fingers, trying to unfold his fist.

His eyes fluttered open, and he focused on me. "Still after my ring, huh, New Jersey?"

"I know who you are and how you got here. You have to give Keir his life back. He's been good to you, and you owe him as much."

"Shhh. Someone might hear you," he whispered. "You don't want people to think you're bonkers, do you?"

"What do you care? If you tell them what you're doing to Keir, they won't."

"How long have you known?"

"Long enough. Why did you lie to me?"

A sly expression broke through the mask of pain on his face. "It was sort of a don't ask, don't tell situation. I always follow the philosophy of when in doubt, say nothing. I wasn't sure you'd be happy to see me, and it turns out I was right." He twisted toward me, winced, and then fell back against the seat. "Ow, it hurts to move. I think I cracked my ribs."

"Be careful. You're hurting Keir." I pried at his hand again. "Let me have the ring before you do any more damage."

Charlie rolled his head from side to side. "No can do, baby. It's my lifeline. I'm having a hard time believing that you, of all people, want to take it from me."

It was time for him to take me seriously.

"First off, I'm not your baby. And secondly, you had your life. One of your own plus three others to be exact, and you chose to waste them all. Now you want Keir's life, too. Well, I'm not going to let you have it."

"Keir is not going to die. He's right here." He pumped his fist against his chest. "And for your information, I never killed anyone intentionally. We all died in accidents."

"Accidents caused by your carelessness. I don't know about your heirs, but Keir valued his life until you stole his mind."

He smiled weakly. "This time, it doesn't have to end bad. I made the jump. No need to do it again. You could still have me all to yourself if you wanted. We could finally have our happy ending."

"What are you talking about?" I asked incredulously.

"It's not too late for you to choose me."

"How could you do that to your brother?"

"He's only holding on to his mind by a neuron or two. He won't be here much longer and then—"

"You've got to stop!" I shook with vexed disbelief.

He hooked his forefinger on the steering wheel and rocked it slightly. "Don't look at me that way. I like the kid and all, but I never had a brother before. How was I to know he would get in our way?"

I glared at him. "The Charlie I loved died on Thunder Road. And it turns out he was only a spirit, and an old one at that. In fact, you're old enough to be my great-grandfather."

"Ha." *Charlie* clutched his ribs. "Don't make me laugh. It hurts."

"I'm not trying to be funny."

"Come on, New Jersey, I've never lived more than eighteen years. I don't know what it feels like to be old. Why can't you just let things alone and be my girl?"

I didn't answer. He'd put me and everyone else through hell, but still, I couldn't bring myself to hurt him.

"Well?" He rolled his hand.

"If I'd have known you were only a body-snatching spirit, I could never have loved you."

A siren rang in the distance. The boys circled the car, demanding I open the door. Sid pounded on the glass again. I hid my face in my hands.

"Obnoxious bunch of lads, aren't they?" *Charlie* muttered.

"Emmy," Sid warned. "Open up before I put my fist through the window."

I swiveled around.

"Don't do it, Emmy, I'm not finished," *Charlie* said.

I huffed and settled back in the seat.

"What will it take to convince you we were meant for each other? If things had worked out the way they were supposed to, you'd be mine, you know."

I covered my mouth and swallowed a sob. "Keir's life is not yours to take. It's time for you to rest in peace before more people die. I can't be with you. Ever. You're evil. Now hand over the ring."

"You got me all wrong. I'm not all about death and doom. I saved your life. You were supposed to die with me that night on Thunder Road, but I couldn't let that happen. Not this time." He brushed my cheek with the knuckles of his first two fingers.

"What are you talking about? Keir stopped me from getting in the car, not you."

Sid pounded on the roof. "Emmy, I'm warning you."

I shushed him.

"Trust me, New Jersey, if I wanted you in that car with me, you'd have been there. But don't think I was on a suicide mission or anything. When I took on the Bump, I had every intention of surviving, but with my track record, I couldn't risk killing you. I'd never felt so strongly about a lady before. Not in my seven decades on this earth."

"So, you killed the mother of your child instead?"

"As I said, it wasn't intentional. Besides, Melody insisted on riding with me." He shrugged.

I'd been right. Charlie had sacrificed his heir for me. In his own twisted way, he must have loved me.

"It still doesn't excuse you. Your time on this

planet has passed."

"Give me another chance. I'll stay away from Thunder Road. I'll treat you like a queen. You loved me before. You can love me again."

"Maybe I could have. But not now. It's over, Charlie. I will never be yours. If you don't let Keir come back, I'll hate you for all eternity."

Charlie clutched his ribs and his eyes faded ever so slightly. His entire body trembled as he attempted to speak.

"Em, he's lying to you. He won't treat you well. He doesn't know how. Don't listen to him, please."

"Keir? Is that you?

He opened his hand until his fingers were rigid. "Take it. Quick."

I steadied his trembling hand and twisted the ring. It stuck on his knuckle. I wrenched it until the edges cut into his skin.

"Ow, New Jersey. That hurts."

"Let go of it, *Charlie*."

His hand curled into a rigid C. "You know, baby, it was supposed to be you and me. It *should* have been you and me."

"No. You're wrong."

I twisted the ring hard, and it popped off. Then I stuffed it in my back pocket. The emotion melted off his face. His eyes were dark and cold. *Charlie* was dying once again. My heart disintegrated, leaving an empty hole in my chest.

"I'm sorry," I whispered.

Then I rested my head on his shoulder and held his ring-less hand in mine. I cried while the strong scent of cinnamon and ashes faded into a pleasant lemony aroma mixed with just the right amount of boy smell.

Keir coughed, and he clutched his ribs. "I hurt real bad, Em."

I brushed the greasy curl off his forehead. "Please hang on. Help is on the way."

"All right, that's it," Sid screamed.

His elbow crashed through the window. Glass fragments scattered across the passenger compartment, pinging off the dashboard and windshield. The door flew open, and the next thing I knew, I was airborne. Sid stormed toward the road with me on his shoulder.

"Put me down." I pounded on his back with my fists and kicked my legs. "I have to help Keir."

"Emmy, I'll help Keir, but I can't until you're safe." Sid climbed the embankment and eased me to the ground. He shot me a look of warning—the kind an angry and frightened father would. "Don't move. Do you understand me?"

"I won't. I promise."

Sid eyed me for a moment as if weighing the truthfulness of my words. Then charged into the field. I didn't want to lie to him, but the task I had to complete was non-negotiable. Sid would have to get over it.

When I reached my car, luck was on my side for once. Chuy had left the keys dangling in the ignition. I hopped in and took off, hellbent on finding Charlie a decent burial place.

And I knew just where to go.

Chapter 29
The Burial

When I reached the Palmetto Trail, I ditched my car on the side of the road. Guided by the moonlight, I crossed the wooden bridge into the forest. The creek, invisible in the blackened woods, trickled in the background. I ignored the eeriness of my solitude and strode forward, focused only on my mission at hand.

After a long hike, I reached the clearing. With my destination minutes away, I upped my pace, leaping over the railroad tracks and scrambling to the top of the sandy dune. Before me, Lake Moultrie spanned across the horizon. The water shone black and swelled against the rock-laden shore. A breeze snaked around me and wailed through the trees, snapping branches and rustling the brush. I sidled down the hill and crossed the dirt road to the water's edge.

Charlie's rock lay like a tombstone in the same place I'd left it that day I'd come with Keir. I balanced on two large boulders lying level with the waterline. My blood raced through my veins as I dug the ring from my pocket.

Memories of Charlie flooded my mind. The day I bumped into him in the hallway, and he broke my fall. The way he swaggered across the shop to ask me to dance. His face as he ignored my pleas, slammed the transmission into gear, and raced off to his death. His broken body hanging from the tree. And finally, pleading with me through Keir's eyes to choose him.

The ring grew hot, nearly burning my fist, and Charlie's voice sounded in my head. *It's not too late. We were meant to be together.*

There was a time I might have believed him, but not anymore. "No, Charlie. You've got to let me go. You don't belong in this world, but I do."

Arguing with my own memory reminded me just how close I was to cracking up. I had to rid him from my life once and for all before I really did wig out for good. I summoned all my strength, drew back my arm, and hurled the ring into the lake.

I stared at the watery horizon and whispered a prayer Sunshine taught me when I was young. A glint of gold light flickered above the water's surface. It fizzed and spit, growing taller and taller, until it formed a fountain of glittering raindrops that radiated outward in an ever-widening circle. The waters around it rippled and rose to an angry boil that rapidly met the shore, rising higher and higher until I was knee-deep in the murky lake.

A scream built in my lungs, but my throat closed. I wanted to run but couldn't will my feet to move. The tether between Charlie and me was too strong. He would never let go.

I closed my eyes. Power deep inside me brewed like a cauldron of liquid over a fire. I willed it upward, and the hot liquid bubbled until hope—or was it faith—burgeoned inside me.

"I said no, Charlie, and no means no. You're not good for me. I know that now. We're done. *Finito.*"

The water rose higher, covering my kneecaps as

steam from my rapid breaths churned in the night air. I'd made my choice. I took one step back and then another until I was on the dirt road.

It was supposed to be me and you, New Jersey. Charlie moaned from somewhere inside my brain. *It's always been me and you.* The wind blew and caressed my cheek the same way he had in one of our stolen moments. I shook it off. No mutant spirit was going to rule my life.

I turned and bolted over the sandy dune across the railroad tracks, my tennis shoes spewing slimy lake water with every stride. Cold air seared my lungs, but I continued onward at a full sprint, through the clearing, and along the footpath into the woods.

In the distance, headlamps flashed. The bridge to the road appeared. Ahead was my escape. Ahead was freedom. Finally, my feet reached the road.

Leaving Charlie Fields behind me forever.

****

I slammed on the brakes. The wheels locked, and my car skidded across the gravel driveway to a dusty stop in front of my little home. Sunshine bounded out the kitchen door, pulled me from the car, and consumed me in her arms.

"Oh, Emerald, where were you? I've been so worried."

I clung to her. "I'm okay, Mom. I took a drive to clear my head. I should have called. I'm so sorry."

She grabbed my shoulders and shook me. "If anything ever happened to you, I would never forgive myself."

"I'm fine. Really." I choked back tears.

Sunshine released me. She placed a hand on her

forehead as she paced.

"When I begged your father to let you stay with me, I convinced him Moncks Corner would be a safer place for you to grow up, small-town living and all. It's been anything but. I should have left you in New Jersey. I'm going to call Frank and tell him to come home from Iraq immediately."

She couldn't send me away. Not after everything was finally the way it was supposed to be. I loved her. I loved Moncks Corner. I loved Keir. I even loved Sid. And as much as I loved Dad, I didn't want to leave.

"He can't come back. He signed a year-long contract."

"If Frank can't come, I'll take you back to New Jersey myself and stay with you there until he can."

I grabbed my mother and hugged her. "Stop it. Can't you see we belong here?"

She stroked the back of my head. "So many terrible things have happened. You've changed. Keir was almost killed today. Poor Elise. What she must be going through to almost lose a second son. What would I do if I ever lost you? I couldn't bear it."

"I'm sorry. I've been behaving horribly, but all that will change. From this moment on, I won't lie. I won't drink. I'll come home early every night, and I won't be a brat."

Sunshine untangled herself from my arms. Her eyes closed, and her face crumpled. She opened her mouth to speak but didn't seem able to form any words. Her lower lip trembled.

"I'll do anything. Please don't make me leave. I need you."

Sunshine snatched me in her arms and squeezed

until I couldn't breathe. It was almost as if we were back to where we started when I'd arrived at the airport. Only this time, I squeezed her back and released a contented sigh.

The kitchen door creaked open. Sid barreled out, arms flying helter-skelter.

"Emmy, too bad this ain't the good old days because if it was, I'd tan your hide. Hell, I might do it anyway."

"And I'd deserve it. I'm sorry, Sid. For everything. The way I treated you is unforgivable. I should have stayed put tonight when you told me to. You've been like a dad to me, and I love you. So, do what you need to do, I don't mind." I cringed.

Sid lowered his spanking hand. His gaze dropped to the ground, and he shifted from foot to foot. "Damn it! Emmy, girl, that's the nicest thing anyone's ever said to me."

Sunshine and I opened our arms, and Sid walked into them. The three of us clung to each other. Sunshine and I cried outright while Sid patted our backs.

"Emmy's home, now. Everything's fine," Sunshine said.

Chapter 30
The Do-Over

Early the next morning, I checked in at the hospital information desk and hopped the elevator to the second floor. I strode down the corridor with walls painted alternately blue and orange and covered with numerous sea creatures. A huge tank full of fish sat in an alcove at the midway point. At almost eighteen, I'm sure Keir found the children's wing mortifying. It certainly wouldn't do anything to raise the bar on his recent self-proclaimed cool factor.

A few yards past the fish tank, a policeman exited a room. He looked like one from Thunder Road. I spun around and admired a decorative soda can someone had crafted to look like a fish, hanging above the nurse's station.

As soon as he passed, I exhaled and turned back around. The nurses stared at me with funny looks on their faces. I blushed. I'd have thought they'd be used to seeing borderline juvenile delinquents in their line of work.

"Excuse me? Could you tell me where I can find Keir Harper?"

The nurse smiled. Her kind brown eyes beamed with unjustified recognition. "You must be Emmy."

"How'd you know?"

Her smile broadened, and she tapped the side of

her temple with her finger. "I make it a point to know my patients, and the young man in 202 gave us explicit instructions that if a pretty brunette with brown eyes shows up, we were to send her right in."

"Oh." My cheeks blazed this time.

"He's down the hall to your left." She pointed to the room where the cop had exited.

My heart sank. I hoped Charlie hadn't ruined Keir's chance of joining the Navy. I stopped short outside the door, almost afraid to go in. If Keir had the same access to Charlie's brain that Charlie had to Keir's, would he still love me after all that happened? I took a deep breath. No matter the outcome, I had to woman-up and face him.

A tan curtain drawn partially around the bed shielded my view, so I knocked on the metal doorframe. "Keir? It's me."

"Emmy, I've been so worried about you."

I stepped behind the curtain. The blood had been washed from his forehead, and a small bandage covered the gash. There were no IVs or hospital apparatus attached to him. He was upright in bed, watching a game on ESPN. He smiled at me, pointed the clicker at the TV, and muted it.

"You look great, considering."

"I'm fine. But they got me on concussion watch. Overall, I'm pretty lucky. I escaped with only ten stitches in my head and a hairline fracture to one of my ribs. They taped me up pretty good." He pulled his hospital gown up, exposing the bandaging from his chest to his navel and his tighty-whiteys.

I cringed and averted my gaze. "That looks painful."

"It's not too bad. They got me on some killer meds."

I allowed myself to smile. "Well, that explains it. Lower your gown. You look like The Naked Cowboy."

He snickered and pulled the flimsy material over his thighs.

I sat carefully on the corner of his bed. "What was the cop doing here?"

"Another bit of luck."

"After what you did, how is a visit from a cop lucky?"

"He came to question me about the accident. But when I told him I planned to enlist in the Navy, he said he'd drop all the charges, as long as I promised not to street race again. He let me off with only a reckless driving ticket." Keir nodded toward a blue piece of paper on the bedside table.

I picked it up, glanced at it without really looking, and put it back down. There were advantages to living in a small town where the community took care of their own. Besides, Keir didn't deserve to be punished for his brother's criminal antics.

"You better keep your promise to him. I've never been so scared in my life. You could have been killed."

"Trust me, that was all Charlie. He had this crazy idea if he broke the pattern of the last sixty years, he could make the jump, and you would be his forever."

I tugged at my collar. "That's the most ridiculous thing I've ever heard. How could he think that?"

"I don't know, but he believed it with all his heart. I could feel it." He patted the bed beside him, and I moved closer. He winced as the mattress dipped.

"Sorry," I said.

"Don't worry about it."

"I haven't told anyone about Charlie yet. Have you?"

"No. We better keep it that way, or we'll both end up in an insane asylum."

He pulled me toward him. The tips of our noses touched before he pressed his lips into mine. He kissed me with such love and tenderness I thought I would burst. I'd missed my friend with the crystal blue eyes.

Something clattered in the hallway. I stiffened and giggled at our behavior.

Keir ran his hand lightly up and down my arm. "I'd forgotten how sweet you tasted."

I dipped my head. "I'm glad you're back."

His lips pressed into a tight line, and he appeared lost in thought. I tried to read the emotion on his face to figure out what he wanted to say, but I waited, allowing him to work it out himself.

"I heard you took off in your car last night." His voice sounded weak. "Where did you go?"

"To get rid of the ring."

His face fell farther, and he heaved out a slow breath. "What did you do with it?"

"I tossed it into Lake Moultrie."

He rubbed his empty finger. "You threw what was left of my brother into the lake?"

"What did you expect? He almost killed you. I couldn't let the ring fall into anyone else's hands or have it land back on your finger."

Keir sipped water from a cup on his bedside table. "Charlie was more than a spirit to me. He lived and breathed. He was my brother, and I loved him."

"I know. I cared about him too. Once. But Keir,

Susan Antony

our Charlie died on Thunder Road. He was gone in body. All that was left was the apparition. And as much as I despise him for what he did to you, I made sure his final resting place was someplace he liked."

"Thanks for that, I guess." He adjusted his bed covers and then looked away. "You know, I remember some of what happened."

Dread as thick as tar pulled at my heart and dragged it all the way into the pit of my stomach. Though the incident with Charlie was bigger than me, bigger than Keir, bigger than the both of us together, he had to be hurt.

"What kind of things?"

"Some stuff that happened while he was in my mind."

"After I figured out Charlie possessed you, I saw glimpses of you shining through. Is that the part you're talking about?" I asked.

He ran his fingers through his hair, still greasy from the day before. "Yeah. But I remember other things too."

The skin on my neck beaded with sweat. "Like what?"

He laced his fingers and thumb-wrestled with himself. "You loved him, didn't you, Em?"

I picked at a loose piece of skin on my finger. There wasn't room for any more lies between us.

"If you count paranormal love as valid, then yes, in a convoluted sort of way, I guess I did."

Keir's eyebrows pulled together. "Jeeze, I thought you'd at least try to lie to me. I was counting on that. Why did you have to tell me the friggin' truth?"

"What's the point? Being of only one mind, I'm at

a total disadvantage in this conversation." I hid a thick swallow in my throat by turning away.

"I tried to stop him from getting close to you," Keir said.

"You did?"

Keir fidgeted. "If I tried hard enough, I could see through his eyes and feel what he felt too. His spirit was powerful. It took every ounce of strength I had to show myself to you when I did. He'd push me out of my head and twist my thoughts until I didn't know if they belonged to him or me."

Charlie had made pawns of us both.

A rich voice sang gospel in the hallway. First far away, then closer, until finally, the nurse who'd directed me to Keir's room poked her head in the door.

"Is everything okay?"

Keir made a happy face. "Everything's great."

She walked over to the bed and slipped a blood pressure cuff around his arm. "Okay. Emmy, you'll have to move from the bed. A cute little thing like you will send his blood pressure through the roof."

I flushed and sat in the hard, wooden chair by the bedside.

The nurse pressed the button on the blood pressure machine. After a moment, it beeped three times. She shook her head.

"See now, I told you. It's high. Not high enough to worry about, but high. Miss Emmy, I need you to keep a respectable distance. One that would make your preacher proud."

"Yes, ma'am, I will."

Keir waited until she left and motioned me closer. I scooted my chair forward and rested my elbows on the

271

mattress.

"Em, do you think it's too late for us to start over?"

"It's never too late, but how do we move forward? Do we tell everyone what really happened? If we stick together, maybe we can convince our parents."

"We can't do that. My mom just started to recover. If she knew what Charlie did to me, it might push her over the edge. I want her and everyone else to have good memories of Charlie."

I nodded. "You're right. It might be better to pretend it never happened."

"I think it's for the best, Em." Keir drew my hand to his heart. "My love for you gave me the strength to let you take back the ring."

"That was you? I thought Charlie gave it up?"

He shook his head, and his blue-eyed gaze locked on mine. "Not without my persuasion. Sometimes good guys do finish first."

Whether it was fate or destiny or the supernatural at play, I wasn't going to fight it. My heart told me not to blow our second chance.

And my head told me the same.

Chapter 31
In the Navy

The day after graduation, the whole crowd gathered in our living room to celebrate Keir's last day in Moncks Corner. The Back Lot Gang and their girls, even Cherie, had come to celebrate. She'd left Paul for Chuy and was now part of our crowd. We didn't discriminate. Dad, who'd arrived a few days earlier from Iraq, looked lean, tan, and happy. He sat curiously close to Elise on the orange sofa.

I was staying in Moncks Corner, the town I was proud to call home. I'd received my acceptance letter to The College of Charleston, which was close enough to commute daily. In a few hours, Keir would be on his way to boot camp in Great Lakes. Afterward, he would be stationed in Florida.

The thought of not having him in my life every day coiled my insides into an achy ball. But Sunshine assured me it was a time for growth in both our lives. If we were going to make it as a couple, this separation wouldn't break us. I had to let Keir go so the two of us could move forward.

Keir held up his wrist and looked at the psychedelic skull head watch I'd given him as a graduation present. "I love it, Em. It's cool and different, just like you."

I laughed. "Maybe now you won't need a skull and

crossbones tattoo on your bicep."

"I think you're right. This is a thousand times better."

He leaned in and kissed me on the mouth. I'd always heard that the first kiss was the hardest, but at this moment, I disagreed. The hardest one had to be the last. Our lips parted, but our gazes remained locked. Could he read the sadness in my eyes?

Keir glanced at his new watch again. "It's time for me to go."

The room quieted, and the many faces that shone with happiness only seconds ago now appeared glum.

Elise hopped up from the couch and skittered over. She wrapped her arms around Keir. "It's still early. Do you have to go right now?"

Sunshine passed her a tissue from the box on the credenza in the hallway. She pulled out another and dabbed at the tip of her nose.

"Mom, I want to give Emmy her graduation present, and I need some privacy," Keir said.

"Ooh." Chuy winked. "I bet I know what you're going to give her."

The gang members gawked, wide-eyed. Sid looked pissed. The corners of Sunshine's lips curled up, and she covered her mouth with her hand. She'd never change.

"Chuy," Keir said stiffly. He nodded at my dad, who shouldered his way toward us.

"Uh, oh." Chuy groaned.

"That's my daughter you're talking about," Dad grumbled.

Slick reached over my shoulder and slapped Chuy on the back of the head. "Now look what you've done.

He's going to kill you. You're not supposed to blurt out stuff like that in front of the 'rents, doofus."

"Sorry, Mr. Russo. I was only kidding." Chuy stuck out his right hand.

Dad stared at Chuy's palm, then at his own. Then he slapped Chuy's hand playfully and offered his to Keir instead. Everyone laughed.

"Good luck, son," Dad said to Keir. "Your mom's real proud of you. We all are."

"Thank you, sir."

Elise sniffled. Keir hugged her tighter to his side.

"I've got to go, Mama. I'll be back to visit in six weeks."

"I know, but I'll miss you horribly." She tweaked his cheeks, then stood on her tiptoes and kissed his forehead.

He pried her arms away one at a time. "I'll write once a week."

"You better." She dabbed at a tear with the crumpled tissue.

The rest of the gang swarmed Keir and pummeled him with farewells. Then we moved to the front lawn.

Keir took my hand and hustled me down the walkway, past the crape myrtle tree, and into the car. Once we were belted in, he turned toward me.

"I'm going to miss you."

My eyes watered, and I wanted to tell him how badly I would miss him but couldn't speak through the large lump stuck in my throat. He lifted my chin, and his warm lips covered mine. I never thought when we moved to Moncks Corner I'd want to stay, much less fall in love. But I was in love, deeply, madly, hopelessly in love. And now my love was leaving.

Cheering came from the direction of the house. I broke away from the kiss, angry at the intrusion but thankful for the distraction. I didn't want to start crying. Keir was finally realizing his dream, and it wouldn't be fair for me to make it difficult for him.

"We have an audience," he said. "We'd better get out of here, or we'll never get a moment's peace."

"Bye, baby," Elise squealed over the chatter.

Keir honked his horn three times. We stuck our hands out the windows and waved as we sped off. When we turned onto the main drag, he took my hand. I squeezed his tight as we rode in silence, past The Olde Soda Shop, the antique store, the tiny barbershop, and all the other family-owned establishments.

Keir hung a hard right onto Highway 52, and we were on our way. The further we drove from Moncks Corner, the tighter the knot in my stomach became. We'd fought so hard to be together that our parting seemed almost insane.

Thunder Road came up on our right. I craned my neck, unable to ignore the place where, if not for a blip in history, my fate would have been sealed. I should have hated the sight of it, but I didn't. While deaths occurred there, it was also the place where Keir and I saved each other's lives.

A semi passed us in a whoosh, and Keir veered into the lane behind it. He slowed down and hung a U-turn at the divide in the road.

"Did you forget something?" I asked.

"Sort of. There's someplace I'd like to visit before I leave."

He took a left at the next divide and sped across the highway onto Thunder Road.

The sunny day and the new growth on the old oak trees made their twisted trunks and moss-covered branches more beautiful than my memory allowed.

"Why are we going back?" I asked. "I thought we agreed to forget about this part of our lives."

"We can't. Because if you ignore history, it will repeat itself. We have to face our past and learn from our mistakes to move forward. At least that's what Mr. Chaput said when we were talking about World War Two in class." He pressed the accelerator pedal, and we shot forward.

I grabbed onto the armrest. "You're not doing anything stupid, are you?"

"Maybe."

The car gained more speed.

"But Keir, what happened to our vow to leave the craziness behind us? Did it mean nothing to you?"

"Em, don't you trust me?" He smiled and punched the accelerator to the floor. After a hard shift, the engine's speed took hold.

Blood pounded through my veins, but I wasn't scared. Instead, excitement buzzed inside me and shimmered across every inch of my flesh. Either I'd turned into an adrenaline junky, or I trusted him.

I stretched my arm out the window and held my hand high. The air beat against my palm and whistled through my open fingers as we zoomed past the clearing toward the tunnel of trees.

I leaned my head out the window and yelled, "Woo hoo!"

The Bump lay ahead in clear view. Just as I trusted he would, Keir let off the gas and eased over to the side of the road. The ruts that The Ghost and The Ghost II had dug on either side were replaced by new growth and no longer visible. It was as if nothing had ever happened here on Thunder Road.

Keir hopped out, ran around the car, and opened my door.

"What are you doing?"

"Get out. There's something I have to do." He straightened, making himself look taller than his nearly six-foot frame.

The air was hot, and the sun burned down. Heat waves rose off the asphalt in a hazy cloud. I gathered my hair in a loose ponytail and lifted it off my neck.

In a fleet-footed move, Keir dropped down on one knee and gazed up at me with his sparkling blue eyes.

There was only one reason a guy knelt before a girl, and we were much too young.

Embarrassed, I glanced around, even though we were in the middle of nowhere. "Get up. What are you doing?"

"Be quiet for once, would you, Emmy? I'm nervous enough as it is."

He wasn't the only one.

"Stop! Neither of us has been to college yet."

He took my hand. "Emmy, until I met you, I was like a vintage V8 running on four cylinders. You can be a challenge, and you can sure be aggravating, but I am up for it."

"We haven't even, you know…" My eyes widened, and I tried to pull away.

"We can work on that when you come to my boot camp graduation. Now, stand still and let me finish. I think about you from the moment I wake up each morning until the moment I close my eyes at night. You make me laugh. You make me cry. You save me from teenage mutant spirits trying to take over my body. You're my best friend. Maybe it's our destiny, maybe not, but in either case, I'm not about to give you up. Because I can't imagine my life without you."

"You won't have to. I'm staying right here in Moncks Corner."

"That's not what I'm talking about. Please let me finish."

"Okay." I nodded.

"Emerald Russo, I know I don't deserve you, but I want to make a promise to marry you in four years after you've graduated college. If you will wait for me." He reached into his pocket and pulled out a small black box.

My trembling hands made opening the lid nearly impossible, but I managed, nonetheless. Inside was a ring with an oval green stone encased in a star frame and tiny diamonds encrusted in the gold points. I carefully slid it on the ring finger of my left hand.

"It's an emerald. I got it to match your nose stud, and for other obvious reasons."

I held out my hand in front of me and turned it from side to side, admiring my new bling.

Keir shifted position. "It's only temporary until I can afford a diamond. And don't worry. I bought it new, so it is spirit-free."

I looked him square in the eye and smiled. "It fits perfectly. How did you know my ring size?"

"Sunshine told me."

"My mother was in on this?"

Keir shrugged. "What can I say? She likes me."

I shook my head. "You do have a likeability factor,

but don't you think we're a little young to be engaged?"

"Emmy, you're only as young as you feel, and we've experienced more in the last few months than most do in a lifetime."

He was right about that. I doubted anyone had ever experienced anything remotely close, at least for two decades.

"Does my dad know about this?"

"I told him this morning. He laughed and said I could ask, but he doubted you'd accept." His brows knit together, creasing the bridge of his nose. "So?"

I reached down and ran my hand through his silky blond locks. "Well, my dad's wrong. I'll accept your proposal of marriage four years from now, but on one condition."

Keir jumped to his feet and grabbed my elbow. "Really, Em. Just tell me. I'll agree to anything."

"I'll marry you, all right, but you've got to do one thing first."

"Anything. Just say the word."

"Put the grease back in your hair."

His face froze, and he blinked a few times.

"Once a rockabilly girl, always a rockabilly girl." I covered my mouth to stifle a giggle.

Keir frowned unconvincingly. Then he swooped me up in his arms like a baby and spun me in a circle.

"You just wait until I get you down the aisle."

His clear skin glistened in the sunlight. He was beautiful, and he was all mine.

I caressed his cheek and ran my finger lightly across his full, red lips. He lifted me higher until his mouth met mine.

Then he kissed me long and hard.

And all of it, every last bit of it, happened on Thunder Road.

A word about the author…

I am an IT by day, hip-shaker and writer by night, artist whenever possible, and an internet addict.

I am also the author of *Cherokee Summer*, published by The Wild Rose Press.

~*~

https://susanantonyauthor.blogspot.com

~*~

If you enjoyed this story, leaving a review at your favorite book retailer or reader website would be much appreciated. Thank you!

Thank you for purchasing
this publication of The Wild Rose Press, Inc.

For questions or more information
contact us at
info@thewildrosepress.com.

The Wild Rose Press, Inc.
www.thewildrosepress.com